Readers love Jamie Fessenden

Billy's Bones

I0659684

"Brilliant. Gripping. Suspenseful. Emotional. Page turner. Go. Buy the book."

—5 Stars, Live Your Life Buy the Book

"There are no words to express my total for love this story and the author's writing. This was an easy 5 stars for me."

—5 Stars, On Top Down Under

"This book deserves well more than five stars. It IS an emotional read. It is also so satisfying. Recommended in the highest way possible."

—5 Stars, Novel Approach

"*Billy's Bones* captures your heart and your mind and carries you in its grip until the final moments. A stunning novel. A recommended read."

—5+ Stars, Reviews by JesseWave

"This is not a steamy, sexy romance, but rather an emotional, disturbing, murder/psychological thriller type story and I highly recommend it. I look forward to reading more from Jamie Fessenden!"

—4.5 Hearts, MM Good Book Reviews

http://www.dreamspinnerpress.com

By JAMIE FESSENDEN

NOVELS
Billy's Bones
By That Sin Fell the Angels
Murderous Requiem
Screwups

NOVELLAS
The Christmas Wager
The Dogs of Cyberwar
Saturn in Retrograde
We're Both Straight, Right?

Published by DREAMSPINNER PRESS
http://www.dreamspinnerpress.com

Screwups

JAMIE FESSENDEN

Dreamspinner Press

Published by
Dreamspinner Press
5032 Capital Circle SW
Suite 2, PMB# 279
Tallahassee, FL 32305-7886
USA
http://www.dreamspinnerpress.com/

This is a work of fiction. Names, characters, places, and incidents either are the product of author imagination or are used fictitiously, and any resemblance to actual persons, living or dead, business establishments, events, or locales is entirely coincidental.

Screwups
© 2014 Jamie Fessenden.

Cover Art
© 2014 Aaron Anderson.
aaronbydesign55@gmail.com
Cover content is for illustrative purposes only and any person depicted on the cover is a model.

All rights reserved. This book is licensed to the original purchaser only. Duplication or distribution via any means is illegal and a violation of international copyright law, subject to criminal prosecution and upon conviction, fines, and/or imprisonment. Any eBook format cannot be legally loaned or given to others. No part of this book may be reproduced or transmitted in any form or by any means, electronic or mechanical, including photocopying, recording, or by any information storage and retrieval system, without the written permission of the Publisher, except where permitted by law. To request permission and all other inquiries, contact Dreamspinner Press, 5032 Capital Circle SW, Suite 2, PMB# 279, Tallahassee, FL 32305-7886, USA, or http://www.dreamspinnerpress.com/.

ISBN: 978-1-62798-659-5
Digital ISBN: 978-1-62798-660-1

Printed in the United States of America
First Edition
March 2014

Dedicated to Eaton House and all the Eatonites who made my time there so magical.

Chapter One

University of New Hampshire, 1996

JAKE COULDN'T remember the last time he'd been so nervous, sitting in the middle of the lounge on a beat-up wooden chair with upholstery like frayed orange burlap. And it was so lame! The three people seated at the table in front of him weren't parents or professors or any other real authority figures. They were just college students like him. But right now he desperately needed them to like him. Otherwise he was fucked.

"I admit," the girl said, "I'm a little puzzled by why you want to move into this dorm." She was small—"petite" might be the word—with long, jet-black hair and olive skin. She looked vaguely Mediterranean, though judging by the way she talked, she was probably as much a New Hampster as he was. Jake thought her name might be Eva.

"Like I said, I love art."

"But you're majoring in business?" She sounded skeptical, as if he might be putting them on. A lot of people reacted that way. Jake seemed so clean-cut, so conservative… so *boring*. How could he possibly be an artist?

It probably didn't help that, with the themed dorms like Eaton House being exempt from the housing lottery, a lot of students tried to get in, even if they weren't particularly artistic. Eaton House was the creative arts dorm and it was supposed to be just for students who were involved in the arts.

"I'm taking an oil painting class."

The chubby guy to her right—Paul, if Jake remembered correctly—asked him, "Have you taken other art classes before that one?"

Jake hadn't. His father hadn't allowed it in his freshman and sophomore years. This was the first year he'd let Jake take a class in something "useless," as he liked to put it. And that was only because Jake had taken more credits last year than he needed to, so he would be ahead of schedule.

Jake had been fidgeting with the sketchbook in his lap, not really wanting to show his work to these strangers. But the other guy on the panel was looking skeptical too. He was going to lose his chance if he couldn't prove he really was an artist. "I brought my sketchbook," he said, trying to dodge the question. "I've been sketching since I was in high school."

He held the book out to them and for one sickening moment, they just glanced at it, seeming disinterested. Then the third boy leaned forward and took it. This guy Jake had no trouble at all remembering. His name was Danny, and he was beautiful. The moment Jake had walked into the dorm lounge, he'd been struck by Danny's delicate features, smooth golden skin, and hazel eyes that seemed smoky and almost gray, smoldering beneath long, unkempt light-brown bangs.

Jake hadn't told anybody he was gay. Certainly not his father—not after what had happened with Tom. His older brothers were just as bad as his father. And he didn't have any close friends now. But the moment he'd seen Danny and been introduced to him, Jake's jaw had hit the floor. He'd probably even drooled a little. Had Danny noticed? Christ, he hoped not.

Danny flipped through Jake's sketchbook slowly, looking at rough sketches of nudes from books of photography taken out of the campus library—sketches Jake had shown to Professor Harriman to get into his oil-painting class but nobody else. To his immense relief, Danny raised his eyebrows as if he was impressed. "Pretty good," he said.

He handed the sketchbook to Eva and she flipped through it a little before saying, "The thing is, Jake, we have one other student who interviewed to get into the dorm this semester...."

Jake felt his heart sink. "In other words, 'no thanks.'" He knew it was a childish reaction, but he no longer cared. He just needed to get the hell out of there before he was humiliated any further.

He could always find other ways to connect to the art community on campus, of course. But he knew, with his tight schedule, it was unlikely. He'd hoped he could spend his last couple of years in college surrounded by the life he'd always longed for, even if he had to spend most of his time in tedious classes he loathed about accounting and business management.

But his hope died as he saw the look of cold disapproval on Paul's face and, even worse, Eva's look of pity. *Poor boring future corporate drone. Isn't it cute that he thought he might have some artistic sensibility?*

Only Danny seemed to be taking him seriously, as if he hadn't entirely dismissed him. Not yet, anyway.

Eva gave him a smile that might have been intended to be reassuring as she handed the sketchbook back to him. Paul didn't seem interested in looking at it. "I'm just saying we need to think it over. We'll let you know what we decide in a day or two."

DANNY WATCHED Jake take back his sketchbook, looking as though he'd just been told his life's work was total shit. But it wasn't shit. Danny wasn't a visual artist himself—music was his thing—but he thought the sketches were really good. And sexy. Somehow, this guy who looked like he'd be more at home in a military academy, who'd been dumb enough to show up to this interview in a *tie*, for goddess's sake, had managed to make the nude men in his sketchbook look amazingly hot. There had been women in the sketchbook too, and they'd been well done from a technical standpoint, but the men….

Jake was gay. He had to be.

"What the fuck?" Paul asked the moment Jake closed the door in the glass divider that separated the lounge from the upper hall and headed down the stairs. "He takes an oil painting class and suddenly he's declaring himself an *artiste*!"

"You didn't even look at his sketches," Eva pointed out.

"I don't need to look at them. Everything about the guy screams 'uptight conservative asshole.'"

"He didn't seem like an asshole to me."

"He was just trying to impress us, so he could get out of the lottery. He should have tried Richardson." Richardson's theme was politics, and it was the odd duck of the minidorms, housing mostly conservative students.

While they bickered back and forth, Danny got up out of his seat and went over to the piano in the corner. Playing always helped him relax, and for some reason he couldn't quite define, the interview with Jake had made him very tense. It wasn't anything the guy had done, really. He seemed nice enough and, despite Paul's assertion, Danny thought he was sincere. The drawings in his sketchbook hadn't been a put-on to get into the dorm. They showed talent and passion.

That passion was part of the problem, Danny reflected. Jake was gay. If the sketchbook hadn't been enough to convince him, the look Jake gave him when they were first introduced certainly was. And the guy was *hot*. Close-cropped red hair and just a smattering of freckles, mixed with handsome features and a tall, muscular physique—the epitome of the all-American boy. Plus soft baby-blue eyes that made Danny want to melt.

Just like Steve's eyes—*too* much like Steve's eyes. Jake reminded Danny entirely too much of Steve. The red hair, the athlete's body... even the freckles were the same. That, in and of itself, was reason for Danny to say "no" to letting Jake move into the dorm. He'd gone to college to escape from Steve and the hell the guy had put him through.

But Jake wasn't Steve. And it wasn't fair to slap him down because of a chance resemblance to someone in Danny's past. Getting into Eaton House was obviously a huge deal to Jake. And Eva had been lying. There wasn't another candidate for the open slot. There *had* been, but he'd apparently been attracted to the dorm, thinking it would be a great place to get stoned all the time. He didn't even have a major yet and really hadn't seemed artistically inclined.

"What about you?" Eva called to him, interrupting Beethoven's *Moonlight* Sonata. "Did you like him?"

Danny played a bit quieter as he mulled the question over. "I suppose so."

"You think we should let him in?" Paul asked incredulously. "Don't forget, Mark's been pushing for the single that just opened up. You could end up with this guy as your roommate!"

The mention of his asshole roommate made Danny stop playing, a sour look on his face. Mark was a homophobic jerk, and Danny hoped he did get into the single. He was sick of Mark's snide comments and looks of disgust. Jake *had* to be better than him.

Of course, if Mark moved into the single, Danny could have his own room. At least for a semester. But then he recalled the look of desperate pleading he'd seen in Jake's eyes....

Oh hell.

"Sure," he responded. "Why not?"

CHAPTER TWO

WHEN JAKE received the e-mail telling him he'd made it into Eaton House, he stared at it in shock for a long time. Then he whooped and danced around his ugly gray-tiled and eggshell-blue-brick room for ten minutes. Fortunately, his roommate was out somewhere, so he didn't need to explain.

The e-mail told him that he'd be receiving his room assignment within a few days, but Jake couldn't sit still that long. He had to walk over to Eaton House this very minute and see if he could sort out which room would be his. Even if he couldn't find it, he'd be able to walk around, knowing that it was now *his* dorm. Maybe there would be people hanging out in the lounges.

The dorm was fairly empty when Jake wandered in. It was still midafternoon, so it wasn't too surprising that most of the students were in classes or otherwise away from their rooms, but he was still disappointed. He'd hoped to find the place vibrant and full of activity—people doing performance art in the lounges, playing music, painting, *something* artistic. Instead, Jake contented himself with wandering through the halls, admiring the brightly colored, and admittedly somewhat garish, murals. Some appeared to be old and painted over in places with new designs. Others were half finished, but somehow that made them even better, because it made them feel like living, growing things.

In the downstairs lounge, Jake came across an empty refrigerator box that somebody had painted to look like a puppet theater, with a cutout front that had curtains hanging in it. There was nobody squatting inside with puppets on their hands—Jake checked. The phone booth had been painted blue and there was a light on top of it. The words "POLICE BOX" were painted in white along the top of the doorframe. The rest of the lounge was dedicated to a couch and two chairs, pulled up in front of a television. Boring.

The upstairs lounge was much better. It held a baby grand piano and an easel with the beginnings of an oil painting on it. The oil painting appeared to be a nude woman, which made Jake wonder if students actually posed naked in the lounge. If they did, would it be blocked off? Or could anyone who wanted to come in and sketch or paint too? That would be incredible.

He didn't know how to play piano, but since he had nothing better to do, he sat down in front of the keyboard and started plunking on the keys, trying to see if he could make a chord. His musical talent was severely lacking. But maybe somebody could teach him some basic stuff. That would be cool.

"Oh, hey."

Jake yanked his hands away from the keyboard like a kid caught sneaking a cookie.

It was Danny. He was standing in the doorway, leaning in as if to see who was violating the piano so brutally. He was also shirtless—less just about everything, in fact. The only thing he had on was a pair of khaki shorts. He was even barefoot. That seemed odd, considering the fact that it was almost October. But then the dorms tended to keep the temperature up really high.

"It's okay," Danny said, laughing. "You're allowed to play it."

"I don't know how to play," Jake replied, sure his pale, freckled face had gone beet red.

"Yeah, I could tell." Danny entered the lounge and walked up to him. He was a small guy and not very muscular, but his body was well proportioned and his skin was perfect—the color of milk and honey, and not a blemish or scar to be seen anywhere. As he drew nearer, Jake couldn't help but notice that the shorts rode awfully low on Danny's hips… and there wasn't any underwear waistband showing. Danny looked down at him with an amused expression, those gray eyes peering out from behind unruly bangs. "That's okay. I can't draw to save my life."

"Can you play piano?" Jake asked.

"It's my major."

"Can I hear something?" Jake wasn't sure if he was being obnoxious. Probably the guy was asked that all the time.

But Danny just shrugged and said, "If you want."

Jake slid off the bench and allowed Danny to take his place. The piece he played was beautiful and mesmerizing, delicate one moment and then flowing rapidly along like water the next, rising to a sweeping crescendo and then falling down like rain. Jake felt himself swept up by the music and carried along with it. He didn't dare say a word to disturb the effect it had on him, even after the music stopped, until Danny set his hands in his lap and said with a shy smile, "Well, that's the piece I've been practicing this week. It still needs work."

"What was it?"

"*Clair de lune*," Danny replied, "by Debussy. It's actually a pretty easy piece. You've never heard it before?"

"No."

Danny laughed, but it was a warm, friendly sound—not at all mean-spirited or belittling. "Well, you'll probably be sick to death of it before too long. I practice a *lot* up here."

Jake couldn't imagine ever getting sick of hearing Danny play, but he just smiled and nodded. "I just got the e-mail saying I was accepted into the dorm," he said.

"I know. I sent it."

"Then thanks."

Danny stood up and said, "Wait 'til you hear the bad news."

"What's that?" Jake asked, suddenly anxious that they'd changed their minds about letting him in after all. Had he left his room too soon to get a follow-up e-mail? *Sorry, bud. We meant to send that first e-mail to the other dude.*

But Danny stuck out his hand, inviting him to shake it, and said, "I'm your new roommate."

A LOOK of surprise flashed across Jake's handsome face, but then he smiled and shook Danny's hand. "Hey, roomie!"

He didn't seem displeased. Thank God. Mark had acted like rooming with Danny was a prison sentence and he couldn't escape fast enough. Of course, Jake hadn't heard the rumors yet. Give it time.

"I wanted to warn you," Danny continued, "because you're probably going to get a letter or something from the bursar's office telling you you got a single. But my old roommate threw a hissy fit and said *he* wanted the single and he had seniority, so...."

Jake shrugged. "Whatever. I don't mind sharing."

"Do you want to see the room?"

The excitement that flashed into Jake's eyes was adorable, like a little kid being asked if he wanted to ride the pony. "Sure!"

His excitement didn't let up, even when he saw that the room was pretty much like any other dorm room: two metal-framed, institutional beds against opposite walls of the room—they could be stacked as bunk beds, but Danny hated sleeping above or below someone—and two desks with chairs. There were a couple of small bookcases, but that was about it.

"This is great!" Jake said.

"It's the same as any other room."

"The rooms in Christensen are all brick and cement. They're ugly as fuck." The walls in Eaton House were plaster, which Danny supposed was better than brick. And they were just off-white, instead of the hideous pastels he'd seen in the other dorms. So maybe Jake had a point.

Only Danny's side of the room had any decorations on the walls—a poster of a piano keyboard with a red rose lying on it and other posters of sword & sorcery wizards like the ones he enjoyed playing in the weekly Dungeons & Dragons game. The one thing he felt embarrassed about was the calendar he'd picked up in Portsmouth with a different naked man for each month. Mark had hated it, but that was the point. Danny had only put it up because Mark insisted on having one with naked women on it.

Now he saw Jake's eyes settle on the stupid thing, and he gave a slightly nervous laugh. "Oh, sorry about that. Um... I suppose this might be a good time to tell you that I'm gay."

Jake just shrugged. "That's cool."

He looked a little uncomfortable. Danny wondered if the initial impression he'd gotten of Jake as a closet case was wrong. Maybe the guy really was straight. Of course, someone who was really closeted might feel uncomfortable rooming with a guy who was openly gay too. Did the fact that Jake didn't respond "I'm straight," mean that he wasn't? Or did it just mean he assumed it was obvious?

Who knows? As long as he doesn't try to beat me up. But that wasn't really the reason Danny was worried about it.

"Are you into role-playing games or something?" Jake asked.

"You mean the wizard posters?"

"And the D&D books."

Danny laughed. "Yeah, I am. Paul—he was the other guy at your interview—is the dungeon master for the game I'm in. Eva's in it too. She's a halfling thief. I have a human mage named Kareth."

"What's a halfling?"

"A hobbit," Danny replied. "But they couldn't get the rights to use 'hobbit' in the game, so they call it a 'halfling.'" Jake still looked confused. Was it possible he'd never heard of *The Hobbit*? It was hard to imagine. Danny plowed ahead anyway, though he was rapidly losing hope. "Do you play?"

Jake shook his head, looking a bit lost. "I guess I'd be willing to try it."

"You don't have to, if you don't want to."

"Would Paul even want me in the game?" Jake asked skeptically. "He didn't seem to like me much."

Danny shrugged and flopped down on his bed, folding his hands behind his head. "Don't worry about it. I think he got beat up by jocks in high school or something."

The moment he said it, he regretted it. Jake pinched his lips together tightly for a moment, perhaps in an attempt to smile, but Danny got the impression that he'd hurt his feelings. "Do I look like a jock?"

"Sorry." Danny suddenly felt self-conscious. "It's just... you're kind of jacked."

"I'm not 'jacked.' I mean, yeah, I play soccer a bit and I like to swim...." Jake sat down on the bare mattress that was to be his. "Is that... I never thought of myself as a *jock*. I don't play a lot of sports, and I don't work out or anything."

"I'm sorry. I didn't mean to be an asshole. I just... I had a bad experience myself with one of the athletes in my high school."

"Did he beat you up?"

"No." Danny really didn't want to talk about this with someone he'd just met. Why did stupid shit always have to come out of his mouth whenever he opened it? He sat up and tried to think of something to change the subject. "Hey, some of our friends down in Mass. invited us to play in their LARP." When Jake's blank expression made it clear he had no idea what a LARP was, Danny explained, "That's a Live-Action Role-Playing game—LARP. If we end up going, and you wanted to join us, you'd probably be a kick-ass fighter."

Jake nodded, but he didn't really seem all that interested. He glanced around at the empty walls and bookcase on his side of the room and asked, "So when do I get to move in?"

Danny shrugged. "They'll probably take a few days to process all the paperwork, but nobody would care if you moved in right away. You could sleep here tonight, if you want."

"I want," Jake said.

It bothered Danny how happy he was to see Jake's face light up in a smile again.

CHAPTER THREE

JAKE MOVED into Eaton House that afternoon. He hadn't planned on bringing everything over that day. He figured he'd just bring his pillow and blankets, toothbrush, shampoo, a few clothes.... But it turned out he didn't really have much stuff after all. It only took about an hour for him to pack everything up into a few boxes and garbage bags. Feeling a slight twinge of guilt, he left a note for his roommate, explaining why he'd suddenly disappeared. But really, they'd barely ever seen each other in the few weeks since the beginning of the semester. He knew the guy's name was Roger and he was a chemistry major, but that was about it. At least he'd been nice enough to let Jake use his computer for e-mail.

Jake ate alone at the dining hall and then came back to Christensen to call Danny on the phone in the lounge. Danny had told him to do that. Eva had a car, and he was convinced he could press her into service. When Jake protested that he barely knew her and didn't want to inconvenience her, Danny shrugged off his objections by saying, "Maybe *you* don't know her, but she's *my* best friend. Besides, I have dirt on her she wouldn't want made public."

True to Danny's word, he and Eva pulled up in front of Christensen about twenty minutes later. The three of them were able to load everything in, haul it over to Eaton, and unload in less time than it had taken to pack it up.

And just like that, Jake was an Eatonite.

Despite her obvious skepticism during the interview, Eva didn't seem to have any issues with him now. She hung out in the room with them as he made up his bed and unpacked his clothes.

"I can't believe Danny already hit you up about our D&D game when you'd only been here, like, five minutes," she commented, sitting cross-legged on the end of Danny's bed.

Danny was sitting on Jake's desk—on *it*, not the chair in front of it—looking through Jake's meager collection of sci-fi and fantasy novels with unabashed curiosity. "I wasn't trying to recruit him," he said defensively. "I was just saying he could join us if he wanted to."

"He probably thinks we're freaks now, or part of a cult."

Jake laughed to hide his discomfort at being discussed so openly. "No...." Truthfully, he did think they were a little weird. But that was good. He needed weird. Ever since he'd fucked up his friendship with Tom, his life had been completely normal and boring and lonely as hell. He knew his time at Eaton House would be way too short. A couple of years from now, he'd be graduating and on his way to becoming a corporate drone with a lot of earning potential and little else that appealed to him. But maybe if he was lucky, he'd be able to pretend his life had some kind of meaning for just a little while.

"So what are *your* hobbies?" Danny asked him.

"I don't know." He really didn't. "I like to read, I guess. And sketch."

"Didn't you say you liked to play soccer and swim?"

Jake smirked at him. "Well, yeah. But just if someone has a game on, or it's a hot day. It's not like they're really hobbies."

"Can you sketch me?" Eva asked. She struck a pose on the bed that might have been intended to be seductive, though it was rather comical. Or maybe she'd intended it to be. Jake wasn't sure if he should laugh or not.

Before he could think of a response, Danny said, "You're not his type."

Jake felt his blood go cold, just as it had when Danny first told him he was gay. The familiar panic welled up inside him, and he felt like he was back in the truck stop with Tom. *Does he know?*

It was all well and good for Tom and Danny to tell the world about themselves, but Jake.... He would have been thrown out of the house in high school, and even now he knew he'd be cut off. The degree he'd spent the last two years studying for, living in this dorm, it would all be yanked out from under him.

"You don't think I'm pretty enough?" Eva asked, pretending to be insulted. At least, Jake assumed she was pretending by the way she was hamming it up, with her hand splayed across her petite breasts. "Jake! You think I'm pretty, don't you?"

Jake forced himself to laugh along with the joke, despite the way his heart was pounding. "Of course I do. I'd be happy to sketch you."

THAT WAS close, Danny thought. The joke had slipped out. He hadn't been thinking. And now it was clear that this was *not* a joke to make around Jake. The combined look of panic and anger that had flashed in Jake's eyes for just a moment... that was a clear "back off" if Danny had ever seen one.

So he backpedaled. "I'm just saying I think he prefers women with bigger breasts, judging by his sketchbook."

"Shut up!" Eva said, pretending to be shocked. "My breasts are perfectly shaped and scrumptious. Aren't they, Jake?"

Jake flushed and busied himself tucking in the bottom corners of his bedspread. "They look fine."

"There! You see?"

"The women in the sketchbook are just ones I saw in a book of photography," Jake added defensively. "I wasn't thinking about their breasts."

No, I'll bet you weren't.

"Well," Eva said, "you can sketch me in the nude sometime, if you want a live model."

"Slut," Danny teased.

"Oh shut up. You're—" He could see where she was going by the look in her eyes. And he knew it would be justified. *Don't say it. Please don't.* As if she could read his thoughts, Eva veered away. "You're just jealous because *you* want to pose for him, but he clearly prefers me."

Thank you.

Danny made a rude noise, but privately he thought posing for Jake could be... interesting. Would Jake be turned on by seeing him naked? Danny mentally kicked himself for hoping he would be. *That's the last thing I need.*

Jake was looking mortified by the whole discussion. "I just met you guys. Do we have to talk about people getting naked already?"

Danny laughed, but he was thinking about the fact that he always slept nude. Would Jake be upset by that? Mark had been, so Danny had done his best to slip in and out of bed without flashing him. But he'd be damned if he'd be forced to wear underwear or pajamas in his own bed. He didn't even like to wear underwear during the *day*.

"If you don't like people being naked around you," Eva said, "You're going to hate the bathrooms."

Jake had been about to sit down on his newly made bed, but now he stopped, his ass hovering a foot above the mattress a second before he straightened up again. He looked worried. "What about the bathrooms?"

CHAPTER FOUR

"YOU'RE FUCKING kidding me," Jake said, looking at the two empty shower stalls as if a naked woman might suddenly leap out of one.

Danny shook his head. "Nope. Co-ed bathrooms. That's why there are no urinals—only closed stalls—and the showers all have curtains."

Jake could see that and it was totally freaking him out. How the hell was he going to take a dump if there were *girls* wandering around outside his stall? "Yeah, but… not at the same time, right? There's some kind of system for when girls are in here and when boys are in here?"

Eva snorted. "Hello?" She gave him a little wave. "You do remember I'm a girl? And I'm standing right here beside you?"

"You're not going to pee in front of me now, are you?" Jake asked, his face screwed up in distaste.

"I don't have to go just now, but thanks for asking."

Danny clamped a consoling hand on Jake's shoulder. "If you really can't hack it, one of the downstairs wings has a bathroom with a little cardboard sign on it, so you can flip it to 'Boy in Bathroom' when you go in."

Jake thought he might just have to do that. This was seriously wigging him out. Had there been anything about this in the description of the minidorms in the student handbook? He couldn't remember. He probably would have skipped right on by it, even if there had been. He'd been too excited by the idea of an art dorm.

Eva took him by the hand. "Come on. Let's get you out of here before you have an embolism or something."

It occurred to Jake at that moment that, with her holding his hand and Danny's hand still resting on his shoulder, this was the most physical contact he'd had in years. Danny's hand felt incredibly hot, as if it might burn his skin, but as Eva pulled him forward it dropped away, leaving a peculiarly cold, empty sensation on his shoulder.

As they left the bathroom, a tall blonde girl walked in, causing Jake to walk a little faster on the way out.

Over the next few days, the bathrooms proved to be a challenge. Initially, he tried following Danny's suggestion to use the downstairs bathroom, but he soon tired of the stupid sign. On one occasion, he walked in while the sign was flipped to "Boy in Bathroom," but apparently the girl in there had forgotten to change it. She went apeshit, as if it was *his* fault she hadn't set the sign correctly. Then one morning while he was showering, one of the girls outside—it turned out the entire wing was occupied by girls—kept shouting at him to hurry up. He really didn't need that shit first thing in the morning.

So he gave up and just used the bathroom down the hall from his and Danny's room. It was embarrassing at first. Eva and another girl named Kelly wandered in one afternoon while he was sitting on the toilet. They couldn't see him, of course, but he was so mortified by the thought of making obscene noises while they were there that he ended up leaving, flushing first to disguise the fact that he hadn't actually gone to the bathroom. Instead, he ran to the bathroom in McConnell before his class.

The first time he walked in on Eva stepping out of the shower—there were tiny changing areas inside the curtains, but nobody seemed inclined to use them—he nearly had a heart attack. His instinct was to apologize profusely and flee, but she smiled at him and said, "Hey," as if it wasn't a big deal. It wasn't—to her. Jake pretended the reason he'd come in was just to wash his hands, ignoring his bursting bladder while Eva toweled off and chatted at him about the D&D game they had scheduled that weekend.

That was another thing. It quickly became clear to Jake that the dorm had several cliques. In high school it had always seemed to him that there were just four groups of kids. There were the popular kids; the jocks, who were also popular, but obsessed with sports; the geeky kids into art and computers and stuff like that; and then everybody else. Here he was finding subdivisions of the "geeky" crowd. First of all, this dorm didn't have a lot of kids into computers. Sure, there was a terminal in the upstairs lounge for connecting to the miniframe on campus—the college had a

VAX/VMS system that a lot of students had e-mail and LISTSERV accounts on—and one student in the dorm was rumored to have a Mac Color Classic that everybody begged for time to play games on. But computers really weren't a big thing here.

Instead, there were rough divisions along majors. The students majoring in art—as in sketching and painting—didn't really distinguish themselves from the music majors, but Jake noticed that the theater majors tended to remain somewhat apart, and as a rule the others regarded them as vain and self-absorbed.

Then there were other less formal groupings. The TV and VCR in the downstairs lounge were in constant use from late afternoon until late at night. The "TV crowd," as Danny and Eva called them, were friendly enough to Jake, but he soon found them dull. He hadn't fought to get into Eaton House so he could sit on his ass all day watching bootlegged copies of *Twin Peaks* on VHS. There was also the "hippie crowd" downstairs. They pretty much avoided everyone else, which might have been for the best, because Jake heard they were on some kind of antibathing kick, insisting water needed to be conserved and soap wasn't environmentally friendly.

Upstairs, there were two groups. One hovered around the guy who owned the Mac. His name was Bryan, and he was clearly the leader of the "popular crowd"—if such a thing could be said to exist in Eaton House. He presided over a constant stream of students going in and out of his room like a king holding court. And then there was Danny and his group of friends, most of whom lived in Danny and Jake's wing.

They were the geeks among the geeks.

Well, more precisely they were called the "gaming crowd" by everyone else in the dorm. And that was certainly accurate. Danny, Eva, and Paul were at the core of it, and they organized one big continuing game of D&D on Saturdays, along with some random one-offs on some Sundays or in the evenings during the week, featuring RPG games like Gamma World, in which everyone was mutated from atomic fallout, and Call of Cthulhu, in which everybody eventually went insane, if they lived that long. Danny and his friends also ravenously devoured fantasy novels—the current favorite was a trilogy by Mercedes Lackey—and Paul had a collection of fantasy movies on

VHS that they watched now and then, on the rare occasions they could pry the TV away from the clutches of the TV crowd.

Not really stuff Jake could relate to, although he agreed to read the first Mercedes Lackey book, after much coercing from Eva. And although everyone in the dorm was friendly and willing to chat in the lounge or even invite Jake to hang out in their rooms a bit, he still found himself drawn back to Danny and Eva. Especially to Danny. The guy was just so… cute. The way he smiled, the way he laughed, the way he peered out at Jake from underneath his unruly bangs, his eyes full of mischief. He was adorable. And the fact that he slept naked was driving Jake insane.

That first night, Danny had stood by his bed in nothing but his shorts—his usual attire whenever he was in the dorm—waiting… for something. Jake had stripped down to his underwear before he noticed that Danny hadn't moved for a while.

"What?" he asked.

"I'm just waiting for you to get into bed so I can turn out the light."

They both had lamps on their desks, so Jake couldn't make much sense out of that. "Just turn out your light and get into bed. I'll turn mine out in a minute."

"I just…." Danny looked really uncomfortable for a moment, finally blurting out "I don't wear anything to bed. Mark always wanted me to wait until the lights were off before I stripped."

Jake's heart fluttered at the thought of Danny stripping—along with a couple of twitches in other parts of his body—but he tried to cover it up by frowning. "That's pretty stupid."

"Well, you seemed uncomfortable about people being naked in front of you."

"That was different!" Jake protested. "That was in the middle of the day. And we were talking about girls showering and stuff like that. I don't care how you sleep."

"You're sure?"

Not knowing quite why he said it, because it was a lie, Jake replied, "I sleep naked too."

"Oh!" Danny looked surprised, as if it had never occurred to him that Jake might do that. "Cool."

With that, he shucked his shorts and kicked them into a corner. Jake watched him out of the corner of his eye as long as he could without being obvious. God, he had a beautiful ass! Like the rest of him, it was smooth and flawless, and it was just a hint lighter than the rest of his golden skin. His dick was nicely shaped too, nestled in a small brown patch of pubic hair, a shade darker than the hair on his head.

Jake found himself stiffening in his boxer shorts and remembered that he was supposed to strip now if he wanted to keep up the pretense that he slept nude. But he sure as hell couldn't do that with a semi!

"I need to take a leak," he said, feeling lame, because he'd just gotten back from the bathroom.

When he reached for his pants, Danny said, "You can just walk to the bathroom in your boxers. Nobody will care."

Jake hesitated but put his pants on anyway. He would have felt too self-conscious walking down the hall in his underwear, especially if he was tenting the front of it. Since he hadn't gotten over his discomfort with the bathroom, he ended up not going in, standing in the hall outside the bathroom door, feeling like an idiot. But it wasn't long before things were under control again. He returned to the room and stripped. He left the light on until after he'd climbed into bed, conscious that Danny was checking him out, even though his eyes were fixed on the wall. Jake wondered if he'd been that "subtle" when Danny had undressed. Probably. But as long as they were both willing to keep up the pretense that they weren't interested, they'd be able to live together.

Lying in bed in the dark, Jake was intensely aware of the feel of the cotton sheets on his bare ass and dick. He'd never slept naked before and the sensations instantly made him hard again.

It was a rough night. Eventually, he fell asleep, but he awoke to the feeling that he was pissing the bed, though it was squirting out of his hard cock in pulses, wave after wave of it. There was no way to stop it and he didn't really want to, despite the fact that he'd have to scrunch against the wall afterward to get out of the wet spot. It was the first wet dream he'd had since he was thirteen.

CHAPTER FIVE

LIVING WITH Jake was pretty cool, especially having endured Mark for a couple of semesters. Not only was Jake a fuckload more pleasant to look at, but he accepted Danny being naked before bed and first thing in the morning without batting an eye. Mark had been a huge pain in the ass about it, even complaining to the resident assistant that Danny kept "waving his faggy dick around." Fortunately, the RA was a stoner who didn't much care for the rules as long as nobody bothered him. He told Mark to chill. Sleeping in the buff was just one of those things you sometimes had to cope with when you had roommates.

Of course, that just made Mark worse. But now the jerk was in a room of his own and more or less out of Danny's hair. If only he could be prevented from passing his poisonous gossip along to Jake.

Yeah.... Fat chance of that.

Jake wasn't perfect. He just stared blankly at Danny and his friends when they talked about their latest gaming escapades and didn't seem interested in joining them. His idea of "music" was country and western, which seemed to consist of two songs—one sung by a man and one sung by a woman—played at varying speeds. And he was still a nervous wreck about the bathroom. He seemed to be okay with showering, though he was careful to stay hidden behind the slime-covered curtain Danny and his friends left open because it was too disgusting to rub up against. But Jake couldn't use the toilet if there was a girl in the bathroom. Danny couldn't decide if it was pathetic or kind of cute.

Danny was finding a lot about Jake cute, unfortunately, and it worried him. Steve had completely fucked Danny's life up in high school, and Jake was entirely too much like Steve. Both gorgeous and athletic. Both sweet, when Danny was alone with them. Both clearly interested, when nobody but Danny was looking. And both total closet cases. Danny had learned the hard way what happened to openly gay kids who got too close to guys terrified of being outed.

Still, Jake hadn't actually done anything that Danny could complain about. He'd been accommodating and easy to get along with. There hadn't been any conflict at all.

Until Danny stole his towel.

The thing was, there was a tradition in Eaton House—sort of an initiation. It had been done to Danny when he'd moved in two years ago, and it had been done to pretty much everybody he'd seen move in since then. Or at least the guys. By unspoken consent, the girls were considered immune to this brand of harassment. It went like this: one day when a guy was in the shower, someone would casually walk off with his towel. Then everyone in the wing would gather in the hall to see if he had the balls to run the gauntlet to his room. Danny wasn't actually sure what would happen if someone refused to do it—nobody ever had. It was stupid and juvenile, but in a dorm where students often posed naked in the lounge for art projects, it wasn't generally considered a big deal.

However, looking back on it later, he realized he should have known that Jake would prove to be the exception.

It wasn't particularly planned. One Tuesday morning, Jake woke up late and had to rush to class without showering. When he returned to the room late in the afternoon, he complained to Danny that he was feeling pretty grungy and wanted to grab a shower before dinner. Danny, Eva, and Paul were camped out in the room, discussing the logistics of getting to the LARP in Massachusetts, but when they saw Jake strip down to his pants and grab his towel, they realized they were being handed an opportunity that might not come back around for a while. It fell to Danny, of course, as his roommate, to sneak in when Jake was under the spray and snag his pants, underwear, and towel.

By the time Jake discovered the betrayal, word had spread and the hallway had filled up with people from both upstairs wings. There was a minute of quiet after the shower was turned off and then Jake's voice bellowed, "Danny!"

Everybody in the hall laughed… except Danny. Suddenly, he was no longer sure this was a good idea. But it was too late. The bathroom door was yanked open and Jake strode into the hall, all traces of shyness forgotten in his fury. He was dripping wet and his skin was beet red from the heat of the shower… and from anger. All traces of Danny's chronically shy roommate had vanished, to be replaced by a guy with a lot more muscle than Danny had realized—a guy seething with fury. He stopped as his eyes fell on the crowd of students in the hall, but then he caught sight of Danny and jabbed his finger toward him. "You!"

Danny ran. He knew that look. That wasn't "Ha-ha, you got me!" That was "I'm gonna kill you, faggot!" There were too many people blocking the exit at the south end of the hall and Jake was blocking the exit in the other direction, so Danny did the only thing he could think of—he ran into their room.

He tried to lock the door behind him, but Jake was too fast. The door burst open, causing Danny to screech and jump away toward his bed. But there was nowhere else to go. In an instant, Jake had slammed the door and twisted the lock shut.

"Jake—"

Jake launched himself at Danny, throwing him backward onto the bed. Danny cried out, but the breath was knocked out of him as he hit the mattress. Jake pinned him down as people began to pound on the door and Eva could be heard on the other side shouting, "Someone get the RA!"

"You fucker!"

"It was just a fucking joke!"

Then something odd happened. Jake grabbed both of Danny's wrists and held him down against the mattress, but the blows Danny was expecting didn't come. Instead, Jake seemed to be rubbing his body all over Danny's. It felt sexual. *Is he going to rape me?*

Danny struggled against him, trying desperately not to whimper in fear. Jake looked down into his eyes, his face still flushed with anger. Then he scrunched up his nose as if he smelled something disgusting. "What are you…?" He stopped moving. "Don't look at me like that!"

"Like what?" Danny asked, his voice trembling.

"I'm not gonna hurt you!"

Terrified, Danny barely managed to choke out, "Then why are you on top of me?"

"To get you wet!"

Danny looked up into Jake's eyes and realized the anger was fading. Now Jake looked more concerned than angry. "I was pissed… but I wasn't gonna *hurt* you. I just wanted to get you all wet."

Suddenly, Danny began to cry. He wasn't quite sure why—it was humiliating as fuck—but he couldn't stop. He rolled his head to the side, trying to hide his face from Jake's gaze, but they were too close together. He could feel Jake's breath in gentle puffs against his cheek.

Then Jake did something else baffling. He let go of Danny's wrists and wrapped his arms around Danny's chest, pulling him into a tight embrace. He breathed into Danny's ear, "Don't…. I was just trying to get back at you, not…. Jesus, I wasn't gonna beat you up or anything."

Jake's bare skin was hot and wet against his chest, his cheek warm against Danny's cheek, and his breath tickled Danny's ear. Danny's fear was subsiding and he was surprised by how good it felt to be held like this. He didn't want Jake to let go. He just wanted to lie like this for a while. Possibly forever.

At this worst possible moment, someone punched the lock combination and threw the door open. Danny felt Jake flinch, but he didn't move.

"Um…. Danny?" It was Sonny, the RA. "Are you okay?"

Jake slowly lifted himself up on his elbows—not exactly off Danny, but enough so Sonny could see Danny's face. Jake didn't acknowledge the RA himself. He kept his gaze on Danny.

Danny blinked his eyes quickly, trying to clear the tears out of them. "I'm fine."

"Jake," Sonny said cautiously, "maybe you should get off him."

Jake was still looking down, and Danny saw a look of panic flash into his eyes. At the same instant, he became aware of just why Jake was panicked by the thought of standing up. "It's okay, Sonny. We just need to talk for a minute. Can you close the door, please?"

"You sure?"

Danny could see Eva and several others trying to peer over Sonny's shoulder. "We're fine. Just give us a minute."

Sonny reluctantly obeyed and once the door was closed again, Jake breathed a sigh of relief. "Thanks."

"No problem."

Jake rolled off onto his back, exposing the massive erection he'd been hiding. Danny took a good look at it, figuring he'd earned the privilege. Like the rest of Jake, it was nicely proportioned and looked... delicious.

"You're still getting my bed wet," Danny commented.

"The mattress is fucking plastic. Don't you have any clean sheets?"

Danny just grunted, still feeling shaken. *It wasn't the same situation. Jake isn't Steve. He's not, damn it!*

"Are you okay?"

"I'm fine." Danny sat up and looked down at Jake, sorry to see that he was deflating. The surprising thing was that Jake didn't seem self-conscious about it. But perhaps he'd felt Danny's own erection through his shorts and figured they were both in the same boat. "Do you want to get dressed before I open the door?"

Jake shook his head. "Screw it. Just give me a minute."

They waited until they were both... presentable, before Danny stepped out into the hall. Everyone was still gathered there, watching the door anxiously, so he spread his arms wide to show them the wet front of his shorts. "He was just horsing around. He wanted to make sure he got me drenched."

As if taking that as his cue, Jake followed him out into the hall stark naked and announced, "All right! You wanted to see it. Here it is!"

He turned around to a chorus of cheers and catcalls. Sonny was still standing there, but he just hooted along with everyone else. How someone with such a complete disregard for the rules had ever become an RA, Danny had no idea. But that was why they liked him.

From that day forward, Jake rarely bothered closing the curtain when he showered.

CHAPTER SIX

"I DON'T know how I'm gonna keep all of this straight," Jake complained.

He'd finally agreed to join the Saturday D&D game, partly to get Eva to forgive him for terrorizing Danny a few days ago—something Jake still felt guilty about. That look of pure terror in Danny's face had really shaken him, and then Danny crying afterward....

Danny seemed to have forgiven him, thankfully. Though when he helped Jake roll a character on Friday night, he told him, "I've decided you're going to be a barbarian—a *wet* one."

Maybe "forgiven" wasn't quite the word.

But Jake didn't really mind being a barbarian. They seemed to be one of the easiest characters for players just starting out. They began the game with a relatively high amount of "hit points," which meant they didn't die as easily as mages and thieves, and they seemed to have a higher strength and did more damage with their weapons. They also had a high THAC0. Jake couldn't remember what a THAC0 was, but supposedly it was good.

But there was a lot of dice rolling, and Jake couldn't keep track of which die to use and what it was supposed to be for.

"Look," Paul explained with exaggerated patience, "just follow along with the story, and let Danny help you roll until you get the hang of it."

Paul was the "Dungeon Master," who was in control of everything. In addition to Danny and Eva, whose thief character was named Mala, the guy who lived in the room across the hall from Jake and Danny was playing. His name was Wallace and he had a paladin named Hastur. A paladin was some kind of anal-retentive religious knight.

The game took place in a land called Al-Qadim, which was like ancient Saudi Arabia or something. Since Jake—or Berengar, as his character was called—hadn't been with the party of adventurers when they first set out on their quest, Paul had to arrange for them to stop in a tavern for the night and bump into him.

Jake had hoped Paul would just have him sitting at the bar drinking, and the others would walk into the tavern and invite him to go with them. But apparently that wasn't exciting enough, so Paul had concocted a little side adventure at the tavern. Jake/Berengar was still sitting in the tavern when they walked in, but unknown to them, he'd been hired as a mercenary to kill Danny/Kareth by some mage who had a grudge against him. Of course, Paul didn't tell anybody about this except Jake, who immediately began to stress out about it. How was Danny supposed to help him if he didn't know what was going on?

Jake didn't care much about the game, but he was finding himself incredibly worried that he would somehow fuck it up—get all their characters killed, or otherwise ruin the "fun." Then they'd all end up hating him. So he fretted while Paul led the others through arriving at the tavern, eating, and settling in for the night.

Then Paul looked at him and said, "I need you to make a stealth roll."

Jake couldn't remember which die he was supposed to roll for that, so he started frantically scanned his character sheet. "Okay...."

"Roll a D20," Danny coached him. "Then add two, because of your dexterity."

Jake did as he was told.

Paul told the others, "You should all roll initiative," though they were already doing so.

Apparently, Eva/Mala's initiative beat Jake/Berengar's stealth, because she woke up and spotted him trying to sneak into their room while they were all sleeping. A fight ensued. The turns went back and forth, with Jake needing Danny's assistance at nearly every step. It was far from a fair fight, with three experienced players ganging up on him, and he felt his frustration mounting. Then after a particularly bad roll, Paul told him, "You lose twelve hit points."

"Damn it! That puts me at negative eleven!"

Paul blinked at him in bewilderment. "I told you to tell me when you got below ten hit points."

"Sorry, I forgot."

Paul groaned and threw his hands up in the air. "Well, now you're *dead*," he snapped, clearly disgusted. "You just screwed up your intro. You'll have to roll a new character."

"What?" Jake had been getting into the game, sort of. Once he'd more or less figured out which dice were for what kind of roll, it had started to get fun. But now that went completely out the window. He couldn't believe they'd kill him off so quickly. Had they just asked him to play for target practice? "That's bullshit! I thought I was supposed to be playing *with* you! You didn't tell me you were gonna kill me off!"

"I didn't *want* to kill you off," Paul protested. "You let your hit points go negative. *Really* negative."

"Because everybody attacked me."

"Of course we attacked you," Eva said patiently. "You were trying to kill Kareth in his sleep."

"Because Paul made me!"

"Just role-play it," Danny said.

Jake glared at him. "How the hell…. Fine!" He stood up and clutched his stomach. Then he toppled dramatically to the floor and sprawled out on the ugly brown-and-white striped lounge carpet, his head lolling to the side, eyes closed and tongue hanging out.

Danny, Eva, and Wallace all laughed—Paul, Jake was rapidly learning, had little sense of humor. Danny said, "Very dramatic, but I meant all of us." He turned to Paul. "There's got to be a way we can save him."

"We'd want to question him," Eva pointed out.

Paul grumbled but responded, "Fine. The barbarian assassin *appears* to be dead. What do you want to do?"

"I cast Cure Light Wounds on him," Wallace/Hastur announced.

"'Light Wounds,'" Paul muttered sarcastically.

Technically, Cure Light Wounds was supposed to be useless on a dead man, and Paul refused to allow the party to drag Jake/Berengar to a temple for resurrection, claiming the nearest one was two days' journey away and the idea of them going to that much trouble for someone who'd tried to kill one of them was ludicrous. But he allowed the healing spell to bring Berengar's hit points above negative five—unconscious and bleeding, but not dead—so they could spend another day at the tavern nursing him back to health.

Jake took his seat again beside Danny, and when he was finally allowed to regain consciousness, he told everyone, "Thanks!"

"Stay in character," Eva admonished him.

"Um… thanketh ye… kind sirs."

He saw Danny trying not to laugh, his gray eyes regarding him with amusement, but it was Eva who asked, "Is your character a Chaucer pilgrim?"

"Not that I'm aware of."

"You can speak normal English," she said with a smile. "Just try not to sound too… I don't know. Colloquial. Try not to use too much slang."

Danny clamped a hand on Jake's shoulder and said, "You'll get the hang of it, my friend."

In that moment, the ribbing and Paul's anal obsession with doing things by the rules ceased to matter. All that mattered was that Danny had called him "friend."

AFTER THE game wrapped up, Danny went to sit down at the piano and began to play Debussy's *The Sunken Cathedral*. Jake hung back, while the others collected all their dice and character sheets and drifted off to other parts of the dorm. Then he approached Danny and said, "I'm sorry if I ruined the game."

Danny stopped playing, regarding him in surprise. "Why do you think you ruined the game?"

"Paul seemed pretty pissed at me."

"No, he wasn't," Danny assured him. "Trust me. He gets like that with all of us when we do things that fuck with his campaigns. He'll forget all about it in an hour."

Jake didn't look convinced. "I was pretty bad."

"I thought you were very entertaining," Danny said truthfully, smiling at him. "And you seemed to be picking it up toward the end. Didn't you have a good time?"

"I guess so. I mean, yeah, it was fun when I didn't feel like I was holding everybody back."

"You weren't holding us back. It's not like we've never had a new player join us before."

Jake nodded, though Danny wasn't sure if he was buying it. Jake really hadn't been that bad, and Danny had been pleased he was willing to try it. Hopefully, he'd play again next weekend.

Jake glanced at the piano and asked, "Could you play that loon one again?"

"You mean this one?" Danny began to play *Clair de lune* and Jake smiled, nodding.

It was sweet, the way Jake listened to the music so intently, as if he'd never heard anything quite so wonderful. He alternated between watching Danny's hands and watching the way the piano hammers struck the strings over the exposed soundboard of the baby grand.

Then they were interrupted by the lounge door opening and Mark walking in with some textbooks in hand. It wouldn't have been a big deal—students came into the lounge all the time—except that Mark seldom entered a room without drawing attention to himself. Today was no exception.

"Thank God the *gamers* are finally out of here!" He put as much contempt into the word "gamers" as he could manage.

Danny immediately stopped playing, and Jake's face clouded over. As far as Danny knew, Jake hadn't had the displeasure of meeting Mark, so he said, "Jake, this is my old roommate, Mark."

Jake nodded and said, "Hey" to Mark, but he seemed more reserved than usual. Perhaps he'd heard rumors around the dorm about how much tension there had been between the two last year.

"So you're the new roommate," Mark said. He flopped down on one of the garish blue couches without extending his hand. He was a good-looking guy in his own way—tall, with blond hair, baby-blue eyes, and a disarming smile—but his sarcasm generally put people off pretty quickly. "I'm glad he found someone… compatible."

There was something in the tone of his voice that Danny didn't like. Clearly, Jake sensed it too, because he narrowed his eyes and asked, "What do you mean 'compatible'?"

"You're into all that D&D shit, aren't you?"

Jake glanced at Danny, as if trying to sort out whether telling the truth would jeopardize their budding friendship. Danny rescued him by saying, "No, he's not. He just decided to try it today."

Mark snorted. "Careful, Jake. That's the equivalent of 'first base' for gamers. You'll be using dice as sex toys by the end of the month." He looked thoughtful for a moment and then added, "Of course, if you're already up to naked humping, it's probably a little late to warn you about *that*."

Danny had expected Sonny or one of the students who'd been in the hall to spread that around the dorm, and he'd prepared himself for it. But from the way Jake blushed, it was obvious he was embarrassed.

"We were just horsing around," Jake said.

"As long as you keep it in your room."

Danny could see the muscles in Jake's cheek twitch as he clenched his jaw reflexively. Then he took a breath and said to both Danny and Mark, "I've got some homework to do." Without another word, he turned and left the lounge.

"See you," Mark said to his retreating back, opening one of his textbooks.

Wishing he could slap Mark for being such a dick, Danny began playing again—Andrew Lloyd Webber show tunes, because he knew Mark hated them. When Mark asked, "Do you mind?" and waved his textbook in the air, Danny ignored him and kept on playing.

CHAPTER SEVEN

JAKE COULDN'T stop thinking about what Mark had said all day. He'd trusted Danny not to blab about Jake getting a hard-on when they were lying together, and as far as he knew, Danny hadn't. But of course Sonny had seen them, as had whoever else managed to see into the room past Sonny. It wasn't surprising that it was all over the dorm. But still, Jake had managed to avoid thinking about it too much, until now.

He was gay. He'd known that since... well, maybe not when everything blew up with Tom Langois, but he'd figured it out not long after that—on those evenings when he'd sat in his room, watching Tom walking by the house, longing to call him inside. And the longing had only gotten worse when Jake's father threatened to take out a restraining order. Tom hadn't come by anymore, and Jake was too frightened of his father and his brothers to try to contact him. He knew then that the longing he felt was for far more than just a lost friend.

But he'd never told anybody. Not even when he went away to college. He hadn't had any friends he could trust those first couple of years. Hell, he'd never even slept with a man. Rubbing up against Danny was the closest he'd ever come to having sex.

He admired Danny's ability to be so casual about it. They hadn't talked about it, but Jake gathered that he'd been out since sometime in high school. Everyone in the dorm knew and all his friends knew. Did his parents? Maybe. How awesome would it be to have everyone know and still be able to go to college and live there? After the way Jake's dad had reacted to Tom coming out, Jake knew he'd never accept having a gay son. They'd already had a huge blowup over the phone, when Jake told him about transferring to Eaton House.

"What the fuck are you doing, moving in with a bunch of *art fags*?" his father had bellowed at him.

It had taken Jake the better part of two hours to calm him down and convince him that Jake wouldn't slack off on his studies. What would he do if he found out Jake was actually living with a gay student? His father didn't often get violent, but he wasn't above backhanding his sons. Jake was about an even match for him now, physically. Not that he'd ever dare hit back, but at least he was no longer terrified of the guy. On the other hand, his two older brothers would just love an excuse to pummel him, and they were both still bigger than he was.

Worse than the threat of physical violence, though, was the likelihood that his father would yank his financial support. Jake didn't qualify for federal loans, since his father made a good amount of money. And from what he'd heard, even if his father refused to pay for his education, the federal government would still look at his father's income and say, "Sorry, kid." He might be able to get some grants. His grades were pretty good. Really good, in fact. But would he be able to get enough grant money to stay in school and live on campus? He doubted it.

If the gay rumors just circulated around the dorm, maybe Jake could live with that. It might even be kind of cool. Would it be possible to be out in the dorm without word of it getting back to his family? It was an intriguing idea. His brothers were already out of school and working, so there really wasn't any way things could get back to them. And the administration wouldn't report anything like that to his father, would they?

Maybe I could come out to Danny. Just to start with.

If Danny was cool about it—and Jake was sure he would be— then Jake could work his way up to telling the rest of the dorm. In all likelihood, Danny already knew. How many straight men got boners when they wrestled with other guys? Well, maybe more than wanted to admit it, but still… there had been *looks* between them. *He probably even knows I'm attracted to him.*

Jake made up his mind to tell him. That night.

But later, as they both stripped naked for bed, he lost his nerve. Every time he tried to open his mouth to bring it up, the butterflies in his stomach flew up his esophagus and choked him. He half expected to spit out a wing. So when Danny climbed into bed and shut off his light, Jake just said good night and did the same.

He lay there for over an hour, unable to sleep and thinking about what would happen if he told Danny he was gay too. Would they end up having sex? Just the thought of what it might be like to kiss Danny made him instantly hard. From there, his thoughts strayed to the feel of Danny's naked chest against his when he'd wrapped his arms around him. He'd never realized how much body heat another man put out. It had been almost scalding.

Jake hadn't jerked off in weeks. In Christensen, he'd been able to relieve the pressure now and then, blowing a load down the shower drain. But that wasn't an option in Eaton House—not with the curtain half open. He'd thought about doing it in bed, while Danny was in class, but so far whenever he'd been in the mood, he'd only had a few minutes to get to class himself.

Now, he cautiously found his dick under the covers and gripped the hardened shaft in his hand. Danny was already breathing deeply and steadily. He tended to fall asleep fast. If he was quiet, Jake should be able to get off without Danny waking up. So he slowly stroked himself, mouth clamped tight against the possibility of an escaping moan, as his hand settled into a quiet rhythmic rustling under the sheets.

DANNY WOKE to the sound of a guy jerking off. It was very quiet, but unmistakable. Every guy who'd ever tried to masturbate in the dark without being heard knew that sound. And Danny was instantly turned on by it.

He'd wondered if Jake was finding time to jerk off. The guy seemed so uptight, Danny hadn't been certain he ever did it. It had been easy enough for Danny. Jake snored. Not too bad, but enough so that Danny could rub one out without being heard above it. And he would know if Jake woke up. But Jake didn't seem to be aware that Danny had woken up now.

He debated making some kind of noise. Was it more ethical to alert him that he was no longer "alone," or to pretend not to notice so Jake could get some relief? If Danny had been straight, he probably would have just let it go, let Jake have some fun, and pretend not to hear. Probably straight guys in dorms did that all the time. But the fact was, Danny was gay, and listening to Jake was giving him a raging hard-on of his own. That made staying quiet and continuing to listen feel kind of creepy. Still, knowing Jake, the guy would shit himself if Danny tried to talk to him right now.

So he moved a bit, as if he was just waking up. The sound of Jake's stroking immediately stopped.

Fuck.

SHIT.

Danny was waking up. Jake was really close, but he froze. His hand still gripped his cock and he was unable to avoid flexing his fingers to give it gentle, rhythmic squeezes, but he didn't dare move his arm. He lay there for a while, hoping Danny would fall back asleep. Though how he'd know, Jake wasn't certain. The bastard didn't snore.

But as he listened in the dark, he became aware that the sounds coming from Danny's bed were no longer just the sounds of someone shifting around in his sleep or waking up. Those sounds had been replaced by a quiet, rhythmic… stroking.

He was jerking off.

Fuck you! I thought of it first!

Jake wasn't sure what to do. Did Danny know Jake was awake? It seemed like a weird coincidence that Danny just happened to wake up horny and decide to beat off at the exact time Jake was doing it. He supposed it was possible, though. And if Danny didn't know Jake was awake, then it wasn't really cool for Jake to just listen to him. That seemed pretty perverted, actually.

So he made a soft, clearing noise in the back of his throat.

The rustling stopped. But then Danny made a similar noise in the back of his throat. And he started stroking again.

Jesus! He knows! More than that, he wasn't stopping!

Jake listened to the sound of Danny masturbating for a minute, realizing that Danny was cool with him listening. And that drove him over the edge. As if it had a mind of its own, Jake's hand began stroking again.

They were both being quiet, but not quite as quiet as before, now that they were no longer hiding it. Jake couldn't believe what was happening. *I'm jerking off with another guy.* It was the first time he'd ever done it and it was incredibly hot. He couldn't really see Danny in the shadows across the room. The windows let in a faint light from a streetlamp way up the hill, but the light cut through the center of the room and left both their beds in darkness. Danny wouldn't be able to see him either.

But just listening to Danny's stroking and increasingly ragged breathing was driving Jake to orgasm. When he heard Danny push his blankets down so he wouldn't spray on the sheets, Jake did the same. They both came at the same time and Jake was unable to stop a soft moan from escaping his lips. But he no longer cared. In fact, he *wanted* Danny to hear it.

THAT SEXY low moan Jake gave out was one of the hottest things Danny had ever heard in his life. *God, if only I can convince you to do this with the lights on!*

That might not happen, of course. Jake might be so mortified by what they'd just done, even without looking at each other, that he might never want to talk about it or repeat it. But as Danny lay there, catching his breath and feeling his come cooling on his belly and chest, predictably but inexplicably losing its consistency and running down his sides in tiny rivulets, he heard Jake clear his throat and laugh nervously. "Was it good for you?"

Danny laughed quietly. "Yeah. Yeah, it was."

He watched Jake's silhouette sit up and reach for something on the floor. Whatever he picked up, it looked as if he rubbed it on himself—probably using a shirt or his boxers as a come rag. Then he tossed it back on the floor and lay down again. "Good night."

"Good night."

CHAPTER EIGHT

MORNING WAS awkward.

They hadn't really had sex, but Jake kind of felt as if they had. Part of him wanted to talk about it, but he couldn't think of anything to say that wouldn't sound stupid or embarrass him even more. He couldn't even look Danny in the eye as they got up, dressed, and hit the bathroom. But somehow Danny was able to act as if nothing had happened, so Jake eventually decided to do the same—or at least try to.

Fortunately, by the time the two of them joined Eva and Paul in the lounge for the trek up to the dining hall, things were starting to feel more normal. As Danny had predicted the day before, Paul no longer seemed irritated about Jake/Berengar's miraculous recovery from death. Whenever he spoke about the game, he seemed to take Jake's continued participation in the campaign as a given.

Jake suspected it was as much to change the subject as real interest on her part that Eva asked, as they settled at a table in the dining hall, "Have you thought about your project?"

"My dorm project?" Jake asked.

"Danny always plays something on piano."

"I'm majoring in piano," Danny protested. "What do you want me to do? Juggle?"

"I didn't say there was anything wrong with that. Everyone loves it. I'm just saying nobody's surprised when that's your project."

Danny raised his eyebrows at her, but she'd already moved on to her next victim. "Paul tried to run a game for the dorm last year."

"They'll never let you do that again this year," Danny told Paul.

Paul frowned. "They're idiots. That would have been a great campaign if more than you two had shown up to play it!"

"Danny's right," Eva said. "You'll have to think of something different this year. I may do face painting. The henna tattoos I did last year were popular, but the girls downstairs were bitching at me for days, because they didn't wash off right away. I *told* everybody before we started—henna lasts about three weeks!"

Paul rolled his eyes. "Idiots."

Jake had been thinking about it since he moved in. The last thing he needed was to be kicked out because he didn't meet the yearly project requirement. But he didn't really know what to do yet, so he fell back on being a wiseass. "I was thinking of running through the dorm covered in nothing but marshmallow fluff and calling it 'performance art.'"

"Oh my God!" Eva exclaimed. "If you buzz the girls' wing, I'll be your friend for life!"

Danny laughed. "I'd love to see that, but it probably won't pass committee approval." The committee, Jake had already learned, consisted of students living in the dorm, so they were pretty lax. But Danny was probably right about them not approving a streaking project.

"I don't really know. Could I sketch or paint something?"

"Sure," Danny replied. "You could do a mural—"

Paul groaned. "Not another mural."

"Or you could do something like gather people in the lounge with a live model for them to sketch," Danny continued. "Or whatever else you can think of."

Jake was still thinking about the mural thing, and that reminded him of a question he'd been wanting to ask since he'd moved into the dorm. "So what's up with that phone booth downstairs, anyway? Why does it say 'Police Box' on it?"

The other three stared back at him for a long moment, as if too shocked by his ignorance to formulate coherent responses. At last Paul said, "Are you kidding me? You have no idea who Doctor Who is?"

"Doctor who?"

BY MIDAFTERNOON, Danny had brought Jake up to speed on the marvel that was Doctor Who—and made certain that he knew Tom Baker was the best doctor. "An argument can be made for Jon Pertwee," he added, "but if you end up preferring Peter Davison, we'll have words. And if you mix up Tom Baker and Colin Baker, you'll have to find another roommate."

"Jesus!" Jake said with a laugh, "I didn't realize this would be so dangerous."

"Doctor Who is serious shit."

They were on the lawn near the dorm, enjoying one of the few warm days left in the season. The leaves had changed and the trees were radiant in hues of red, gold, and orange. It was beautiful and peaceful. *Almost romantic*, Danny thought before shoving that into the back of his mind.

Jake was stretched out on the grass, looking up into a blue sky streaked with wispy, fast-moving cirrus clouds, while Danny sat cross-legged beside him. "So when are you going to start doing things *I* like to do?"

He sounded a little petulant, as if they were boyfriends rather than just roommates trying to build a friendship. It made Danny a little uncomfortable that they were settling in so quickly—particularly because he did feel something growing between them and he wasn't sure if it was a good idea—but he covered his discomfort with highly inappropriate humor. "I thought we did that last night."

Jake blushed, but he smiled and gave him a playful punch to the leg. "Fuck you," he said lightly.

Danny rubbed the spot on his leg. He wasn't really hurt, but he wondered just how hard Jake *could* hit someone if he were angry. "Well, what do you like to do?"

Jake seemed to be mulling it over. "I don't really have a lot of specific interests. I like movies and TV—*Seinfeld, Home Improvement*. I like sports." He lifted his arms over his head and stretched, causing his shirt to ride up and expose a delicious-looking patch of firmly muscled stomach with an adorable pink belly button nestled in the middle. Danny had to force himself not to stare at it. "I don't know," Jake continued. "I like to be outdoors, and you guys are always hanging out in the lounge or in your rooms."

"True," Danny admitted. "Do you want to go for a walk? The college woods are just over the railroad tracks." The tracks ran right by the minidorms behind Richardson.

"Sure!"

So they just got up and started walking. The minidorms were loosely clustered around a circular drive, so they had to cross this and climb the hill to Richardson, and then continue uphill past that to the railroad tracks. Trains still used these tracks, but they were fairly infrequent. It was possible to walk along them at certain times in the day without seeing a train for two or more hours. On the other side of the tracks, a path led down to a service road and then split off from that to enter the woods.

They hadn't walked far into the forest before the path forked. Jake turned to Danny and asked, "Which way?"

"That would be cheating."

Jake gave him a sour look. "You've never been here before, have you?"

"I've been here," Danny answered truthfully. "Dozens of times. We used it for a LARP Paul made up last summer based on Norse mythology, and I like walking around in here when I want to be alone."

"So which way?"

Danny shook his head. "Uh-uh. You wanted this adventure. Lead on! If the sun starts to go down before you've found the exit, I'll start tossing out suggestions."

"You're a nutjob." The corner of Jake's mouth quirked up and the look in his clear blue eyes was disturbingly affectionate. Although perhaps it was only disturbing because he was the first boy to ever look at Danny that way.

It wasn't really difficult to navigate through the woods. The paths were well traveled and there were just a few main ones. They were long and could take a while to hike, but it was difficult to really get lost. The main path followed the river, past a hollow tree that had enough open space in its trunk to hold a full-grown man, even though the tree was somehow still alive, and an enormous boulder that had probably been deposited there by a glacier twenty thousand years ago. At another fork, one direction led toward the river and a wooden bridge that spanned it. Jake was drawn to the bridge. They ended up sitting on it for a while, dangling their feet above the shallow, slow-moving water and talking.

"I love being outside," Jake said. "I mean *really* outside, away from houses and cars and noise."

"I do too. But you have to remind me that I do. Otherwise, I'll stay inside reading or playing piano all day."

Jake laughed and said, "I'll remember that. Not that I'd ever want to stop you from playing piano. You're fucking brilliant!"

It wasn't often that Danny was embarrassed by compliments, especially about his music. He knew he was good. He'd always had a talent for music, ever since he was a little kid, and people frequently told him how good he was. He tried not to be arrogant about it—he knew he wasn't good enough to compete against students from Berklee or the New England Conservatory—but he knew he was one of the best pianists at UNH. Still, Jake's effusive praise embarrassed him, perhaps because it mattered to him that Jake liked his music.

He decided to reflect some of it back. "Your sketches are really good. Why don't I see you doing more of that?"

"I'm doing it," Jake said defensively. "Just in class or in the library."

"Dude, you moved into a creative arts dorm. You should be sketching in the lounge or setting up an easel somewhere and oil painting."

"I know. I just feel awkward when other people are watching me draw."

"You shouldn't ever feel awkward around me," Danny said, realizing after he'd said it that it sounded a bit... gay. Certainly a bit hyperbolic. But Jake didn't seem to mind.

"Yeah, you're right. It's kind of lame for me to be afraid of doing it in my own room."

"Especially when you seemed perfectly fine with doing it in your room last night."

All right, that was twice now. *Why am I being such a dick?*

Fortunately, Jake was able to see the humor in it. "Dude!" he said, laughing and shaking his head. "Why do you keep bringing it up?" His face had turned bright red again.

"Sorry. It just slipped out."

"You did it too!"

"I know. I'm just an asshole who likes to tease people. I'm sorry. It was a stupid joke."

Jake groaned and let himself fall back onto the wooden bridge, bringing his hands up to cover his face. "I'm never going to whack off again."

"That'll be a challenge."

Jake sighed and dropped his hands. He looked up at Danny and asked, "So what am I supposed to do? The showers aren't exactly private."

Danny shrugged. "Do what you've been doing."

"I haven't been doing *anything*. That was the first time I tried since moving in, and you caught me right away."

"I do it when you're sleeping at night. There's no reason you shouldn't do the same."

"You'll catch me again."

"So what?" Danny asked. He stretched out beside Jake and looked up at the sky through the overhanging trees. "If I hear you doing it, maybe I'll join you again."

"This doesn't embarrass you at all, does it?"

"Nope." *Excite me, yes. Embarrass me? No.*

Jake sighed and was silent for a long time before he said, "All right. But you'll have to start next time. I'll be way too self-conscious."

Danny felt his dick go instantly hard in his shorts. *Jesus.* It was almost as if Jake had propositioned him. "You mean tonight?"

"Whenever. Just… you start first."

"Okay."

There was another long silence between them. Then Jake asked, "You know I like to sketch nudes, right?"

"I saw the pictures."

"Would you ever consider posing for me?"

"Are you kidding?" Danny asked. "I'd love to! Anytime you want."

Jake moved his arm toward him and for a weird moment Danny thought they were going to hold hands. But Jake just tapped the back of his hand against Danny's arm—a mildly affectionate gesture, but not a gay one. "Thanks."

CHAPTER NINE

JAKE LAY in bed that night in the dark, horny as hell, hard dick in hand and feeling like a total perv as he listened intently for the sounds of his roommate jerking off. He wasn't sure how much time had gone by since they'd turned off the lights, but it felt like hours. How the hell was he supposed to sleep if his erection wouldn't go down?

At last he heard it, the gentle rhythmic rustling of Danny's hand under the sheets. That was all he needed. He started going at himself, no longer really caring if he made any noise. He'd just needed to know Danny was doing it before he could find the courage to do it too. But now that the okay had been given, Jake surrendered himself to his pleasure. It was amazing, knowing that Danny was masturbating less than fifteen feet away, and it might have been his desire to *hear* Danny that made Jake noisier than usual, sighing and making low guttural sounds in his throat.

He was pleased to hear Danny respond in kind. When he neared orgasm, he held back just long enough to make sure that Danny would reach it at the same moment. Then Danny's groan as he came drove Jake over the edge and he exploded all over his stomach and chest.

While they were both cleaning up, Danny laughed softly and said, "You're a much more fun roommate than Mark was."

Now that his dick was no longer overriding his brain, Jake was again embarrassed by what he'd just allowed himself to do. He rubbed his stomach dry with his underwear and grunted. "I doubt my old roommate would have done this with me either."

"You're totally wigged out now, aren't you?"

Jake tossed the underwear on the floor. "Not... totally. But it is kind of weird. I don't think most roommates are this... open with each other."

"We don't have to do it if you don't like it."

"I do like it. But maybe we shouldn't talk afterward. That just makes it feel awkward."

"Sorry. I always like to have everything out in the open. Maybe that's not always a good idea, though. I'll try not to talk next time."

Jake stretched out on his mattress and pulled his blankets up. But as he lay there in the darkness, thinking over what Danny had just said, he knew that wasn't really what he wanted. It felt weird to talk openly about jerking off together, but on the other hand it was kind of cool that they could do that. He'd never had a friend he felt this close to. Not even Tom. And he'd only known Danny for a few weeks.

"Fuck it," he said. "We can talk about it. It's not like anybody's gonna kick down our door and arrest us."

"Not unless you keep moaning like we're filming a porno in here."

Jake rolled over and buried his face in his pillow. *Just when I think he can't embarrass me any more than he already has....* He lifted his head and told the dark silhouette across the room, "Fuck you, asshole. Now go to sleep."

THE NEXT day was Monday, and although Danny was looking forward to posing for Jake, he knew it was unlikely to happen that afternoon. Jake had a pretty full schedule on Mondays. He and Danny generally had dinner together, but it wasn't unusual for him to be gone right up until then.

Danny wasn't sure why it was so important to him to pose. Maybe it was because nobody had ever thought he was worth sketching. He'd offered to pose in the lounge for drawing sessions once when people were suggesting art projects for the dorm, but nobody had taken him up on it. In fact, the resounding lack of interest had stung a bit. Mark had sneered at him when they were alone after the meeting, saying, "Nobody wants to look at that."

But Jake did. Danny couldn't be absolutely certain, but he suspected Jake might even be attracted to him. Danny supposed he must be at least moderately attractive—he'd had plenty of guys proposition him for quick fucks. But once they heard the stories or simply found out how experienced he was, they rarely came back for seconds. If they did, it was because they figured he'd be a good, easy lay. Danny had learned how to give them what they wanted, and he'd long ago given up any hope of anyone actually caring about him.

Wanting to sketch him wasn't exactly caring about him. But Jake did seem to like him. Danny realized, as he went through his day unable to deny that he was looking forward to meeting Jake at the dining hall for dinner, that this relationship was starting to feel romantic. Jake was still acting straight, but Danny found it harder and harder to believe. True, some straight guys got off on masturbating with friends—or so Danny had read somewhere. And some straight guys formed close, affectionate bonds with other men. But there was just something about the way Jake looked at him that just felt… gay.

Or maybe I'm just seeing what I want to see.

When dinner finally rolled around, he went to the dining hall to meet up with Jake. Instead, he ran into Eva standing in line. He had a momentary desire to dodge her so he could be alone with Jake, but he knew that would be stupid. He had plenty of time alone with Jake. And the dining hall wasn't exactly a great place for conversation anyway.

He and Eva went through the line and grabbed a table in the corner of the room they always ate in. Jake came along and joined them just a few minutes later.

"Do you have some time after dinner?" Jake asked him.

Before Danny could respond, Eva asked, "For what?"

"I want him to pose for a sketch."

Eva's jaw dropped and she gasped in a comical imitation of a person who'd been utterly betrayed. "Danny? I thought you were going to sketch me!"

"Yeah," Danny said. "Turns out you were the only one who thought that."

Jake looked uncomfortable, still not quite in tune with Eva's idea of humor. Danny had known her far too long to be disturbed by the theatrics. "He's my roommate," Jake said, as if that explained it.

"But he doesn't have perky bosoms. Don't you want to sketch perky bosoms?"

"Well… maybe sometime…."

Danny decided to rescue him with a change of subject. "If we're going to go to Worcester, we're going to have to make up our minds soon. The weather's starting to get cold."

"I know," Eva replied, her bosoms forgotten. "Karl says there's an event this Sunday if we want to go."

"What's in Worcester?" Jake asked, confused.

"The LARP we've been talking about," Eva said. "They do still get together for indoor events in the winter, but the first time we play, we'd like to see what it's like to actually be out in the woods."

"But this weekend is Thanksgiving."

Eva shrugged. "So we'll go home for a couple days and drive down to Mass. on Saturday."

"That would be fine with me," Danny said. "I can only spend so much time with my mom."

"Your mom's terrific," Eva said in her defense.

"I know. She just fusses. Anyway, she won't be too traumatized if I leave on Saturday. We could see if Karl can put us up. Maybe he'll help us create our characters ahead of time."

"Paul will probably be happy to get away from his grandparents for a couple days."

Danny noticed that Jake was stirring his mashed potatoes with his fork, looking unhappy, so he asked, "Did you want to come with us?"

"I don't have a car."

Eva rolled her eyes. "Yes, we know that. But how far from here do you live?"

"Concord."

"Well, that's a little out of the way," she admitted, "but we can swing it. Could you be ready to leave early on Saturday morning?"

Jake was suddenly all smiles. "Sure."

CHAPTER TEN

TRUTHFULLY, JAKE wasn't sure that he'd enjoy "LARPing," as Danny and Eva called it. He still hadn't made up his mind about D&D in the lounge. But spending time with them sounded infinitely more fun than spending time with his family. He was actually dreading going home. He hadn't seen his father since moving into the dorm.

After dinner, Jake took his books into the lounge to study for an exam the next morning, while Danny practiced a piece he said was by Brahms. Jake didn't know Brahms from Bach, but the music was pretty, even though it got a little monotonous by the tenth time Danny played it through.

Beginning yet another repetition, Danny suddenly stopped playing, dropped his hands in his lap, and sighed. "I'm bored," he said, looking accusingly at the piano.

"You could play something else," Jake suggested.

"No. I'm tired of playing."

As usual, he wasn't wearing anything but one of his numerous pairs of shorts—this one was pale green. Jake had been admiring his smooth, golden skin and the soft blond hair on his arms and legs, but now he sensed that he was beginning to grow stiff in his jeans. He forced himself to look away. "We could.... Do you have time to pose for me?"

Danny looked at him and smiled. "Sure."

Jake felt himself stiffen even more. *I'm such a pervert. This is supposed to be artistic, not for me to get off on!* He stood up, hoping his jeans wouldn't show his erection too blatantly. From the way Danny's eyes immediately settled on his crotch, he suspected they'd betrayed him. But fuck it—Danny had seen it already. "Come on."

Danny followed him silently into the dorm room, as if Jake had just announced that they were going to have sex. With Danny dropping his shorts the moment the door was closed, it really *did* feel like that to Jake, and judging by the way Danny smirked at him, he knew it.

"Where do you want me?"

Sitting on my face. "Um… why don't you just find a comfortable position on your bed," Jake said, feeling awkward. He went to his desk to gather his sketchbook, pencil, and eraser.

Danny sat down on his bed while Jake moved one of the desk chairs to the center of the room for him to sit on. But when he looked at the position Danny had taken up, he was confronted by a new problem—he didn't like it. Of course, that wouldn't normally be a problem. He could just ask Danny to move. The problem was the *reason* he didn't like it.

Apparently, his disapproval could be read in his face, because Danny asked, "What's wrong? Do you want me to move?"

"Yeah, I guess so. It doesn't seem right."

Danny unfolded himself from the cross-legged position he'd taken up and stretched out on his stomach. "Yes? No?"

Jake tried to smile. "It's fine."

Danny laughed and sat up again. "In other words, 'no.' So what do you want?"

"I don't know." Jake shrugged. "How about if you sit back against the wall?" Danny did so, leaning back against the wall with his legs spread and bent at the knees to support his arms. "That's perfect," Jake said.

I'm going to burn in hell, he thought. He knew full well that what he'd been aiming for all along was a good view of Danny's crotch. He cleared his throat, which had suddenly gone dry, and bent over his sketchpad, hoping he could settle into the drawing and stop thinking about licking Danny's beautiful penis.

DANNY WATCHED Jake as he sketched. He seemed intent on the pad of paper in front of him, glancing up frequently at Danny, but always quickly, never lingering. Nevertheless, Danny wasn't fooled. He knew why Jake had wanted him in this pose. The only way he could have put his dick more blatantly on display would have been if he stood in front of Jake and stuck it in his face.

You want me. How long are you going to pretend you don't?

Not that Danny really minded. This little game of cat and mouse was the most exciting thing that had happened to him in years. He could keep playing ignorant, if that was what Jake wanted—keep pretending that Jake wanting to jerk off together in the dark was just some straight guy's kink, that wanting to see Danny naked and sketch him was just curiosity. But Danny was as sure Jake was gay as he was sure Paul jerked off to the nearly naked women in *The Savage Sword of Conan*.

But the longer the game dragged out, the longer Danny could pretend Jake liked him and wanted him for more than just a fuck. He had no desire to end that pleasant fantasy.

"You can talk if you want," Jake said, after a long time had passed in silence.

"About what?"

"I don't know. I just meant that you don't have to be quiet when I'm sketching you."

"I don't know what to talk about."

Jake looked up at him for a moment and smiled. "What do you plan on doing after you graduate?"

"I was planning on playing keyboard in the food court at the mall. You can get awesome tips doing that."

Jake's hand stopped midstroke as he debated whether or not Danny was serious. "See, I would have thought you'd be good enough to play in a bar."

"Well that's the dream. Playing in a bar with a bunch of half-full beer bottles lined up on the piano lid to give it that beautiful jingly sound you can't get anywhere else. But I'll have to do the shit gigs for a while before I work my way up to that."

"A man's gotta have dreams."

"What about you?"

Jake frowned and sighed. "I'll start out as some low-level manager at my dad's company—he's the CEO of 4Tran."

"Dude!" Danny exclaimed. "Seriously?"

"Yes."

Danny's first thought was *Your family must be loaded!* But he had enough manners not to say that out loud. Though he did wonder why the son of a prominent business executive didn't have his own car. "Then you're planning on rising up through the ranks and taking over?"

"One of my brothers will probably do that—after they duel to the death to see who gets top position. They're twins, and they're insanely competitive. I'm doomed to be middle management until I either go to another company or put a bullet in my brain."

The thought of Jake killing himself didn't strike Danny as particularly funny, so he changed the subject. "When did you first start drawing?"

"In high school," Jake replied, "I had a really cool art teacher—Mrs. Dougherty—who thought I had some talent. She really encouraged me."

"But your father didn't want you to 'waste your time' on it in college?" Danny guessed.

Jakes eyes flicked up at him briefly. "No." He paused for a moment to erase something with the gum eraser he had on the desk beside him. Then he picked up the pencil and returned to sketching. "I once spent a week sketching a little potted rosebush Mrs. Dougherty brought into class so I could give it to my mom for her birthday. I even spent my lunch breaks working on it. I'd never shown my mom anything I'd drawn before and I wanted it to be perfect. She said she loved it, and she put it on the fridge. Then a few days after her birthday, it disappeared." Jake looked up at Danny with a peculiarly cold expression in his eyes. "My mom asked us all at dinner if anybody knew what happened to it. My father told her it was past her birthday... so he threw it away."

"Nice" was all Danny could think of to say, though he was thinking *What a fucking asshole.* "I just live with my mom. My dad left when I was a kid—I have no idea where he is now—and I don't have any brothers or sisters."

Jake nodded and closed the sketchbook. "I guess I'm done. You can relax."

"Can I see it?" Danny asked, standing up to stretch his cramped legs.

Jake looked reluctant, but he opened the sketchbook again and let Danny come over to look at it. Danny leaned over his shoulder, conscious of the fact that he was still naked. If he leaned an inch or two closer, his dick would be resting on Jake's elbow. But though it was... interesting... to be naked and this close to Jake, Danny didn't want to totally wig the guy out.

"It's really nice," he said, and it was true. For one thing, it was a very good likeness, unmistakably Danny. But Jake also had a beautiful soft touch that Danny found appealing. It made Danny look ethereal and... beautiful. *Is that really how I look to you?* he wondered. But instead he said, "That's really awesome! You've definitely got talent."

"Thanks." Jake didn't seem to believe him, but he smiled as he put the sketchbook aside.

When he moved his arm, his elbow nudged Danny's penis.

"Oh, sorry!" Danny said, pulling away quickly. It was one thing to tease Jake a little, another to actually rub up against him.

"Don't apologize. I'm the one who touched you."

"I shouldn't have been standing so close."

Jake laughed quietly, though he still seemed distracted. "Dude, I'm not freaked out about you being naked. If I was, I wouldn't have asked you to pose for me."

"I'll put my shorts back on." He bent to pick up the shorts he'd kicked off near the door.

"Don't."

Danny stopped, the shorts in his hand, and glanced up at him. Jake looked puzzled, as though he wasn't sure exactly why he'd said that, and Danny was sure he looked just as confused. But before either could say anything, there was a loud knock on the door. Eva called to them. "Hey! Come on, you guys! Holly and I are going for ice cream!"

"Ice cream," Danny said, almost as if it were an apology.

Jake nodded. "Yeah."

CHAPTER ELEVEN

JAKE HAD almost told Danny right there. The difference between "I don't mind if you're naked" and "I like it when you're naked" had seemed so slight. What normally seemed like a giant, epic announcement had suddenly seemed casual and easy. Just a shrug and a few words. *I like looking at you.*

I think you're beautiful.

But… ice cream. It was actually pretty chilly at night for an ice cream run, being late November and all. But Jake was learning that people in Eaton House often did things precisely because they were bizarre. The ice cream bar at the train station had closed for the season, but there was a combination coffee shop and ice cream parlor in downtown Durham that was open year-round. Since there was no permanent parking near the minidorms, Eva's car was parked in A Lot, which would take longer to walk to than it would take to just walk directly to the ice cream place.

But that meant fifteen minutes of walking across campus in the dark, when the temperature had dropped to just a wee bit under freezing. By the time they got to their destination, Eva was the only one who still insisted upon ice cream. Paul, Danny, Wallace, Jake, and Holly—a theater major who lived in the room opposite Eva's—all opted for coffee or hot chocolate.

"Eva," Danny said, warming his hands on his hot chocolate cup, "have I ever told you you're insane?"

"Frequently."

"Just so we're clear on that."

"So I was thinking," Eva said, "since tomorrow night is our last night in the dorm—"

"Until Sunday."

"—we could have a party."

"How brilliantly original," Paul murmured, sipping his decaf coffee.

Holly seemed to consider the idea while she attempted to fold her napkin into something. Jake couldn't tell what—maybe a bird. "We shouldn't just have a party. That's boring. We should do something original—have a theme."

"Like what?" Eva asked.

"I don't know. Costumes?"

"Come dressed as your favorite nudist!" Danny exclaimed gleefully.

Jake laughed, even as he felt his dick stiffening in his pants again. *Jesus.* Danny didn't even have to actually take his clothes off to get Jake hard. All he had to do was *mention* taking his clothes off. Jake had had an erection the entire time he'd been sketching him.

"I like it!" Wallace said, giving Danny a high five.

Holly grimaced. "You would. Guys are always willing to get naked if it will get girls naked too." Eva nodded in agreement.

"Not me!" Paul exclaimed. He looked panic-stricken. "I don't want anyone looking at my fat ass naked."

"I keep telling you," Eva said, "you're not as bad looking as you think. You probably have an adorable ass."

"What if I pop a boner?"

"There might be a definite risk of bone-age," Wallace agreed.

Holly and Eva both snorted and had to take a minute to stop snickering. At last Holly said, "Erections can't always be helped, so I think we can overlook them."

"As long as nobody starts masturbating or humping furniture," Eva added, giving Paul a stern look.

Paul looked scandalized. "Don't look at me! I won't even be there!"

"Oh come on, Paul. You have to be there."

"What if Holly and Eva lose control and start having wild lesbian sex?" Danny asked Paul. "You wouldn't want to miss that, would you?"

"I *already* have a boner," Jake said, causing everyone to laugh. But he felt stupid for making the joke. At this point, he doubted he was fooling anyone with his masquerade of heterosexuality. Certainly he wasn't fooling Danny. He could tell by the way Danny smirked at him.

THE PARTY was held the next evening in Danny and Jake's room. They were the only ones in the group with a double. In addition to Eva, Holly, Wallace, Jake, and Danny, Holly's boyfriend Kevin had joined them. He actually lived in Hall House, the outdoor activities minidorm, but they could hardly tell him he wasn't invited to a nude party with his girlfriend. Fortunately, he was cool. He didn't even act jealous of Wallace—and for all he knew, Jake—ogling his girlfriend's breasts. Danny also couldn't say he objected to a buff, physically fit guy stripping down with them. Wallace was okay—just an average-looking guy, not unpleasant to look at—but Kevin was definitely hot.

Paul did show up, reluctantly. He tried to just strip to his underwear at first but finally had to cave to Eva and Holly's badgering and take those off. He then promptly grabbed a pillow and hid his crotch under it for most of the evening. That was fine with Danny, even though it was *his* pillow Paul was rubbing his crotch against. Paul wasn't exactly disgusting to look at—more just pudgy and kind of shapeless—but he was a bit on the grubby side. One of those college students who took advantage of the lack of parental oversight to avoid showering except when absolutely necessary. Not at all appealing. Eva had launched a campaign to cure him of this behavior, but it didn't appear to be having much impact.

By far the most attractive man in the room was Jake. Kevin was sexy, but Jake was… unbelievable. Sure, Danny had seen him naked a lot lately, before bed and in the mornings, but he never got tired of looking. Jake wasn't really "jacked," as Danny had accused him of when they first met, but he was definitely well-defined and muscular, his pale skin making him resemble a Greek statue carved out of marble—except for patches of red hair in interesting places.

The comparison to a marble statue was apropos in another way was well, since it turned out the only guy present who seemed to have a problem keeping his erection in check was Jake. Well, Paul might have had trouble, but nobody could tell, thanks to the pillow. But Jake's was right out there on display. Considering how chronically shy he'd been about showering a few weeks ago, he no longer seemed to give a damn. He smiled shyly when the girls teased him about it, but he made no move to cover himself. And that made it very hard for Danny to keep himself under control.

They pooled their money and ordered four large pizzas and three two-liter bottles of soda. They debated flashing the pizza delivery guy, but if one of the guys did it, they'd be brought up on sexual harassment charges. Holly argued that one of the girls might be able to get away with it, but ultimately Danny and Jake dressed for a few minutes to go out and retrieve the pizzas from the end of the hall.

They did, however, all end up streaking through the dorm in a long conga line—all but Paul—which horrified the people in the downstairs lounge who were trying to watch *Blue Velvet* for the tenth time. Somebody fetched Sonny, who put on his best stern-parent voice and ordered them back to their rooms if they didn't want to be written up. But he was having so much trouble keeping a straight face they obeyed more because the novelty had worn off and they were getting cold than for fear of disciplinary action.

Overall, though it had consisted of little more than eating pizza and enjoying being naked around other people, the party was declared a huge success. Wallace and Kevin seemed to have been hoping for some kind of orgy to break out, but they were willing to call the party "fun" even when that didn't happen.

Jake remained naked while their friends all dressed and left, and since he clearly didn't care, Danny stayed naked too.

"You still look ready for action," Danny teased as he picked up the pizza boxes their friends had kindly left scattered all over the floor.

Jake had sprawled out on his own bed, and now he raised his head to look down at his disobedient erection. "The stupid thing won't go down."

"Must be all those hot naked girls you were surrounded by," Danny replied. He didn't bother hiding the sarcasm in his voice.

Jake didn't rise to the bait. All he said was "Must be."

Danny decided he didn't need to be a jerk about it. He was getting a nice view of a gorgeous man with an erection. He might as well just appreciate it. Jake could decide to come out or not as he saw fit.

After the pizza boxes had been cleared out of the center of the room, he tried to make some kind of order out of his bed. People had been sitting on both his and Jake's beds all night, so the blankets were all messed up. But the big thing was his pillow. He picked it up and noticed a dark pube on it. Yay. Not knowing why he was stupid enough to do so, he took a tentative whiff of the pillowcase. Yep. That was crotch smell all right. Not really bad, but knowing it had been Paul's crotch, he decided against resting his face on it. He stripped the pillowcase off and turned to pull a new one out of his drawer.

That's when he caught sight of Jake lying on his bed, watching him and… jerking off.

Okay, are we going to pretend straight guys do that *now?*

Jake wasn't going full at it. He was just holding himself and slowly moving his hand back and forth. But it wasn't subtle enough to fool anyone into thinking he was just scratching himself or something. Now that Danny was looking directly at him, he asked, "Do you mind? I'm really horny."

"Do I mind what?" Danny asked. For a moment, he wasn't sure if Jake was asking him to *do* something.

"If I jerk off. I mean… I can wait 'til the lights are off, if you don't like me being this blatant about it."

Danny thought about it for a second. Not because he minded—it was really starting to make him horny too, which would be difficult to hide in a minute—but because he wasn't sure where this was going. "If you don't mind me watching," he said finally.

"I want you to watch," Jake said. "I'm hoping you'll do it too. We've never done it with the lights on."

"Jesus, guy. If I didn't know there hadn't been anything in that soda, I'd swear you were drunk right now."

Jake smiled. "Not drunk. Just… so horny my judgment's kind of flown out the window."

"All right. Sure. Why not?"

IF JAKE thought jerking off with Danny in the dark was hot, this was completely over the top. Danny had grown hard while they were talking about it, and then he'd moved to lie down on his bed and grab hold of himself. Then they went at it, occasionally closing their eyes when the pleasure was intense, but mostly watching each other.

Jake had never watched another guy masturbate. Not even Tom, though he'd desperately wanted to. He'd heard classmates in high school joke about circle jerks—usually as something *other* kids did, but not *them*—and he knew his older brothers had done stuff like that with each other. But before tonight, Jake had never even seen another guy's dick hard, except for glimpses in porn magazines.

He still couldn't see Danny's that well. It was across the room and mostly covered by a hand. But that didn't stop this from being the hottest sexual experience of Jake's pathetic virgin life. He timed his orgasm to coincide with Danny's, and they both watched each other splash come on their chests.

Jake lay there for a long time, thoroughly sated and breathing heavily. Danny seemed content to do the same. Eventually, when the silence had dragged out longer than he could stand, Jake took a deep breath and asked, "You've figured out by now that I'm gay, right?"

His heart was racing. He hadn't intended to say that. Not yet. It had just kind of come out on its own.

"I thought you might be."

Another long silence fell between them, until Jake took another breath and said, "I've never told anyone before."

"I figured that too. Thanks for telling me."

Jake's heart was still pounding in his chest, but the relief he felt was amazing. He felt better than he could remember having felt in a very long time. He wanted to whoop and run across the room, maybe crawl into bed with Danny and say, "Fuck me!" But no, he wasn't really ready to take things that far. Not even with Danny. Even though part of him wanted to.

Baby steps.

He didn't even know if Danny would be interested.

"I just…. Can we keep this to ourselves? I mean, I know everyone's probably figured it out already, but…." He didn't know what to add. He couldn't think of anything that would make sense. If everyone already knew, why did he still want to keep it a secret?

But Danny sat up and looked at him with a serious expression. "Jake, anything you tell me… anything that happens between us… is just between us. Okay? Just us. Until you say otherwise."

Anything that happens between us? The implications behind that statement turned Jake's throat dry, and he was forced to swallow so he could talk again. "Cool. Thanks."

Danny found his discarded T-shirt from earlier in the evening and used it to wipe himself off. Then he tossed it down and got into bed, while Jake continued to lie there like an idiot, still covered in come. Danny reached up and snapped his light off. "Good night, buddy."

"Good night, Danny. You're awesome."

FUCK ME, Danny thought. *I might as well have offered to be his new sex toy.*

Was that where this was headed? Danny didn't think Jake was necessarily thinking that, but come on! He'd just come out. He might never have even had sex before, or at least not with another guy. Of course he was going to want to do some "experimenting." Who wouldn't?

And Danny would probably give him whatever he wanted, because he was still a sucker for a cute guy saying, "I just want to know how it feels. Just once. And we're friends, aren't we?"

He needed to learn how to say "no." Just because a guy acted sweet and vulnerable, and looked like Danny's idea of a god, didn't mean he wanted more than sex. It didn't even mean he *liked* Danny.

He was vaguely aware that Jake hadn't necessarily asked him for anything. Maybe he wouldn't want to do anything with Danny, after all. But Danny's mind had spiraled off into the familiar black hole of anxiety and memories he managed to avoid recalling during daylight, but which often engulfed him during the night. Unbidden, the high school guidance counselor's words came back to torment him now.

I'm sorry, but I can't find it in myself to have any sympathy for you. None at all.

Those boys gave you exactly what you'd been wanting.

CHAPTER TWELVE

NEITHER OF them really knew what to say about Jake's dramatic—and in the light of day, somewhat embarrassingly raunchy—coming out the night before, so by mutual consent they simply didn't bring it up. Instead, they hung out in their room after eating breakfast, showering, and packing to go home. There were some classes on Wednesday, but the residence halls all closed at 6:00 p.m., so Jake skipped his classes to pack. Danny sat on his bed watching him. Whether he had classes too, Jake didn't know, but he didn't seem concerned about them.

"So I'll get to meet your brothers?" Danny asked as Jake debated whether to bring his sketchbook home.

"I guess so." He thought about the naked picture of Danny in the sketchbook and decided against it. Instead, he slipped it into his desk drawer.

"What are their names?"

"Robert."

"What about the other one?"

"They're both named Robert." Jake laughed and zipped up his backpack. "Seriously. My dad named them both Robert because they're identical twins."

Danny shook his head and quirked one corner of his mouth up. "How do you tell them apart?"

"We call one Robbie and the other Bobby."

There was a loud bang in the hall, as the outer door that led to the handicapped access ramp opened and a voice called out, "Yo! I'm looking for Jake Stewart!"

"There they are," Jake muttered. Then his eye fell on the calendar of naked men behind Danny's head. "Jesus! Get rid of that!"

The door to the room shook as someone pounded on it and then, before Jake could answer, it flew open. "Hey, faggot!"

While Danny scrambled to yank the calendar off the wall and drop it down between the wall and his bed, Jake frowned at his older brother. "What the fuck? What if this wasn't the right room? You could have walked in on a couple girls."

Bobby grinned and darted in low to give Jake what he considered a "love tap" to the stomach. Jake tried to block the jab but missed and ended up doubled over for a minute. "Still too fuckin' slow." Bobby straightened up and ruffled his hair affectionately. "You said you were in room 202. God, this place is small." He glanced over at Danny and stuck his hand out. "You his roommate?"

"Yeah," Danny said, grimacing slightly as Bobby shook his hand. No doubt Bobby was squeezing the shit out of it, but the moron was too stupid to notice.

"Good to meet you."

Still holding his aching stomach, Jake made a halfhearted attempt to introduce them. "Bobby, this is Danny—

"We gotta go," Bobby interrupted, already having forgotten Danny's existence. "Robbie's waiting in the car. Grab your shit." He remembered to wave briefly at Danny on his way out the door. "Good to see you."

Jake sighed and looked at Danny's shell-shocked expression. "He's always like that," he said apologetically. "I'll see you on Saturday."

"I'll see you."

Jake grabbed his backpack and a garbage bag of clothes and then headed downstairs.

They found Robbie at the wheel of his metallic-gray BMW, revving the engine impatiently. As soon as Bobby opened the back door to let Jake in, Robbie started bitching. "That goddamned campus cop keeps coming around giving me the hairy eyeball. We need to get out of here before he comes around again, so I don't punch the little shit."

Jake didn't bother asking him to open the trunk. He just tossed his bags onto the seat beside him and got into the car. Bobby hopped into the front passenger seat and they took off.

The trip was about an hour, which meant that Jake was expecting his brothers to ramble on interminably about stuff he didn't care about—their jobs, the stock market, whichever girls they were fucking this month until things started to get too serious, what expensive hi-tech toys they'd just bought....

What he hadn't expected was for them to be grimly silent while Robbie navigated the car off campus until they hit Route 4. Jake was beginning to get paranoid, wondering if somehow they'd found out about him being gay—though he couldn't imagine how—when the twins exchanged a look and Robbie said, "Mom's filing for divorce."

That hit Jake harder than any punch the twins might have thrown at him. Their mother had always been his only ally in a house full of straight men hopped up on testosterone. How would he be able to stand it there without her?

He glanced out the window and muttered, "Fuck."

DANNY WAS playing piano in the lounge when his mother arrived to pick him up. She was a small woman, pretty and always smiling. She'd been a flower child once and the whole hippie mystique still clung to her like perfume—not just the faint smell of the amber-and-jasmine cologne she liked, but the faint jingling of her copper bracelets and hoop earrings, and an almost-tangible aura of calm that accompanied her. Danny found her difficult to be around, not because she was unpleasant, but because he felt filthy and unpleasant by comparison.

She walked into the room and waited quietly for him to finish the piece he was playing before asking, "Are you ready to go?"

"Yeah. Just let me grab my bag."

"Is your new roommate here? I'd love to meet him."

Danny shook his head. "His brother picked him up. And trust me—you're better off not running into *him*."

"You like your roommate, don't you?" Danny had told her a little about Jake the last time they'd talked on the phone.

"Oh yeah. He's great." He didn't mention anything about Jake being gay, not only because he'd promised not to, but also because she would have assumed some kind of romantic relationship between them. That was the last thing Danny wanted.

"Well, maybe you can invite him over sometime."

"Sure."

THANKSGIVING DINNER in the Stewart household had always been chaotic and loud, with the twins shouting over each other at the table and later roughhousing in the living room until their mother ordered them outside. Jake's father largely ignored everybody, reading through the ever-present mound of paperwork he always had with him, while Jake and his mother did their best to talk about innocuous things and dance around any topic that might set his father off—politics, religion, money, art—basically anything that might come across as "liberal."

"So I met Jake's new roomie," Bobby announced at one point. "He seemed like kind of a hippie."

Robbie snorted. "Was he wearing a tie-dye?"

"He wasn't wearing anything, hardly. Just shorts and bare feet."

"How does that make him a hippie?" their mother asked, looking perturbed. "If he was in their room, perhaps he just hadn't fully dressed yet."

"His hair was all long and scruffy too. You should know, Jake. Is he a hippie?"

Jake frowned at him. "If you want hippies, check the downstairs wings in the dorm. Danny's just a guy. He's probably my best friend now."

Robbie gave him a smirk and said, "Let's hope he doesn't try to get in your pants like your *last* 'best friend.'"

Tom had been a terrific best friend. It was Jake who'd failed by panicking and running away when Tom came out to him. If he'd had the balls to admit he felt the attraction too, that he'd *loved* Tom too....

But that had been three years ago and it was too late to fix it. Jake's family had moved to Concord after he graduated from high school, and he heard Tom had moved away too. Jake wasn't even sure where. It was all ancient history now. Jake had found new friends, and hopefully Tom had too.

Now Danny was beginning to move into that empty space Tom once occupied. Jake didn't know where things were going with him—maybe nowhere. Maybe they'd just end up being friends. But he was excited to find out.

"I liked Tom," his mother said, looking down at her mashed potatoes as she scooped some up on her fork. Jake cringed when she said it because he knew that tone of voice. She was challenging Robbie—challenging both the twins and their father, since they were one of a kind. She was in the mood for a fight.

"Tom Langois was a little pervert," Mr. Stewart said, stirring like a bear coming out of its winter hibernation. He put his paperwork down for a moment and glared at his wife. "And he'd set his sights on your son, in case you've forgotten."

"Tom was half Jake's size. I'm sure Jake was quite capable of defending himself if he needed to."

"He probably didn't want to," Robbie said. He snapped the back of his hand at Jake's face, making contact with his cheek. "Did you, faggot?"

Jake flinched when Robbie's hand hit him. "Jesus!"

"That's enough!" their mother shouted, slamming her hand on the table. "I've had enough of you two hitting Jake all the time just because he's younger than you!"

"I thought you said he could defend himself?" Jake's father observed.

Furious, Mrs. Stewart threw her fork onto her plate, causing gravy to spatter onto the tablecloth. She stood up from the table and stormed out of the room. The twins just snickered and jabbed at Jake as if he'd somehow caused the fight. He did his best to pretend they didn't exist, though it wasn't easy, especially when Bobby got in a good poke to his ribs. Their father muttered, "Christ" under his breath and went back to his paperwork.

After a few minutes, Jake got fed up with his brothers and left the table to see where his mother had gone. She wasn't in the kitchen, but the door to the back porch was open, so he went out there. He found her sitting on the porch swing, smoking a cigarette. He hadn't even known she smoked.

She was still a lovely woman, though she looked out of place to him now. He saw for the first time that the style of her hair, piled up on top of her head, and the skirts she wore were from another decade. He'd always felt that his mother was like one of those moms from television when he was a kid, and now he could see that in a way it was true. She was beautiful, her blonde hair not yet turning gray and her skin still free of wrinkles, but she was old-fashioned, conservative.

"I quit smoking when I married your father," she said when she glanced up and saw him standing over her. "He forced me to. Now I keep taking cigarette breaks when I want to piss him off."

Jake didn't know what to say to that—he couldn't even recall ever hearing his mother use language that crude before—so he just sat down on the swing beside her. She took a long drag on the cigarette, exhaled, and then stubbed it out in a metal jar lid she was using for an ashtray.

She held the cigarette up in her hand and examined it. "I can't say I really like smoking anymore."

"Then maybe you shouldn't do it."

"Maybe not." She set the cigarette down in the lid. "I assume your brothers told you?"

"About the divorce? Yeah."

"It's just…." She took a deep breath and looked out over the quaint suburban neighborhood with its freshly painted white houses and neatly manicured lawns. "I just need to get away."

"From us?"

"Not from you." She smiled at him and took his hand in one of her own. "I always felt like you and I understood each other. I love your brothers—" She laughed gently. "—despite the fact that they drive me crazy. But you were the one who kept me grounded, who made me feel a little less isolated in a house full of boisterous male egos."

Jake wasn't quite sure how to take that comment. "You don't think I'm masculine?"

That made his mother laugh more than he'd seen her laugh since he was a boy. "Oh, honey! Of course you're masculine. I didn't mean that at all. But you're quiet and thoughtful. That's a good thing. And with you out of the house now, I've missed that."

It occurred to Jake that perhaps she felt about him the same way he felt about her—that they had been allies against the onslaught of his brothers and the autocratic attitude of his father. Now that they were apart, living in the house must be as bad for her as it would be for him. "The past couple years… you've been alone with Dad for the first time since the twins were born."

"That's right."

"And you don't like it?"

She gave him a sad look and shook her head gently. "He hasn't changed… but I have. I'm no longer the docile young woman he married." She paused. "And I no longer recall what I used to love about him."

THERE WAS no Thanksgiving dinner at Danny's house. His mother considered Thanksgiving and Columbus Day to be celebrations of the oppression of Native Americans by European settlers and refused to do anything festive. Danny could understand not wanting to celebrate Christopher Columbus—the guy had been a total jerk—but he didn't see what was wrong with some settlers celebrating the fact that they'd survived a harsh winter. There was little point arguing over it with his mother. The pilgrims hadn't been his ancestors anyway. He was Irish. His mother's family had arrived in New York sometime in the eighteen hundreds.

Regardless of that, he had a pleasant day. He'd always been close to his mother. Coming out to her in his high school freshman year had been easy. She'd even supported him when the school guidance counselor had called her in to discuss his "promiscuous behavior." She'd stood up to the jackass and said bluntly, "Mr. Allen, what you appear to be saying is that my son was raped—" Danny could hear the trembling in her voice, a mixture of horror and rage. "—but you think he deserved it."

"'Rape' is a strong word, Mrs. Sullivan," the bastard had replied calmly. "According to the other boys, Danny agreed to it beforehand."

And he had. That was why he'd been too ashamed to tell his mother. The difference between what he'd agreed to and what had happened was enormous, but still, he'd let it happen. If Mr. Allen hadn't decided to humiliate him further by calling her in, Danny might never have told her.

She had threatened to sue the school, although the school hadn't really done anything other than ignore the name-calling and the daily humiliations heaped upon Danny. It was his music teacher, Mrs. Kelly, who'd gotten indignant enough to talk to the guidance counselor. She thought she was helping him, but Mr. Allen had been unsympathetic.

In the end, Danny had begged his mother to let it go. Everybody already knew about it. Taking it to court would just increase the humiliation, and they would lose anyway.

Still, he loved her for trying. And he was grateful to Mrs. Kelly for trying too. But there was nothing that could be done.

His mom did cook him a nice lunch—"Not because of that stupid holiday, but because I haven't seen you for a while and it's nice to have you home"—of stir-fried vegetables and brown rice, sesame noodles, and vegetarian steamed dumplings. They drank it all down with jasmine tea and, after dinner, they had a little sake. Danny wasn't twenty-one yet, but that had never mattered to his mother. For his eighteenth birthday, she'd baked him pot brownies.

They sat around in the "sun-room" while they talked over cups of hot sake. The sun-room was a small room on the side of the house that his mother had fixed up with warm hues of gold and terra cotta on the walls, a fake oriental rug, and huge cushions to sprawl on. She used it for yoga and meditation, and Danny had to admit it was a very cozy space to chill in.

"So…," his mother said, after they'd settled in. "Are you seeing anybody?"

Danny rolled his eyes. "Have I ever answered 'yes' to that question?"

"There's always a first time," she replied with a dismissive wave of her hand. "Please tell me you're at least getting laid occasionally."

"Not recently." He left out the fact that he expected that situation to change soon. Not because he intended to *seduce* Jake, but simply because he felt that was where Jake wanted things to go, and he was totally down with that.

His mother sighed and took a sip of her sake. "I really don't think it's healthy—"

She was cut off by a loud *thud* coming from the front of the house. They both set their cups down and scrambled up as another *thud* came. It sounded as if something was striking the front door. Danny reached the door first and foolishly yanked it open.

Something clipped his shoulder—something hard and *wet*—and bounced up in the air. In the street, tires screeched as an old blue Camry pulled away from their house while some jackass screamed "faggot" out the window. Before Danny could react, his mother shoved her way past him and threw something overhand. It struck the back of the car and splattered into pieces on the back bumper.

"Karma is a bitch!"

The kids just laughed as the car took off, but Danny was amazed. His mother turned back to the house, wiping something off her hands in disgust, and he exclaimed, "Jesus! Have you joined pro baseball since the last time I was here?"

He could smell something now. Something that smelled like… rotten apples.

"Are you okay, hon?"

He rubbed the wet spot on his shoulder. It hurt a bit, but not too much. "Was that an apple?" Looking around him, he could see that two other apples had left wet spots on the door and exploded into brown, pulpy fragments on the front stoop.

"I caught the one that hit you," his mother said. "Too bad I couldn't crack their windshield with it."

Danny pulled off his soiled T-shirt and handed it to her to wipe her hands on. He was as pissed as she was—more. But it was just a stupid prank, and there was nothing they could do about it now. He hadn't recognized the car, though he was pretty sure it had been Randy Woodman shouting the word "faggot." He remembered the sound of it. But they'd had to call the town cops so many times for vandalism in their front yard that every call was now met with heavy sighs. Nothing ever came of the reports.

He did his best to smile. "That's not very centered and life-affirming of you."

She shook her head and smiled back at him.

CHAPTER THIRTEEN

GOING FROM Concord to Worcester only took about an hour and a half, so it wasn't particularly necessary to start out early in the morning. But Jake got the impression his friends were all glad to be escaping their families. Certainly he was. Danny had called the evening before to tell him they'd be arriving at 10:00 a.m., which gave Jake time to shower and dress and eat the usual large breakfast his mother insisted on preparing for him and his brothers. When Eva's car pulled up, nobody bothered to get out—she just popped the trunk for him to toss his bags in. Then Jake climbed into the backseat, where Danny was lying half-asleep against the opposite door, and they drove off.

Jake's sense of relief, once they were on the road, was enormous. He let out a huge sigh.

"Fun time?" Eva asked with amusement, glancing at him in the rearview mirror.

"It was interesting."

"Yeah. Mine too. My younger brother just got fired for hitting on his manager. Dumbass. Now he's got our father lecturing him for being an unemployed deadbeat and our mother chewing him out for being a sexist pig."

"Ouch."

"Well, at least it kept them off *my* case. I should get him something extra nice for Christmas."

Jake was relieved that she didn't pry into his own holiday. She and Paul started discussing the rules for the LARP, leaving him and Danny to fend for themselves. Danny didn't seem to be in a very talkative mood, though. He looked at Jake through half-closed lids, nodded briefly, and then went back to his nap.

So Jake just sat there in silence, staring out his window at the leafless trees along the edge of the highway as they drifted past. He noticed that Danny was kind of twisted, his legs at an odd angle to the rest of his body to keep them on his side of the car. So Jake said, just loud enough for Danny to hear, "You can put them in my lap."

Danny opened his eyes slightly to give him a long, evaluating look. Then without a word, he lifted his bare legs and placed them across Jake's lap. He adjusted the jacket he had balled up under his head and closed his eyes again. Jake rested his hands on Danny's legs, uncertain if Danny might pull away, but he didn't. He was wearing his usual khaki shorts and the feel of his skin was hot against Jake's palms. The skin was covered in soft, blond hair that was nearly invisible, and felt silky to the touch. Without thinking, Jake caressed it lightly, barely moving his hands. Danny didn't appear to mind. He'd never imagined touching someone's legs could feel so sensual, but he felt his crotch stiffening as he slid his palms against Danny's skin. The temptation to slide his hands up along the inside of Danny's thighs was strong, especially when his eyes traveled upward and he found himself looking up one of the legs of Danny's shorts. At a glimpse of pubic hair, Jake quickly lifted his eyes... only to find Danny watching him, a faint smile across his lips. Danny raised one of the hands resting on his stomach and gave Jake a thumbs-up before letting it fall back into place and closing his eyes again.

Jake wasn't sure if that meant it was okay to look, or if Danny simply forgave his lapse of manners, but he felt himself blushing regardless. He went back to looking out the window. But of their own volition, his hands continued to caress Danny's legs.

They stopped for lunch at a Friendly's, even though they weren't far from their destination. Jake was all for the opportunity to stretch his legs and use the restroom. He wasn't very hungry, considering the size of his breakfast, but Danny didn't seem to be either, so they shared an order of fries and a chocolate malt. There was something intimate about the way they ended up using the same straw—Eva noted it with a raised eyebrow, though she didn't comment. Jake liked it, liked the feeling of being so close to another guy that swapping something back and forth between their mouths would feel completely natural.

But he could tell that something was bothering Danny, and that bothered him too. When they got back in the car, he waited until they were back on the highway and then leaned in close to talk.

Apparently, it was a little too close because Danny asked him, "Are you going to kiss me?"

"Huh? Oh. No." Jake backed off just a bit, wishing he *could* kiss Danny. He said in a low voice, "I just wanted to ask you what's wrong without broadcasting it to everybody in the car."

Danny smiled sadly at him. "I'm all right. Just the same shit I've been dealing with since I was in high school."

"You have a fight with your mom?"

"No. She's awesome. It's just… other stuff."

Jake nodded. He didn't know what to say and he was probably already prying. "Sorry. It's none of my business."

"Can I lie down again?"

"Sure."

To Jake's surprise, instead of placing his legs across Jake's lap, Danny curled up in a fetal position on the seat, resting his head in Jake's lap. It was insanely adorable, and Jake couldn't resist draping his hand across Danny's shoulder. He felt his dick stiffening a bit and worried that Danny might feel it against his face. But if Danny hadn't figured out by now that Jake got hard at the slightest contact, he'd have to be a complete moron. And he wasn't. So hopefully it was cool.

IF HE wasn't careful, Danny knew, he could easily end up falling in love with Jake. The guy was attentive and sweet, and they weren't even dating. And that was on top of being gorgeous and perpetually horny. Danny could feel Jake's cock stiffening in his blue jeans directly under Danny's cheek, and the urge to nibble it through the rough fabric was almost overwhelming. Danny was resting his left hand on Jake's leg, just above the knee. Just to be a dick, he slid the hand upward a bit, tracing his middle finger along the inside of Jake's thigh, until he came into contact with something that was definitely not Jake's leg.

Jake gave him a light slap to the top of the head and whispered, "Bad boy!"

Danny snickered but moved his hand back to Jake's lower thigh. At least he was no longer brooding about his past continuing to dog him. Still, it was probably a good thing that they arrived at the house in Worcester a few minutes later.

Karl's house didn't really belong to Karl. He wasn't even the only person living there. He just happened to be the only one Danny knew well. They'd met at Dragon Con two years ago and, yes, they'd ended up in bed. But Karl wasn't really Danny's type and vice versa. Danny had visited him—and fucked him—once last year, but that was it.

One of Karl's housemates came out of the house when they pulled into the driveway, directing them to a spot in the back where they could park. Serena was a large, olive-skinned woman in her midtwenties. She might have been part Hispanic, but Danny had never asked. She hugged him warmly when he climbed out of the car and said, "It's good to see you again. We've been trying to get you back down here for ages!"

"I have returned," Danny said dramatically. He gestured to his friends. "And look! I brought exotic slaves from the north!"

Danny and Karl had been relaying messages between their two groups of friends for ages, trying to get them all together for the LARP, but this was the first time any of them had actually met face-to-face. He introduced everybody, and Serena insisted upon hugging them all. Eva was fine with that, but Paul looked as if he might have a seizure. *Jesus*, Danny thought, *we really need to get him laid.*

After she'd hugged Jake, she stepped back and admired him. "Is this a new boyfriend? He's handsome!"

Jake immediately turned beet red and Danny hastily told her, "He's not my boyfriend. He's my new roommate, but he's straight." He hated lying to her, but he was afraid Jake would think he'd outed him in one of the phone calls to Karl. He hadn't. He'd never said one word about having a new boyfriend or Jake's orientation.

Serena smiled. "Oh, that's even better!" She hooked an arm through one of Jake's and turned toward the house. "Come into my parlor, said the spider to the fly."

The house was huge—the kind of place Danny and Eva had often talked about renting together after college, where friends could come and go as they pleased, crashing in empty rooms, and gaming 24/7 if they wanted to. Karl was, in fact, currently camped out in the living room with his other two housemates, Tara and Becky, amid piles of medieval-style clothing and weaponry.

Karl jumped up the moment they entered the house and ran up to Danny to give him a hug and a rather familiar kiss on the mouth—with tongue. "I'm so glad you could make it, sweetheart!" he said, when he finally broke the kiss. He stepped back and got a good look at Jake. "Oh my God! You've brought me a present!"

"He's straight, Karl," Serena admonished him. She patted Jake's arm comfortingly, "Don't worry, I'll protect you."

Jake did, in fact, look as if he could use some protection. The poor guy had probably never been exposed to a flamboyantly gay man in his life, Danny guessed. He might not be afraid of Karl turning him gay, necessarily, but he'd put so much effort into appearing straight, someone like Karl was still a little intimidating. But Jake smiled, if a little uncertainly, and extended a hand. "Hey. I'm Danny's roommate, Jake."

"Sweetheart, we don't shake hands in this house." Karl opened his arms. "Come along. I won't bite you."

Jake hesitated but submitted to the hug. Then Danny introduced Eva and Paul. To be fair to Jake, Paul looked even more uncomfortable with the idea of everyone hugging him, but Danny was reasonably certain it wasn't discomfort with Karl being gay—Paul seemed uncomfortable with *anybody* touching him. Serena then introduced them to Tara and Becky and bustled off to the kitchen to scrounge up something for everyone to snack on.

"Can any of you sew?" Becky asked.

"Don't look at me," Eva answered immediately. "I skipped Home Ec."

To Danny's surprise, the only person who raised his hand was Jake. When he noticed Paul giving him a curious look, he said defensively, "Boy Scouts. You have to sew your merit badges on your uniform."

Danny tried not to look amused, but Karl put a fluttering hand to his chest. "He's even a former boy scout. How could destiny be so cruel to me?"

Tara rolled her eyes. "It's not all about you, Karl."

"Don't be silly. Of course it is."

"Jake," Becky said, patting the carpet beside her, "come be my new best friend. I have a ton of garb here that needs to be repaired before tomorrow, and Karl and I are the only ones who can sew."

"I have to repair these swords!" Tara protested.

"I understand. I'm just saying, unless Jake and his friends brought their own garb, they'll probably have to borrow some of these."

"We didn't bring anything," Eva confessed. "Is there anything else I can do to be helpful?"

"I have to pee," Paul said petulantly.

While Karl showed him to the bathroom, Serena returned from the kitchen with a large tray of herbal teas and cookies for everyone. Jake took his place beside Becky, and Eva and Danny settled down beside Tara to help with the weapon repair. The "weapons" turned out to be constructed largely of PVC pipe covered in insulating foam and then wrapped in colored duct tape and electrical tape. The pommels of the "boffer swords," as Becky called them, were wrapped in cloth grip tape—the kind used for tennis rackets. Most of the repairs had to do with taping up tears in the duct tape or rewrapping the grip tape.

When Paul returned from the bathroom, Serena drafted him to help her in the kitchen, where she was baking shortbread and other food for tomorrow's event.

The rest of the day was largely spent preparing for the LARP— referred to as The Shires by everyone in the house. Not that Karl and his friends weren't good hosts. There was plenty of food and conversation, and everyone was welcoming to the newcomers. But the conversation rarely strayed from The Shires or the specific "shire" the household belonged to, known as Griffinmyre. Everyone even used their LARP names in casual conversation, such as when Serena called for "Lord Merek" to assist her with something in the kitchen and Karl responded. Danny had stayed here during spring break the year before, and it had been the same back then, but he was much more conscious of it with Jake there. If people in the dorm had thought Danny, Paul, and Eva were hardcore gamers, that was nothing compared to the denizens of Griffinmyre.

During the course of the day, several more people arrived until the house was bustling with activity. Danny learned that they would all be staying the night, camped out wherever they could find a spot in the many rooms of the house. "Is there a guest room we can crash in?" Danny asked Karl, worried that he and his friends would end up on the floor somewhere.

"You can sleep in my bed, sweetheart."

"What about Jake?"

"Well," Karl said reluctantly, "if your gorgeous friend doesn't mind, I suppose there's room for him too. It's a queen-size futon." Danny knew the reason for his hesitancy—he'd been hoping to get laid. But Danny wasn't really in the mood to have sex with Karl.

Jake overheard them and interjected, "I guess I don't mind." He was looking down at his stitching, concentrating on it perhaps a bit more intently than necessary.

"Dibs on the middle," Danny said quickly, before Karl started getting ideas of being the filling in a Jake and Danny sandwich. He was apparently too late, because Karl gave him a sour look.

Back off, buddy. You're not getting your hands on him.

"Where am I going to sleep?" Paul asked.

"You can share my bed," Tara said. "It's a double." Paul looked scandalized, his eyebrows jumping up so high they threatened to pop off his forehead like in a Looney Tunes cartoon, but before he could say anything, Tara grimaced and said, "Don't worry. I'm a dyke. I'm not going to molest you."

"Oh," Paul said uncertainly. "Okay."

"Do you mind sleeping with me?" Becky asked Eva.

"Only if we have wild lesbian sex."

"It could be arranged."

Despite the joke he'd made while planning the nude pizza party, Danny had no idea whether Eva would seriously consider having sex with a woman or not, but he quickly decided he didn't need to know. At least everybody was accounted for. And he'd just arranged to spend his night sleeping beside Jake in a bed that wasn't all that roomy for three people.

I'm not going to get a wink of sleep.

CHAPTER FOURTEEN

JAKE HAD to wonder if he wasn't cramping Danny's style by saying he'd share a bed with him and Karl. He'd seen the way Karl kissed him. They'd slept together before, he was pretty sure. The thought of it made Jake... well, he had to admit he was jealous. But he knew he didn't have any right to be. Danny wasn't his boyfriend. He could sleep with Karl if he wanted to. Or anyone else, for that matter.

Even if the thought of it made Jake want to storm out and walk all the way back to New Hampshire.

By evening, the repair work and other preparations for the LARP were finally done and the gathering evolved into a party. Everyone pooled their money for pizza and soda, and Serena broke out the mead. Jake had never had mead before—he wasn't even sure what it was until Karl explained it to him. It was basically an incredibly sweet alcohol made from fermented honey instead of grapes or grain. "Don't let the sweetness fool you," Karl warned. "The Vikings used to drink this. It's very butch."

It was definitely sweet but also very strong. Jake had to admit it tasted wonderful, though after a few glasses, he was feeling a little nauseous.

"We have to get some of this stuff," he told Danny.

Danny laughed and touched his shoulder in a gesture that seemed halfway between a friendly pat and a caress. "Liquor stores can't sell it in New Hampshire. But maybe we can grab a bottle before we leave Massachusetts."

People started winding down and finding places to crash by one or two in the morning, but unfortunately for Jake, his friends had decided this was the perfect time to work on their characters for the event. They gathered together in Karl's bedroom with Karl and Tara to go over the details. There was considerably less involved in creating a Shire character than there had been in rolling a character for the D&D game, and with the exception of Paul, who didn't have a character in that game, everybody decided to just use those characters as their starting point. So Jake was once again a barbarian named Berengar, Danny was an elvish sorcerer named Kareth, and Eva was a halfling thief named Mala. Paul decided to be a human bard, hoping that would prevent him from getting hit.

That was about it. There wasn't the obscenely complicated rolling up of stats, which Jake had loathed. If he got hit in the arm, he lost his arm. If he got hit in the chest or the head, and wasn't wearing armor, he died. If he had armor, a good hit would destroy it, and the next good hit would kill him. It seemed simple and Jake liked that.

What wasn't simple—what was absurdly complicated in this gaming world—was getting dressed. Everybody put massive amounts of time and energy into their garb, armor, weapons, and makeup. It was like they were all preparing for a run on Broadway. Eva and Danny tried on a dozen combinations of tunics, breeches, cloaks, hats, pantaloons, robes, you name it. It meant they were in their underwear half the time, something Jake still hadn't gotten used to. In high school, he'd always gotten the impression that the geeky kids were chronically shy about their bodies. Certainly they'd always hated undressing in gym. But with the exception of Paul, these people were totally comfortable tossing their clothes off no matter where they were. He couldn't figure it out.

At one point, Eva ended up in some kind of diaphanous harem girl outfit—which Jake had to admit she looked great in—but she decided it would be far too impractical to run around in the woods like that, especially in late November. Danny found a cool-looking gray robe with a burgundy cloak, and Paul settled for a rather plain brown tunic and breeches. Apparently, he was going to be a bard who blended into the background and didn't talk much.

Jake wasn't really into the whole dress-up thing, so he was having trouble picking something out. Unfortunately, that gave Karl an opportunity to swoop in.

"I have just the thing for you, sweetheart." He got up from the futon and went to rummage through his closet, eventually pulling out something that looked like a big plaid blanket. "Ta-da!"

Tara and Eva laughed, but Danny groaned and rolled his eyes at Karl. "Will you stop trying to get into his pants?"

"This isn't a pair of pants. It's a kilt. And I think it would be perfect for his character."

"You're just hoping he'll wear it regimental."

Jake hadn't heard the expression, but he knew enough about kilts to guess what it meant. "What? You want me to wear it without underwear?"

"Of course," Karl answered. "That's the proper way."

Jake laughed at him. "You're such a perv. They'd kick me out the moment a gust of wind blew it up."

"It's actually very heavy wool," Tara interjected. "It would take a really strong wind to lift it up."

"What if I spin around too fast or kick something?"

"They're designed to lift up just enough to flare out around the bottom of your butt but still keep you covered, unless you get really carried away."

"What happens then?"

"The rest of us will probably be very entertained."

"Won't I get in trouble for flashing everyone?" he persisted.

Tara shrugged. "If you're doing it deliberately, someone might complain. But the occasional accidental flash is part of the fun of wearing a kilt and being around people who wear kilts."

"So if I deliberately flash people, that's creepy and disturbing," Jake said. "But if I wear something that I know will probably lead to me flashing people *accidentally*... that's okay."

"Better than okay. It's encouraged."

"Don't forget the 'Are you regimental?' dare," Eva pointed out. "If someone goads you into it, you're allowed to deliberately flash. But only your butt."

"Oh yeah," Tara agreed. "Deliberate dick flashes are highly inappropriate."

Jake shook his head. "That's fucked up."

Danny was laughing so hard he flopped down onto his back on the futon. When he'd calmed down enough to speak, he said, "You don't have to wear the kilt, Jake. We'll find something else for you."

Karl looked as if were about to protest, but before he could open his mouth, Jake went over to him and took the kilt out of his hands. "Fuck it. You guys all think I'm too chicken, so… fine. I'll wear it."

That was easy, Danny thought. *I wonder what else I could accuse him of being too chicken to do?* He wouldn't really do that, of course, but he knew the gears were already churning away in the sleazy recesses of Karl's mind. The guy could be managed, if he was given clearly defined boundaries, but he'd take advantage of any openings. Danny would have to keep an eye on him or they'd be playing Truth or Dare soon.

"How do you wear it?" Jake asked.

Karl clapped his hands together gleefully. "You're going to love this. First you strip naked. Then we all ogle your penis for about ten minutes. Then we wrap the kilt around you."

"That sounds like fun," Jake said wryly, but he didn't seem particularly upset by Karl's comment.

"I admit I added the leering at your private parts for my own benefit," Karl confessed. "I suppose we can leave that out, just this once."

"Thanks."

Putting on the kilt did require Jake to get naked, though, and he didn't seem to mind the fact that there were five other people in the room—two of them women. This particular type of kilt had to be laid out on the bed and accordioned up in the middle, since it was over six yards of fabric. Then Jake had to lie down on top of it, so Danny and Karl could wrap him up in it and cinch it around his waist with a belt. It wasn't really a two-man job, but Danny was mostly trying to prevent Karl from finding an excuse to grope Jake during the whole process. He'd never minded Karl's lecherous behavior when it was directed at *him*. It had even been flattering. But seeing it directed at Jake was really getting his feathers ruffled. Jake could probably take care of himself, but Danny still felt responsible for subjecting him to this harassment.

The kilt looked good on Jake, but it had a section that draped over one of his shoulders, and without a shirt he looked more like a caveman who'd just killed and skinned some enormous plaid beast than a medieval warrior.

"Hmm," Karl said, regarding him critically, "I must have a poet shirt here somewhere."

"Poet shirt?" Jake asked skeptically.

"It's what they're called. You don't have to write poetry in it. It's just a big, blousy white shirt."

"Aren't we getting a little off track from the whole 'barbarian' theme here? Do barbarians wear shirts?"

"Just say you're a Scottish warrior, then," Karl said, waving his objection aside. "You'll thank me when you're hacking your way through tree branches in December."

He found a shirt in his closet that would fit Jake and tried to get him to take the kilt off again, so he could put the shirt on first. But Danny intervened.

"How about we just lower this part?" he asked, slipping the cloak part of the kilt off Jake's shoulder. "Then you can just tuck the bottom of the shirt down into the kilt for now. Tomorrow you can put it on properly."

But it was Jake who thwarted him by laughing and shimmying out of the lower part of the kilt. "Dude, if he wants to see my dick, he can see my dick. He's gonna see it when we sleep anyway."

"What?"

"Oh really?" Karl asked.

"Danny doesn't have any underwear on—he never does—so he's gonna have to sleep naked. And if he gets to, why shouldn't I? I always do in our dorm room."

"Indeed." It couldn't have been lost on Karl—or anyone else in the room—that Jake was starting to get aroused.

Paul moaned. "All right, that is *way* more information than I needed, and I don't need to see that thing jutting out at me again. Can we please get him back into some clothing?"

"I think maybe your friend's had a little too much mead," Tara suggested, eyeing Jake with amusement.

Danny shook his head as he helped Karl pull the shirt down over Jake's head and shoulders and then try to pull it down over his growing erection. "No. He just gets like this sometimes." It was pretty clear to him that being naked in a room full of people *really* got Jake turned on. And as Danny had begun to learn, when Jake got turned on, his judgment got a little cloudy.

They wrapped Jake up in the kilt again and this time he looked like a Scotsman—a damned sexy Scotsman. Which was in fact what he was. The outfit was declared a success by all in the room save Paul, who just wanted to go to bed. Since it was past 3:00 a.m. and they had to be up by nine, bed sounded like a good idea to everyone. Danny was still convinced that Karl might try to push Jake a little further, though. And the state he was in, Jake might let him.

The girls left the room, dragging a half-asleep Paul with them, and Danny got a moment alone with Jake while Karl went to the bathroom.

"Please tell me you aren't going to take this any further tonight."

Jake looked a little hurt by that. "What's wrong?"

"It's not exactly that there's anything wrong," Danny said as he pulled the kilt off Jake's shoulder and helped him push the lower part down past his hips. "But... I think I know you well enough to see where this is going. You've got yourself all worked up again and you really want to get off. But you're not really attracted to Karl, are you?"

"No."

"Do you really want him going down on you?"

Jake sighed in frustration, pulling his arms out of the sleeves of the poet shirt. "You've fucked around with him, haven't you?"

"Yes. A couple times."

"And if I wasn't here, you'd be fucking him right now."

"Maybe."

Jake stepped out of the mass of material pooled around his feet and pulled the shirt over his head, leaving him standing there stark naked again and beautiful, his cock jutting out from his body in all its horny splendor. "So I'm kind of in the way," he said. "But maybe the three of us...." He trailed off, as if he didn't really know where he was going with that.

But Danny knew. And he didn't like it.

"Jake," he said, stepping closer. "Karl's not horrible. He's a decent guy, when you get past the lecherous comments. But do you really want your first time to be a three-way with someone you really aren't into?"

Jake looked directly into his eyes and Danny wondered if the mead was still affecting him, because he seemed to be sinking into those pools of aqua blue. "If you were there too," Jake said. "I want my first time to be with you."

Nothing in those words was a surprise, yet it still sent a ripple of warmth throughout Danny's entire body, pooling in his chest and in his tightening crotch. Unable to stop himself, he pulled Jake close and kissed him hard on the mouth, delighting in the softness of those lips and the sweet taste of mead. Jake whimpered and crushed him in his powerful arms, holding Danny tight against his naked body. Danny held on to him, caressing the hot skin of Jake's back with his hands.

But a tiny part of Danny's brain was still aware enough to scream at him about what a bad idea it would be to start fucking on Karl's bed. Karl probably wouldn't mind, of course, but he'd want to join in. And Danny wasn't in the mood to share.

He pushed Jake away, gently but firmly. "I want to be your first. But not here and not with Karl coming along for the ride. Let's hold off until we're back in the dorm."

Jake actually growled at that, low and quiet and deep in his chest, like an animal. "As soon as we're back in the dorm. You promise?"

"I promise."

CHAPTER FIFTEEN

KARL DIDN'T seem at all happy about both Jake and Danny claiming to be too tired for anything sexual, even though they were both naked when they got into bed and there wasn't any way for them to hide their erections. He offered to give them both blowjobs—which Jake had to admit was tempting—but Danny said "no thanks," and Jake backed him up. He knew he'd be insanely jealous of anyone going down on Danny in front of him anyway.

But God, he was horny!

A much bigger deal than his throbbing cock, however, was the fact that Danny had kissed him! It was the first time he'd ever been kissed. Things had never gotten there with Tom, even though Jake had fantasized about it. He'd always thought another man's lips would be hard, like muscle, and dry. But not at all. Danny's lips were full and warm and incredibly soft, like satin. And the mead they'd just drunk made his mouth taste sweet and faintly of honey. It had been... beautiful. One of the most beautiful things Jake had ever experienced. He would have written a poem about it, if he had the ability to string two words together in any artistic way. Or a song, if he had any musical talent. Maybe he could sketch Danny's mouth....

Even more amazing than his kiss was his promise. *I want to be your first.* God, it was going to be nearly impossible to wait. They had all day tomorrow to get through and then the car ride back to UNH. It would be excruciating.

Danny allowed him to slide up behind as they lay in Karl's bed, curling the front of his body up against the back of Danny's, pressing his swollen cock against Danny's naked ass and draping his arm around Danny's waist. It did nothing to ease the tension in his groin, but it felt wonderful nevertheless. He lay there for what felt like hours, unable to sleep, but eventually he must have dozed off, because he suddenly woke to a pulsing sensation in his cock and realized he was coming—all over Danny's ass and legs.

Shit. I'm such a fucking loser!

His hope that Danny might sleep through it were dashed when Danny moaned and whispered, "Oh fuck. Are you awake?"

"Yeah. I'm sorry."

"It would be really hot, if it weren't like four in the morning."

Then, just to make matters worse, Karl said from the other side of the bed, "Why the fuck are you two having a conversation at this hour?" He sounded groggy and irritable, as well he should be.

Danny didn't say anything, perhaps not wanting to embarrass Jake, but Jake decided he might as well man up. "I, uh… I just had a wet dream."

"Jesus. Are you like thirteen years old?"

"Adults do it too," Danny defended him. "Can we just find something to mop it up before it gets ice-cold?"

Grumbling, Karl turned on the lamp beside the futon, which made them all flinch. "Sleeping next to the biggest come whore in New England—me—and he wastes it by spewing it all over the bed sheets." He rummaged around in a pile of dirty laundry, while Jake slipped out of the bed and held the sheets aside so Danny could get up without rubbing the mess all over them.

"Would you like to lick it off my ass?" Danny asked Karl.

"Tempting, but I'll pass."

Jake stood there, hugging himself in the chilly early morning air while Karl wiped Danny's ass and between his thighs with a dirty shirt. He felt utterly pathetic and wished he could curl up in a fetal position under a pile of blankets and never come out again. His face must have been completely red—he could feel the heat in his cheeks.

"I suppose you were dreaming about a woman with enormous tits while you were hosing down your roommate's ass?" Karl asked him.

Jake shook his head. "I don't know what I was dreaming about."

"Stop picking on him, Karl." Now that he was dry, Danny knelt down on the futon to examine the sheets. "There's a little wet spot, but it'll dry. Let's just get back to bed."

Karl tossed the shirt back onto the laundry pile, and they all climbed back under the sheets. When the light was off again, Jake lay on his back, afraid to spoon Danny again and feeling like a complete ass. But then Danny rolled back toward him and said over his shoulder, "You can go back to cuddling."

"Thanks." Jake rolled onto his side and pulled him back into his arms, reveling in the warmth of Danny's back and ass against his front. He sighed contentedly and breathed in the clean smell of Danny's hair. Danny wasn't mad at him and was back in his arms. Life was good again.

From the other side of the bed came Karl's quietly sarcastic voice. "Yeah, all straight guys like to cuddle with their male roommates. It's totally butch."

THE LARP event was held in a nearby state park. This particular event was actually being put on by the Shire of Griffinmyre, so Karl's household was in charge of it, which meant Danny and his friends were more or less on their own. The Griffinmyre people were far too busy watching over things to babysit the newbies. Other participants were friendly and helpful, but Danny soon discovered the gamers were loath to drop out of character. This made finding things in-game, such as the location of an inn or a place to get spell components easy enough, but asking for clarification of the rules or other out-of-character information could prove challenging. When they found themselves standing around feeling helpless at the beginning of the game, finding someone who could tell them where they were expected to go took far too long.

Being out in the woods was nice. The weather was beautiful and still fairly warm despite the fact that it was officially December. Because it was a state park, the gamers had to contend with "mundanes"—ordinary people not participating in the game—as they walked along the paths, and the Griffinmyre people were adamant about not pissing anybody off if they ever wanted to game in that park again. But for the most part, the woods were crawling with people in medieval/fantasy garb, and that was really cool. In that way, the immersive element was everything Danny, Eva, and Paul had hoped for.

But in other ways it was lacking. Danny had known that he'd be starting his sorcerer over from scratch, but he hadn't been prepared for just how powerless he'd be. He had one spell. One. And it proved to be useless. No attack spells were available at his level, so he'd chosen Identify. Alas, nothing needed to be identified.

Eva's thief character turned out to be pretty useless too. There were strict rules about taking people's possessions—probably a good thing—so a thief was only allowed to steal certain items, and the rules for what could or could not be taken and *when* it could be taken were so confusing Eva just didn't bother. She kept asking if she could check for traps, but if there were any, she never found them. Paul was doing his best to stay on the sidelines, but he got smacked in the eye with a magic missile—a bean bag—and killed. When he was told he'd have to wait until they found someone to resurrect him, he went back to the picnic tables that represented the inn and hung out there for the rest of the afternoon, reading a *Forgotten Realms* novel.

Jake, on the other hand, appeared to be having a blast. Perhaps Danny shouldn't have been surprised, but role-playing game or not, The Shire was largely a game for athletes. There was an enormous amount of walking, hiking, running, even climbing... and then there was fighting. Everything seemed to revolve around boffer combat, even for those classes that supposedly weren't fighting classes. Because everyone was fair game for being *attacked* by boffer swords, whether they carried one or not.

As a sorcerer, Danny was allowed to carry a moderate-sized boffer weapon, but he was pathetic. The guys he fought against had clearly been doing this for ages, and they had no trouble at all deflecting his blows and bypassing his feeble attempts to defend himself. Both fights he got into ended in less than a minute.

But even with his lack of experience, Jake was a killing machine. He whirled that blade like it was an extension of his arm. The marshals had to rein him in when he got too enthusiastic, but he never actually hurt anybody—no more than any of the other warriors did, anyway. Getting whacked upside the head with a boffer sword hurt, no matter how safe the marshals insisted they were. But the experienced fighters laughed their wounds off and accepted Jake as one of their own.

He seemed tireless as the day progressed, running around and hooting like a maniac. During one of his fights, he executed a dramatic somersault which elicited cheers, catcalls, and a round of applause—he appeared to have forgotten that he was wearing Karl's kilt. Or maybe he knew perfectly well what he was doing. Danny wouldn't put it past him. Jake seemed to be developing an exhibitionist streak. Technically, that violated Tara and Eva's rules of kilt flashing, but Danny doubted anyone would complain. That somersault was probably the highlight of several gamers' days. Certainly Danny enjoyed it. And he enjoyed seeing Jake laughing and playing like a big, excited puppy.

The kilt flash also reminded Danny of how nice it would be to get back to the dorm. Unfortunately, it wasn't logistically possible to do that quickly. Eva's car was back at Karl's house, which meant they were forced to hang around the park at the end of the event, helping with cleanup. They didn't mind helping out—although Paul grumbled privately to Danny about how tired he was—but they were definitely exhausted by the time they piled into Karl's car.

"The others want to meet up at Denny's for a late dinner," Karl informed them. "Is that okay?"

Danny really just wanted to go home, but Eva pointed out, "The dining hall will be closed by the time we get back."

"All right," Danny said.

The trip to Denny's with the Griffinmyre household and some of the others who were part of their shire might normally have been a lot of fun. But even Jake was starting to wind down, and Paul had more or less turned into a whiny two-year-old. By the time they got back to the house and got on the road, it was almost eleven. Eva had to do all the driving because she was the only one who knew how to drive a standard. Danny was worried about her nodding off at the wheel, but she insisted she was fine, and none of them wanted to stay another night.

Once they were on the road, Eva said, "Well, that was fun." She didn't sound completely convinced.

"I hated it," Paul muttered from the front passenger seat.

Danny was lying on the back car seat with his head in Jake's lap again. The darkness partially obscured the fact that Jake was running his fingers through his hair and had his other hand inside Danny's shirt, resting against the skin of his abdomen. He would have been content to just drift off to sleep like that, but he felt obligated to participate in the conversation, if for nothing else than to keep Eva awake. "It was okay. Maybe if I get up to a higher level as a sorcerer, my spells will be more useful."

"I hated it," Paul said again. "If I wanted to get pummeled by jocks, I would have stayed in high school."

Danny had to admit he kind of felt the same way. The game was completely dominated by the fighters. And unlike table D&D, where anyone could eventually become a kick-ass warrior by building up his or her stats, someone like Paul would never be able to excel as a fighter in The Shires, because he'd never have the physical prowess necessary.

"I thought it was awesome!" Jake said.

"That's because you were good at it," Eva pointed out. "*Really* good at it. And you totally rocked that kilt."

"Kilts are great. I need to get one."

Danny smiled at the thought. "We'll see what we can do."

They pulled into the dorm parking lot around 1:00 a.m. and dropped their bags off in their rooms. But Eva couldn't leave her car there overnight without getting towed, and it wasn't safe for a young woman to walk alone on campus at night, so they all rode with her to A Lot. Then they had to walk fifteen minutes back to the dorm, freezing their asses off the whole way. By the time Danny and Jake were finally alone in their room, Danny said, "I know I promised, as soon as we got back…."

"I'm too fucking tired to do anything," Jake said.

"Me too."

"Will you sleep with me, though?"

Danny considered it. The beds were pretty small, but if they spooned, they might be able to pull it off. "Okay. But try not to spooge all over me."

Jake smirked at him and reached out to pull him close. He wrapped his arms around Danny, making him feel at once warm and safe and protected. "I'll try," Jake said. Then he lowered his face and kissed Danny full on the mouth.

It was nice, but Danny ended up interrupting it with a yawn. "Sorry. Warrior needs sleep, badly."

They managed to fit into Jake's bed, with Jake practically wrapped around Danny's naked body, his hard cock firmly wedged between Danny's ass cheeks. Danny wasn't sure how they'd be able to sleep like that, but they were both so exhausted sleep overcame them quickly.

CHAPTER SIXTEEN

JAKE WOKE with his erection wedged between Danny's thighs. Overall, he considered that a pretty nice way to wake up. Danny was asleep, but he figured it would be acceptable to caress his shoulder and side, and maybe even his smooth ass a bit, under the circumstances. Of course, the moment he started touching him, Danny said, his eyes still closed, "Hmm. I wonder who could be fondling my butt?"

"I have no idea," Jake said. "That's pretty ballsy. Maybe you should report him to the RA."

"Nah. I think I'll just fuck his brains out."

Danny rolled backward into Jake's arms and they kissed, but any plans for hot sex were interrupted by a knock on the door and Paul's voice grumbling, "Are you guys awake? Eva told me I had to get you for breakfast."

Jake looked over at his clock and discovered it was actually pretty late. The dining hall would stop serving breakfast soon. Danny sighed and said, "I guess I am kind of hungry."

"All right, but right after we eat, we're coming back here so I can lose my virginity."

Neither bothered showering for breakfast, since hardly anybody in their group of friends did. Even Eva and Holly looked disheveled as most of the wing gathered in the lounge for the trek to the dining hall. Paul looked half dead. If anybody had early morning classes this Monday, they appeared to be skipping them.

They ate together at one of the long tables and even though Danny sat right beside Jake on the bench, neither of them seemed inclined to speak. They just listened to their friends' grumbling about being awake and banter about how their holidays went. Eva told Holly and Wallace about The Shires, with Paul injecting a sour note about how his eye puffed up when someone tried to put it out with a bean bag.

Abruptly, Danny set his second cup of coffee on his tray and said, "I've got stuff to do back at the dorm." He glanced down at Jake and asked, "Are you coming?"

"Sure," Jake replied and quickly gathered up his tray to follow Danny to the tray return. Then they walked down the hill together, not really knowing what to say about the fact that they were going to be fucking soon, until they neared the dorm. At that point, Danny announced, "I'm going to take a shower."

"I probably should too."

"Okay."

Back in the room, Jake watched out of the corner of his eye while Danny stripped out of his clothes. He'd seen Danny naked more times than he could count by now, not only in the mornings and just before bed, but whenever Danny came back from class and insisted on changing into the shorts he wore around the dorm. But today it felt much more erotically charged. Danny wrapped his towel around his waist, grabbed a bottle of castile soap, and then stood there, waiting for Jake to finish stripping and get his own towel. Then they walked to the bathroom together.

They had the place to themselves, at least for the moment. Danny stepped up to one of the two shower stalls, set the castile soap on the shelf, and reached in to turn the shower on. While the water was heating up, he removed his towel and Jake saw that he was already erect. It was the first time Jake had seen his dick in that state, at least close enough to get a good look. Jerking off across the room wasn't at all the same.

Danny's hard cock was beautiful. Like the rest of his body, it was perfectly proportioned, satiny smooth—at least, to all appearances— and golden. It was also uncut. That part Jake had known about. He'd seen it soft and thought the foreskin gave it a nice, sleek shape. But now the foreskin had slipped back so that the tip of Danny's glans protruded just a bit, and it glistened with precome.

Danny was watching him closely, as if trying to gauge his reaction. The expression on his face wasn't lecherous or teasing, merely attentive. It was if he were presenting himself for inspection and waiting to see if he passed muster.

He certainly did.

Jake's own erection was straining against his towel, and he felt obligated to reveal it, though Danny had certainly seen it hard several times now. But fair was fair. Jake licked his lips nervously, glancing at the closed door for a second before pulling his towel off.

Danny looked him over and nodded appreciatively. "Two showers or one?"

It wasn't really possible for Jake's cock to grow more erect than it already was, but it sure as hell tried. It almost hurt. "What if somebody comes in?"

"We'll keep the curtain closed and be quiet." Danny looked up at him through his tousled bangs and his mouth quirked up in a mischievous smile. "Unless you're not interested in how I feel when I'm all soapy."

Oh God. "I'm interested."

Danny stepped under the spray and looked back to see if Jake was following. Jake hung up his towel and pulled the curtain closed. The damned thing didn't want to close tightly, but he managed to block as much of the gap as possible before stepping under the shower.

Danny poured a small amount of the liquid soap into his hand and rubbed it between his palms. Then he moved closer and wrapped his arms around Jake's middle, pressing their naked stomachs and crotches together while he ran his soap-covered hands up and down Jake's back and ass. The feel of his hands sliding along Jake's skin was amazing, but it paled in comparison to what Jake was feeling up front. He'd pressed himself against Danny's naked ass a couple of nights in a row, and that had been amazing, but this was the first time they were dick to dick, and both hard. Jake felt Danny's erection pressed between their abdomens, sliding along the length of Jake's cock. But it wasn't enough. He needed to *feel* it, to *touch* it.

"Can I touch you with my hands?" he asked breathlessly.

"You already *are* touching me." That was true enough. Jake had his arms around Danny's shoulders and was caressing his back, just as Danny was caressing his. But that wasn't what he meant.

"I mean, can I touch your dick?"

Danny laughed. "Oh yeah. Touch anything you like."

"Can I *lick* anything I like?"

"Please."

So he did. He started by pawing at Danny's cock in a way that probably wasn't all that erotic for Danny, but at least he got to thoroughly explore what another guy's cock felt like. It was kind of weird, how hard it was. He should have known that, since he had one of his own, but the sensations were coming in differently than they did when he jerked off—all through his hands. Was this how *his* dick would feel to another person? Probably, except for the foreskin. That was strange, but he loved the feel of it, the smoothness of the wet skin over the hard shaft. And he loved rubbing it between his fingers, especially when he accidentally stumbled across the spot on the underside of Danny's cock that made him moan involuntarily, his eyelids fluttering closed. Jake tried it again. Danny moaned again.

This is awesome!

But he needed a kiss. He wanted to taste Danny's mouth so badly his whole body was quivering at the thought of it. He lifted his hands to Danny's shoulders and held him there, as if afraid Danny might try to duck away. But when Jake leaned down, Danny raised his face and met Jake's lips, returning the kiss without hesitation. Jake explored Danny's mouth and he opened himself to Danny's tongue, which still tasted faintly of coffee.

After they'd kissed for so long that Jake was growing dizzy from lack of oxygen, Danny pulled away and panted, "Wash me now. All of me. And then I'll do you."

Jake was happy to comply. Neither of them had thought to bring shampoo, so he used the castile soap to wash Danny's hair and then his face. Jake wouldn't have thought that touching another man's face would be erotic, but he shuddered with arousal the moment his fingers brushed against Danny's cheeks. It was the first time he could recall doing it. He'd roughhoused with his brothers and friends in high school, grabbing and poking just about every part of their bodies *except* the face. He'd grabbed asses and even crotches, but not the face. That was too personal. And now it was driving him wild, caressing Danny's nose and cheeks and eyelids. Slipping his fingers through the crevasses of Danny's ears felt almost like *fucking*. And from the way Danny closed his eyes and grunted when Jake did it, it seemed to feel that way to him too.

Jake moved down Danny's back and chest, washing his armpits and feeling like a pervert when he couldn't resist licking them once he'd rinsed the soap off. Danny giggled but made no move to stop him. Jake relished washing his beautiful, round ass cheeks, but hesitated when his fingers slipped into the hot crevasse between them.

"Go ahead," Danny breathed. "Just soap up your fingers and slide them along the crack."

"Inside?" Jake asked, not sure he really wanted to go that far. Not yet.

"No. Not with soap. Just brush it."

Jake did so, delving a little deeper with each stroke, until he was brushing against the puckered skin of Danny's anus. He should have been grossed out. Sure, he'd been washing his own ass his entire life, but someone else's? But it actually felt kind of soft and silky under his fingers, and his throbbing cock certainly didn't seem turned off. Danny had pushed himself forward and lifted one leg to give Jake better access, and now he was pretty much rutting against Jake's thigh.

"You really like that."

"Wait until it's your turn," Danny gasped.

Jake wasn't sure if he was excited or freaked out by that idea, but he trusted Danny to go easy on him. He'd never thought of himself as particularly delicate—twenty years of being pummeled by older brothers had toughened him up pretty well—but this was different. Awesome and amazing, yes, but also a little frightening. All he said was "I want to wash your crotch first."

Danny stepped back and let him do that but stopped him when his "washing" began to resemble "jerking off." He put a hand on Jake's and said, "Not yet."

It was his turn to bathe Jake, and as his hands slid over every inch of Jake's skin, Jake finally understood what people really meant by the word "ecstasy." When Danny at last slipped a finger in between his ass cheeks and drew it slowly and caressingly over his anus, the sensation sent waves of pleasure throughout Jake's entire body, especially his dick.

Jake barely had time to gasp out, "Oh shit!" before he came, his swollen cock squirting out ropes of come against Danny's abdomen. Danny settled his finger on Jake's puckered hole and gently vibrated it to carry him through the orgasm. Jake thanked God nobody had come into the bathroom yet because he couldn't stop himself from moaning as he spasmed again and again.

When it was finally over, Danny's stomach and crotch were covered in semen. Jake struggled to catch his breath and was forced to pant heavily into Danny's mouth when Danny drew him down for a long kiss.

"I'm sorry," Jake said when they broke the kiss. He felt like a lightweight, since Danny hadn't come yet. Still, it had been fantastic.

Danny smiled mischievously up at him, his bangs plastered to his forehead and rivulets of water running onto his face. "It's not over yet. Let's rinse off and go back to the room."

DANNY HAD been convinced when he woke up that sleeping with his roommate would be a phenomenally bad idea. What if Jake fell for him? What if *he* fell for Jake? The whole thing could blow up in their faces and then they wouldn't be able to share a room anymore.

But he'd woken up with an erection that hadn't died down while watching Jake dress. His dick had remained at least semierect all through breakfast, until he'd found himself asking Jake to follow him from the dining hall and then more or less threw himself at him in the shower.

God, he's gorgeous!

He'd almost lost control under the spray and shot his load while Jake was playing with his ass, and then again when Jake came all over him. *Jesus, that was hot.*

But he wanted Jake in bed, where they could stretch this out for a while—hours, if necessary. He wanted to taste that perfectly formed cock and teach Jake the glory of a nice, leisurely sixty-nine. He wanted to *make love* to Jake.

And so he did.

After they'd toweled off, Danny had Jake stretch out on his bed and then he climbed on top. He was pleased to discover that Jake wasn't at all squeamish about sucking cock. In fact, he was extremely enthusiastic about it and not half bad, once he'd figured out how to keep his teeth out of the way. Although he did use his teeth to nibble gently on Danny's foreskin, which drove Danny wild.

Danny felt his orgasm building and he tried to pull his cock out of Jake's mouth, but Jake grabbed his ass and held him in place. "I'm going to come in your mouth," Danny warned, panting, but he was too far gone to put up any more resistance.

His cock pulsed and spewed deep into Jake's throat. Jake didn't react except to pull Danny closer and try to swallow more of his cock as it squirted more times than Danny could ever remember it doing before. Jake swallowed all of it and continued sucking and licking until the last of it oozed out.

Danny had been avoiding something, though he desperately wanted to do it, because he wasn't sure how Jake would react. But now he lost all control and pushed himself forward, pulled Jake's legs up on either side of his shoulders, and spread them with his elbows so he could duck his head down to meet Jake's upturned ass.

"You're not...," Jake gasped, but whatever he intended to say was lost in a drawn-out moan. "Oh my God...."

It didn't take long before Jake came without touching himself for the second time, erupting between their pressed-together bodies. When Danny lifted himself up and sat down on the bed beside him, Jake had his hand covering his eyes. "I can't believe something that gross is the most intensely hot thing I've ever felt in my life."

Danny laughed. "A lot of people like it. I certainly do."

"But you're sticking your tongue up someone's ass!"

"Don't worry. I won't make you do it to me."

Jake sighed and dropped his hand from his face. Looking up into Danny's eyes, he said, "If it feels half as good to you as it does to me, I'll do it for you."

Danny smiled back at him. "You're very sweet."

"Your come tastes totally awesome, though," Jake added. "I definitely want more of that!"

"Luckily for you, I have an unending supply."

Jake looked so adorable that Danny couldn't resist leaning down to kiss him, only hesitating when he remembered what he'd just been doing. But Jake grabbed him and pulled him down to kiss him passionately, any squeamishness he might have had apparently forgotten. He was a good kisser, considering his lack of experience—at least with men. Perhaps he'd kissed girls. Though, if he had, that was the last thing Danny wanted to think about at the moment.

When Jake finally allowed him to sit up again Danny said, "I'm totally safe, but… in general, I wouldn't recommend swallowing on a first date."

"Oh." Jake's eyes widened. "I guess that wasn't very smart."

"Don't worry about it. I'm clean. The clinic on campus has free screenings for HIV and other STDs." He quirked an eyebrow. "I wouldn't normally recommend *believing* it when some guy tells you he's clean, either. But I'm telling the truth."

"I trust you." Jake looked a little uncomfortable when he added, "And you don't have to worry about me."

"Virgin?"

Jake nodded. "You knew that, didn't you?"

"I knew I was your first guy. You said you'd never told anyone you were gay before… that night, and it's a little hard to keep that a secret from a guy when you're fucking him. Plus that comment about losing your virginity was a dead giveaway. But I thought you might have had sex with girls—just not men."

"God, no." The expression of distaste that accompanied that statement made Danny laugh. "I flirted with girls a little, when my friends were around...."

"Keeping up appearances?"

Jake flushed a little. "Yeah. You know how it is."

Not really, Danny thought. But he kept it to himself. He leaned forward to look at the clothes Jake had tossed on the floor, doing his best to ignore Jake's finger sliding up his leg to poke gently at his entrance. *God, I hope he gets it into his head to fuck me later.* Danny found Jake's discarded shirt and snatched it to use as a come rag.

"Dude!" Jake laughed. "That's my shirt!"

"It's your spooge," Danny said, wiping his belly dry, "so it can go on your shirt."

"I'm gonna have to wash that before it stains," Jake grumbled, but he allowed Danny to wipe him off with it too.

When they were both dry, Danny tossed the shirt back onto the floor and stretched out to lie beside Jake, his arm draped across Jake's chest and his head nestled in Jake's armpit. Jake pulled the sheet over them and they lay together, sleepy and content. Danny listened to Jake's even heartbeat and relaxed into the gentle rise and fall of his chest, enjoying the faint scent of masculine musk Jake exuded mixed with the smell of castile soap.

Just as he was about to drift off to sleep, he heard Jake ask softly, "So what happens now?"

"We take a nap?"

"I mean with us. Are we... boyfriends? Or just roommates who fuck around?"

Danny sighed and rubbed Jake's chest slowly. "I won't rule out being boyfriends. But... maybe it would be better to just be fuck-buddies for a while."

"Why?" He sounded hurt. Of course.

"Because we just met, really. I like you, and I think you're really hot. But I've had bad luck with relationships—"

Suck that cock, faggot....

"—and I'd just… like to take it slow."

"But you want to keep fucking me."

Danny raised his head so he could look Jake in the eye. Their faces were inches apart and to his horror, he could see Jake's eyes glistening, as if he were fighting back tears. *God, don't cry! I won't be able to take that.* "It's entirely up to you. I'll understand if you don't want to sleep with someone who isn't going to commit. But I really enjoyed it, and I'd like us to keep doing it."

Jake blinked hard and looked away. "So you're going to keep sleeping with other guys?"

Fucking faggot whore….

"Do you want us to be monogamous, as long as we're sleeping together?" Danny asked. "I'm fine with that if it's what you want."

Jake nodded. He looked so vulnerable at that moment it took all Danny's strength not to wrap his arms around him and swear to love him forever. And for all Danny knew, he *could* love Jake. But could Jake love him? Even after he found out the truth? Danny wasn't sure he could handle falling for Jake just to see his affection turn to disgust.

"Okay. Monogamous sex partners," Danny said, trying to sound cheerful about it, as if he didn't know they were both craving so much more. "At least, until we get to know each other. Then maybe we can take it further, when we're ready."

Jake sighed. "Okay."

CHAPTER SEVENTEEN

IT WASN'T easy for Jake to go back to ordinary reality after that weekend. For one brief moment, he'd thought the universe might have forgiven him for what he'd done to Tom—for what he'd done to *himself*. But all Danny wanted was sex. What a fucking kick in the teeth. Jake had thought....

Well, probably everybody thought they found true love the first time they had sex.

And the sex was still there, beautiful and hot and sweet and fucking *epic*, whenever he and Danny could find a moment alone. Which was a *lot*. Several times a day. It was hard to find time to study.

Not that Jake was complaining.

The first time he gave Danny a rim job—Jake hadn't even known there was a term for it—he'd been really nervous that it would smell bad or the taste would make him gag or something. But Danny had showered and he was clean. The smell and taste had just been... kind of musky. Not bad at all. And once he got into it, he couldn't get enough. Especially when he heard the way it made Danny moan.

Danny had warned him that rimming wasn't exactly safe sex. It was debatable how risky it was, in terms of HIV—supposedly saliva and stomach acid killed the virus—but HIV wasn't the only potentially fatal STD. And there were other STDs that were incurable and unpleasant, even if they weren't fatal. So Jake knew he was being a bit foolish, trusting that Danny was telling him the truth about not having any of the STDs the school clinic tested for. But he couldn't help it. He instinctively trusted Danny.

He knew Danny wanted to be fucked. And Jake did want to try it. But the thought of it made him nervous. He wasn't even sure why. It just seemed so... intense might be the word. Or hardcore. He was perfectly willing to admit that he was a little naïve about sex, but the idea of sticking his dick in someone's ass really grossed him out. Yes, he'd heard of it before. And yes, he'd seen some pictures of it in a porn magazine. But still, licking the *outside* of Danny's asshole was one thing; going *inside* was another.

Fortunately, Danny didn't pressure him. Danny never made him feel like he wasn't good enough in bed or tried to make him do things he wasn't comfortable with. But Jake was desperate to make him happy, and part of him was convinced it was his inexperience that made Danny reluctant to commit to a relationship.

But he didn't really know. He thought of Danny as his best friend, and as far as he could tell, Danny thought of him the same way. The sex hadn't changed that. They still hung out together all the time, talking about whatever random shit came to mind, going on increasingly chilly walks in the college woods, playing D&D—which Jake was beginning to enjoy, despite the baffling rules…. And Jake pretty much had every inch of Danny's body, including parts Danny himself couldn't see, committed to memory. Eva had joked that they were beginning to *act* like a couple, even if they weren't having sex, not knowing of course that they *were*.

But despite all that, Jake was beginning to sense there was something Danny was holding back from him—something he never wanted to talk about. Something dark. Something that made him cry when he didn't think anyone could hear.

Jake had only caught him a couple of times, though he suspected it happened other nights as well. It had happened the night after they'd first had sex. He'd awoken to find Danny crying very softly. They were lying together in Jake's bed, Jake spooning Danny's warm, naked body with one hand draped around Danny's waist. The moment Jake stirred, Danny seemed to freeze, but Jake had the weird impression that something was wrong.

"Are you okay?"

Danny didn't answer, but Jake knew he wasn't sleeping. He raised himself up on his elbow so he could look down at Danny's face. Even though he was turned away and covering his eyes with his hand, Jake could see the shimmer of wetness on his cheeks. "Are you crying?"

"It's nothing."

"What do you mean 'nothing'? Why are you crying?"

With a frustrated snarl, Danny wiped the tears away with his hand. "Go back to sleep, Jake."

"What the fuck?"

"Jake!" The warning in his voice was clear, so Jake let it drop. But as he laid his head back on the pillow, he felt unsettled and worried. He couldn't escape the thought that he must be doing something wrong if Danny wasn't happy in his arms.

The second time was about a week later. Danny was sitting up in bed when Jake woke. He didn't actually see tears this time, though he saw Danny wipe his face quickly. Jake didn't try to force him to talk but lifted his hand to stroke Danny's naked back. Danny tensed for a second before relaxing into the caress. After a few moments, he lifted the blankets off Jake's body and leaned down to take Jake's cock into his mouth. Jake was surprised, and he suspected Danny was doing it to distract him. But it worked. Within seconds, Jake was no longer able to think coherently about anything.

THE ONE thing Danny hadn't expected when he got involved with Jake was that the nightmares would grow worse. He hadn't been having them that often since he'd arrived at UNH. Hardly at all, in fact. Everything was different here.

Well, mostly. There were students from his high school at UNH, so he hadn't completely escaped from them. Mark was the worst. There had been no way the college could have known not to put Danny in with someone from his old school, but it had been like a slap in the face nonetheless. Things had seemed okay at first, as though Mark might be willing to let things lie. Then Danny made the mistake of trusting him.

But all of that aside, Jake was the complete opposite of Mark— sweet, considerate, amazingly handsome, and gay, of course, even if he was still in the closet. Danny had no doubt Jake wanted him, at least sexually. So things should have been good.

Except that now the nightmares came almost every night. And it was harder to hide it when they were sharing a bed. Jake hadn't woken up often—thank God he was a sound sleeper—but when he did he tried to comfort Danny, which just made it worse. If Jake really understood what was going on, he'd drop Danny in a second. Well, Danny had to admit, maybe he wouldn't be quite that cold about it. Jake was a good guy. He'd try to be sympathetic, perhaps. Maybe they'd stay friends. But he'd certainly give up this silly fantasy he had about there ever being anything serious between them.

There were times when Danny wanted to tell him the truth, times when he thought he was just being an asshole by letting it all drag out. It would be better for Jake if he nipped this relationship in the bud. It was already too late to avoid hurting the guy. The longer things went on, the more painful it would be for Jake when he realized Danny wasn't what he'd been hoping for. But every time Danny thought about ending it, Jake would smile at him as if he loved him, or give him a gentle caress, and his resolve would melt. The fantasy was too beautiful, too seductive.

But he knew it was just a matter of time.

Chapter Eighteen

Jake's first snowfall at Eaton House was magical. It came down in fat, downy flakes and blanketed the landscape like his best Christmas fantasy. By midafternoon all classes were cancelled, and the snow was still coming down hard.

Jake was ecstatic. He loved the snow. He dragged Danny and Eva outside for a brief snowball fight until they both started grousing about being cold and having snow melting down their necks and went back inside. Paul, of course, never set foot out the door. But Jake didn't care. He stayed outside by himself, trying to build a snowman. It wasn't quite deep enough yet—his snowman had as much dirt and dead leaves embedded in it as it did snow—but he found a couple of pebbles for eyes and then ran into the dorm to beg for a carrot to use as the nose. Nobody had one. The dorm had a small kitchenette, but most of the students used it for cooking ramen noodles or macaroni and cheese out of a box. Nobody had a supply of fresh vegetables on hand. Not even the hippies—he checked.

Eventually, someone turned up a fluorescent-orange plastic kazoo. About ten students followed Jake outside to watch him plant the silly thing in the middle of the snowman's face. A cheer rose up and the snowman was declared a masterpiece of postmodern art—whatever the hell that meant—before everyone scurried back inside to warm up.

A short time later, as the sky was beginning to darken, the campus carillon proclaimed the hour. Jake had thought the carillon was beautiful when he'd first arrived at UNH as an eighteen-year-old, but like most students he soon grew tired of it—it was programmed to play just a few songs, and some of them had mistakes in them. But with the snow falling softly all around him, the carillon bells sounded ethereal and magical. Jake went inside to see if he could catch his friends before they trudged up the hill to the dining commons.

What he found in the lounge took his breath away.

It was Danny, looking magnificent in a black tuxedo. There were other people in the lounge, all dressed to the nines in tuxes and evening gowns, but Jake was only dimly aware of them. He'd never seen Danny like this, and Jake was amazed by how beautiful he was—hair slightly damp and combed back from his high, smooth forehead for once and tucked behind his ears. He was turned profile when Jake first saw him, eyebrows furrowed as he seemed to be scanning the crowded room. Then he turned and saw Jake, and his face lit up with a radiant smile. For one brief moment, Jake fantasized he was walking down the aisle with Danny standing at the altar dressed like that, smiling, waiting for him....

"There you are!" Danny exclaimed, coming up to him. "Shane thought we should all commemorate the first snow by dressing up and processing to dinner in *style*." Shane was one of the theater majors living on the first floor.

Jake was enthralled by the way the waves of Danny's golden-brown hair shimmered like satin when he moved his head. But he brought his attention back to what Danny was saying. "I don't have a tux."

Danny shrugged. "You kind of have to have one if you're a music major. A lot of the theater majors have them too. The girls have evening gowns. Everyone else is just dressing up in their best clothes."

Jake wasn't poor. He had all the clothes he needed, but generally his wardrobe consisted of jeans and T-shirts, with some athletic wear thrown in. He did own a couple of business suits, but he hated them. They would make him feel even more out of place in this gathering of musicians and actors and artists than his current, somewhat sweaty attire.

"Don't worry about it," Danny said, reaching up to put his hands around the back of Jake's neck, inside his winter jacket. "There isn't time for you to change anyway."

Jake thought he might be moving in for a kiss—though he'd never done anything that bold in public before. Jake was still technically in the closet, despite the fact that rumors were probably running rampant, and Danny was doing his best not to out him. Danny brought his hands around to the front and fastened something under

Jake's Adam's apple. Then he stepped back and gave him an appraising look.

"Perfect!"

Jake lifted a hand and found a bowtie fastened around his neck.

"Let's go, people!" Shane called from across the room, waving a silver candelabrum in one hand. "Break a leg!"

They processed up the hill, about forty of them, wearing boots—they weren't dumb enough to wade through half a foot of snow in dress shoes and high heels—but heedless of the snowflakes accumulating on their jackets and wraps. Shane, tall and lanky in his tux, brandished the candelabrum like a sword and led the charge. When they entered the dining hall, shivering but fabulous, the students there gawked at them, then laughed and applauded.

Jake executed a dramatic bow alongside his dorm mates, struggling to keep his expression solemn, though inside he was bursting with joy. For the first time since he'd moved in almost two months ago, he felt like he belonged. His shitty, mind-numbing major no longer mattered. He'd found his true home, among people he'd always been told were "weirdos." Well, if this was what weird was like, then bring it on! He was an artist! He'd just built his first postmodern snowman—whatever that was—and he'd just made his first *entrance*!

DANNY WATCHED Jake all through dinner, marveling at his energy. He was grinning from ear to ear. The Eatonites had more or less taken over one of Philbrick's dining rooms—the one that overlooked the dorm—and violated the rules by moving all the tables into a giant U. When they began competing with each other to see who could make the most pompous, affected toasts, Jake jumped up more than once to play along. Danny had never seen him happier. It was adorable.

"That kid needs Ritalin," Paul grumbled under his breath.

"No," Danny replied, looking up at Jake—who was standing beside him, going on about lunching with Princess Diana that afternoon—and smiled fondly. "No, he doesn't."

When Jake finally wound down long enough to take his seat again, Danny said in a fake British accent, "I say, old man—where did you get your bow tie? It's quite dashing."

"You're too kind. I believe my valet purchased it at Victoria's Secret."

"Oh! They have such *lovely* negligees!"

"Quite. I own several."

Danny noticed Eva watching them from across the table with a smug expression on her face. *Oops. She's on to us.* Not that Eva would seriously think they were cross-dressing. But there was something about the way she was smiling at the two of them that made it clear she regarded them as a cute couple.

Hopefully Jake wouldn't freak out if she said something. But really, they hadn't exactly been secretive. They were inseparable, they touched each other a bit too much in public, and the way Jake looked at him when Danny played piano in the lounge was pretty much a dead giveaway.

After dinner, they all went back to the dorm. The mood that evening was too mellow to do anything productive, so homework was tossed aside for hanging out and watching videos of Christmas specials in the downstairs lounge—after they had changed into more comfortable clothes, of course. Danny wasn't at all surprised to discover that Jake adored the specials and could recite the dialog of *Rudolph, the Red-Nosed Reindeer* and *A Charlie Brown Christmas*. But it was also clear that Jake wanted to get outside again. He kept going to the glass sliding doors and sticking his head out.

When the snowfall hadn't stopped by ten o'clock, Jake suggested taking a walk in it to anybody within hearing. Danny wasn't sure he felt like trudging through a foot and a half or more of accumulated snow on the ground, but he could see the excitement and anticipation in Jake's eyes. So they ran upstairs and donned their winter jackets and boots and then gathered in the lounge. This idea had met with less enthusiasm than the march to the dining commons, so in the end there were only about fifteen people. Eva decided to come along, but there was no way anyone was dragging Paul back out into this weather. Unfortunately,

Mark was one of those tagging along, but Danny could handle that as long as he didn't start anything.

The snow had transformed the landscape into something beautiful and ethereal, and as they crossed the minidorm circle and climbed up to the train tracks, they barely spoke, reluctant to disturb the silence. Or near silence—their footsteps made muffled *chump*ing sounds in the fallen snow, they were panting a bit, and the faint sound of traffic on Route 4 could be heard in the distance. There was also a dog barking at one of the farm houses on the edge of the college woods. But there was no wind, no nearby traffic, no laughter or shouts coming from the dorms.

Just a lonely band of explorers with snow drifting down around them like a veil from a low-hanging slate-gray sky.

As they crossed the tracks, Joe, one of the theater majors, laughed and said, "All right, everyone keep an eye on Mark."

"Shut up," Mark said.

"We've managed to make it this far without fatalities."

"I said shut up."

"Mark decided to stick his tongue to one of the railroad ties last year," Eva explained to Jake, since he was the only one there who hadn't been at Eaton during the incident. "It was a pretty cold night and it froze there."

"I was shitfaced," Mark growled. He had been, Danny knew. Danny had been pretty drunk that night too, and he didn't feel like taking that little trip down memory lane any more than Mark did.

But Kevin wasn't done ribbing Mark. He told Jake, "The train started coming, and he practically ripped his tongue off to escape."

"Jesus," Jake said.

"It was just the tip," Mark protested. "I had a…" He waved a hand in the air as he tried to think of the word. "…canker sore for few days. That was all."

Eva grimaced. "Sounds lovely."

They continued down the path on the other side of the tracks, heading past the transformers and some small brick buildings Danny had never bothered to learn the identity of, until the road turned off into the college woods. Nobody was in the mood to go trudging through the forest in the snow, especially at night. So they turned around.

Jake did something odd on the way back—he reached out and took Danny's hand in his. He didn't say anything, or even really look at Danny, beyond a quick glance and a shy smile. But the others saw it. Everyone pretended it was perfectly normal, but Danny could see the surprise they were struggling to mask. Except for Eva, who merely looked smug.

It was sweet and it felt very romantic to be walking hand in hand on this beautiful evening, but Danny knew that it was a big deal to Jake. He'd just outed himself, not just to Danny, but to the entire dorm.

It shouldn't have bothered Danny. He'd been out himself for years, and he rarely thought much about it. And Eaton House was pretty much the most gay-friendly dorm on campus. So Jake should be perfectly safe. But Danny saw something in Mark's eyes, something calculated and malicious in that brief look at Danny's hand in Jake's, and he couldn't help but worry.

CHAPTER NINETEEN

"I'M GOING to die."

"No," Jake said patiently, "what you're gonna do is have fun."

Paul frowned at him, the ear flaps on his brown knit hat making him resemble a fighter pilot. A petulant one. "Fun? Look at how *steep* that is!"

They were at the top of the hill beside the college library, which had a nice long stretch of even lawn and was probably the best sledding hill on campus. With all the snow that had accumulated the night before, it was swarming with students on cheap plastic sleds and saucers. Jake had already been down the hill more times than he could count, and so had Danny and Eva. But Paul had been standing at the top of the hill for almost two hours, griping about the cold and threatening to go into the library and do something productive.

Finally, Jake had had enough and practically picked him up bodily to shove him into the sled.

"It's not that steep," Jake countered. "Christ, Paul, haven't you ever gone sledding before?"

He was on the sled with Paul, partly to reassure him and partly to keep him from bailing. He had his arms around Paul's middle and his legs on either side, which forced Paul's butt into his crotch. The position might have been sexy if it was Danny in the sled with him, but Paul didn't stir anything in him except perhaps a sense of protectiveness. The guy needed friends to drag him out of his safe little world of D&D and fantasy novels now and then, kicking and screaming if necessary. And Jake felt obligated to do his part. The gaming and the novels were okay—Jake had finally finished book one of the Mercedes Lackey trilogy and been forced by Eva to start book two—but they could all use a lot more fresh air and exercise, and as far as Jake was concerned, that was *his* contribution to the group.

"Yes," Paul grumbled, "and I hated it."

"Well, today you're gonna *love* it!"

And with that, Jake pushed off.

Paul screamed. It would have been surprising if he hadn't. But Jake ignored him and concentrated on steering the sled around the few large bumps on the hill and other sledders who were moving too slow. Jake didn't fuck around when it came to sledding. He went *fast*. If Paul hadn't been there, clutching Jake's knees in terror, he would have hit all those bumps and tried to get airborne. In fact, as they approached the bottom of the hill, it occurred to Jake that this might be the only time Paul would get on a sled with him, and there was one small outcropping left he'd been planning to steer around....

Fuck it. They were going over. Paul was going into space. This would be a sled ride to remember, damn it! Not some wussy attempt to avoid all danger.

Paul apparently figured out Jake's evil plan just as the outcropping swung into their path. He screamed, "Nooooooo!"—all drawn out like in a cartoon—and then they were *flying*! It was unlikely they got more than three feet off the ground, but it was marvelous. For a moment, they were weightless, and then they slammed down in a spray of snow and barreled down the rest of the slope. Jake contemplated tilting the sled over, because that was the sort of thing *he* found fun, but he suppressed the urge, digging his heels into the snow instead to bring them to a more or less graceful stop.

He climbed out of the sled and turned back to see if Paul needed a hand getting up. Paul wasn't moving. His face was red and he was glaring up at Jake, his arms folded across his chest.

"You did that on purpose!"

"Yee-*up*!"

"What if we'd flipped over?"

Jake was panting a bit, though less from exertion than adrenaline. He shrugged. "We would have rolled into the snow. It happens. Life goes on."

"You're an asshole."

"Wanna do it again?"

Paul's mouth opened, hung there for a minute as if the suggestion was so absurd it had caused his brain to short circuit, and then snapped shut again. He climbed out of the sled and began trudging up the hill, looking ridiculously childlike in his sweater, winter jacket, scarf, hat, and two layers of pants. After a few steps, he turned back to look at Jake impatiently. "Well, come on."

Jake had to carry the sled, of course.

Danny and Eva were waiting at the top of the hill. They only had the one cheap plastic sled between the four of them. The Durham Marketplace—affectionately known as "the DuMP"—had put them out a couple of weeks ago for just a few bucks each, and Jake had picked one up in anticipation of snow. The others hadn't been quite as enthusiastic, and this morning, with ten thousand students hitting the local stores for anything resembling a sled or a saucer, the town was pretty much tapped dry.

Eva had named the sled "The Blue Ballistic Bomber," and they were all hoping it would survive until at least the end of the semester, if not the whole winter.

Paul went down the hill again, and even a third time, though he insisted upon Jake going with him each time, and nothing could cajole him into making a fourth trip. Eva and Danny both grumbled that nobody was protecting *them* from a possible sledding fatality, so Jake took a turn with each of them. Then he took one more turn with Danny, because he liked the feel of Danny's butt snuggled up in his crotch.

NOBODY HAD commented on Jake quietly coming out the night before, at least not in Danny's presence. Of course Eva had probably guessed and Paul most likely didn't care. Hopefully the rest of the dorm would be cool. Nobody had ever bothered Danny, except for Mark. But if Jake started holding Danny's hand in the lounge or kissing him in front of everyone… that might test some boundaries. Danny wasn't particularly worried about himself, but he was fretting about what it could do to Jake if some people reacted badly.

At least nobody would be dumb enough to threaten him physically. After a naked Jake had chased Danny into their room, word had gotten around pretty fast about how muscular he was—and how scary he could be when he was pissed. Even Mark was liable to think twice about antagonizing him.

Apart from his concerns, Danny was pleased that Jake no longer felt he needed to hide. And the way he'd announced it…. Well, after that gesture, everyone would pretty much assume they were a couple. Even though they weren't.

But it's a nice fantasy.

When they'd gotten back to the room that night, neither had said a word. They'd simply undressed, lit the illegal sandalwood candle Danny kept in his top drawer, and turned off the lights. The sex had been sweet and gentle—the closest they'd ever come to "making love." Unfortunately, that voice of warning in the back of Danny's mind had refused to be silenced, and later when they fell asleep, the nightmares had punished him for daring to hope.

It wasn't for him, this cozy, almost domestic, fantasy. It would never be for him.

But daylight and Jake's enthusiasm for getting outside to take advantage of the snow had temporarily banished the darkness. The hill by the library was one of the traditional spots for sledding on campus, so by the time they'd arrived, it was packed with students. But Jake had been undaunted. He plowed into the fray, dragging his three more socially challenged companions behind him—including Paul, who'd only come along under duress. And they'd all had a wonderful time. The crowd didn't seem that big a deal, once they were going down the slope. Even the occasional collision or near miss just added to the fun.

When Jake convinced Paul to go down the hill with him, Eva had proclaimed it a miracle. After the *third* time, she declared Jake a saint, pending acknowledgement from the Vatican. But Jake wasn't impressed.

"I'm not Catholic," he told her as they walked back to the dorm.

"Would you like to be? I get to count conversions in my own list of miracles."

In response, he emitted an enormous, resonant belch.

"I'll take that as a yes."

"If she hands you a cracker or a glass of wine," Danny warned his roommate, "don't take it. It might seal the deal."

They dropped off the sled in the lounge and went to lunch. But immediately afterward, Jake was outside organizing the Eatonites to build a snow labyrinth. Eva and Paul sat that one out, but Danny sighed and went out to be supportive. Sonny was one of the participants, and by the time the maze started to show some real promise, he shouted across it to Jake, "Dude! I think we should make you the official winter activities coordinator!"

A general cheer of "Huzzah!" went up among the twenty or so maze-builders.

"Is there such a thing?" Jake asked Danny, who was helping him roll snowballs for the two snowmen Jake wanted to guard the entrance to the maze.

Danny shook his head. "Not really. At least, not until now. I think you just got elected."

"Great." It was hard to tell if he was being sarcastic or if he actually liked the idea.

Danny shouted back at Sonny, "I think this project should count as Jake's dorm project!"

"Don't look at me," Sonny replied. "I'm just the RA. The committee has to vote."

It turned out the members of the committee were all present, so a quick vote was taken. It passed.

"Seriously?" Jake asked, looking completely broadsided. He'd been struggling to come up with an idea ever since Danny pointed out that posing naked in the lounge for art students to sketch might be deemed "pornographic," considering Jake's usual reaction to being naked in front of people.

"Congratulations, roomie! You've just gotten credit for your project."

Jake grinned broadly, surveying the labyrinth taking shape on the dorm lawn. It was certainly a work of art, albeit a temporary one. "Cool," he said.

CHAPTER TWENTY

THE LAST two weeks of December and the first two of January were Christmas break. Or, as Jake preferred to think of it, The Longest Month of the Year. It was going to be made worse by the fact that he would now be enduring his father's cold silence and his brothers' pummeling while pining for Danny—and without the support of his mother. She'd moved out just after Thanksgiving.

"She's staying with Aunt Helen for now," Robbie told him over the phone when Jake called home to arrange a ride. "Dad's acting like a bear in a bee's nest. Christmas is gonna suck—no decorations, no dinner, he won't even let us put up a tree."

Apart from being impressed by his brother's use of an analogy—neither twin was particularly fluent in English, despite it being their only language—Jake was miserable to hear that things were developing so fast. Though he supposed it only felt fast because he was away so much. To his mother, it probably hadn't been nearly fast enough.

After he hung up with Robbie, he dialed his aunt's house and spoke with his mom.

"I'm sorry to spoil your Christmas, sweetheart, I really am," she told him. "Your brothers' too. But once I told your father I was leaving him, things got very tense between us. He does *not* handle rejection well."

Jake felt sick in the pit of his stomach. A thought had just occurred to him that he'd never had before. "Mom... he didn't... hurt you, did he?"

"No, Jake," she answered evenly. "That was never an issue. I could say a lot of things about your father—not that I will—but he never raised a hand to me. Trust me on that."

Jake breathed a sigh of relief. "I don't blame you for needing to get away, Mom. It doesn't matter about Christmas. You need to look out for yourself, for once."

"Thank you for understanding, sweetheart. I'd like it if you could swing by sometime over the holidays. It doesn't have to be Christmas Day."

"I will."

He told Danny about the situation, of course, not expecting anything but a little sympathy. Danny surprised him by saying, "Why don't you spend Christmas at my house?"

Jake stared at him like an idiot for a minute. Then he asked, "You mean Christmas Day?"

"I mean the whole four weeks. If you want to. It doesn't sound like you really want to go home this year."

That was an understatement. Jake shrugged, for some reason feeling he shouldn't appear overeager. "That would be cool, if your mother doesn't mind. Four weeks is a long time for a houseguest."

"True," Danny agreed. "Come on."

He got up from his bed and led Jake downstairs to the TARDIS phone booth. Jake felt awkward standing there and listening in on Danny's conversation, but Danny was the one who'd told him to tag along. Everything seemed to go okay, at first. Danny asked his mother if it would be okay to have a friend come home for break—all four weeks of it—and she seemed cool with it.

Then he said, "No, don't bother putting him in the guest room. He'll just sleep with me."

Jake nearly choked on his own tongue. "Dude!"

"Hold on, Mom. I'll call you back in just a minute." Danny hung up the phone and leaned against the wall of the booth. Fortunately, nobody else was in the lounge at the moment. "Sorry, I wasn't thinking. I assumed if you were out here, you'd be out at my house."

"Not necessarily."

Danny grimaced. "I'll tell her you're going to sleep on the floor. We have an air mattress that's pretty comfortable."

"It's too late *now*," Jake protested. "She already thinks we're fucking!"

"She might believe me, if I tell her we just like to talk—"

The phone rang and Danny picked it up. "Hello? No, Mom. We're not fucking."

Jake groaned. "Screw it! If you want her to know, go ahead and tell her."

"Scratch that. We *are* fucking." Danny paused a minute. "I can't help it if he's indecisive. But he's cute, so I put up with it."

They talked a bit longer, arranging the details, while Jake quietly hyperventilated and paced back and forth in front of the booth. On the one hand, it was kind of cool that Danny's mother seemed okay with them sharing a bed—and having sex. They wouldn't have to sneak around, grabbing a kiss or a caress when her back was turned, and then go to sleep in different rooms, about to explode from sexual frustration. On the other hand, Danny had just *outed* him—to his mother!

Asshole.

When Danny hung up the phone, Jake stood there a moment, glaring at him.

"I said I was sorry," Danny said, spreading his hands in surrender. "I tell my mom everything. And I thought you'd want to keep sleeping together. I mean, it's four weeks, man."

Jake frowned and shook his head. Then he sighed. "Fine. I just think you should have asked me first."

"Yes. I'm sorry."

"Okay."

Danny stepped out of the booth and put his hands on Jake's hips. That kind of gesture had been more common lately, for both of them. So far, nobody in the dorm had objected. Danny raised his face, and Jake leaned down to kiss him. That was something they hadn't been brave enough to try when there were people around.

"Would you like to have makeup sex?" Danny asked him, smiling impishly.

"Okay."

Danny turned to go upstairs, with Jake trailing behind him, but he stopped on the first step and turned around, a look of distress on his face. "Oh. I forgot to mention... we don't really do Christmas."

"Don't… *do* Christmas?"

"We don't celebrate it. We're Wiccan, so we celebrate the Solstice and Yule instead."

Jake knew Danny's mother was into Reiki and meditation, and Danny had described her as "kind of New Age," but he hadn't thought much about it otherwise. "What's 'Wiccan'?"

DANNY WAS surprised to learn that Jake had never even heard of Wicca. There were about a million books in the stores about it. Then again, he couldn't imagine Jake browsing the occult section at Barnes & Noble, so maybe it wasn't so unlikely after all. He spent some time explaining the basics—how it was an earth-based religion, honoring both a god and a goddess, and following the cycles of the moon and the seasons.

"*Which* god and goddess?" Jake asked.

Danny shrugged. "Pretty much any of them. Mom's coven likes Herne, the god of the Wild Hunt, and Brighid, the goddess of the hearth."

"The hearth?"

"The home," Danny explained. "Well, technically the fire that warms it. The point is, different covens honor different gods, depending on who they feel an affinity for. But they have two, because they believe there has to be a balance between male and female."

Jake regarded him for a moment, his brow furrowed. "Do you believe all this?" he asked finally.

"I'm kind of agnostic, but I'll roll with it in a pinch. It's what my mom raised me with."

"I think my parents are Baptist. But we never went to church."

They were lying naked on Jake's bed, spent from sex and a little on the sweaty side. Danny rolled on top of him, feeling Jake's cock almost instantly harden between their abdomens. The guy was inexhaustible. "Look, you don't have to believe it. You can think it's silly, if you want. Just don't make fun of it in front of my mom, okay?"

"I'm not a complete barbarian," Jake grumbled. "I know not to insult my host and not to pee on the carpet."

"Glad to hear it."

Danny didn't hover around the phone when Jake called his brother back to beg off going home, but Jake was in a foul mood when he returned. "He's pissed" was all he said. Danny tried to pry more out of him but gave up when it was clear Jake didn't want to get into it.

The dorm was nearly empty on their last night of the semester. Sonny was downstairs in one of the empty rooms hosting a drinking party, despite the fact that half those present weren't quite twenty-one yet. Danny, Jake, Eva, and Paul were the only ones left in their wing, and Eva technically shouldn't have been there, because her last final had been two days before. But she'd convinced Sonny she needed to stay in order to drive the three boys home.

They decided to have a D&D campaign in the lounge. Wallace wasn't there, so that meant they couldn't continue the main campaign they were on, and Paul had to improvise a side adventure for the three of them while Wallace's character, Hastur, made a pilgrimage to a local temple. It was fun but not very eventful.

Danny found it more interesting to watch the subtle changes that had come over his friends in the past couple of weeks. Jake was openly affectionate—even flirtatious—with him now, not caring that Eva and Paul were watching. He poked Danny, made playful grabs at his knee, caressed his shoulder. After a particularly good roll that saved Jake/Berengar's neck from a worg, Jake even kissed his cheek. It was a little unsettling, given that their relationship had been in the closet for Danny as much as for Jake. He was relieved they were no longer hiding it, but he hadn't quite adjusted to being openly affectionate and kept glancing around to see who might be watching.

Eva and Paul acted as if it were perfectly ordinary, which made it easier. Paul had changed recently too. On the surface, he was still petulant and antisocial, but ever since Jake had taken him down the hill on the sled, he no longer made subtle jibes at the "jock" in their midst. It was a bit too early to say for certain, but Danny thought he saw a hint of admiration in Paul's eyes now whenever he looked at Jake.

And that pointed out another change. Even though Danny was sure—well, *pretty* sure—that Paul was straight, he found himself feeling a bit… proprietary whenever he caught Paul giving Jake that look. As if Jake was *his*.

Not good. Yet who had been the one to suggest spending a month together, more or less just the two of them?

The next morning, Eva dropped him and Jake off at Danny's house in Peterborough before heading on to Keene, where she and Paul lived. Danny had to admit, he loved his house. It was warm and welcoming, with small herb gardens flanking the door in the light half of the year, and a dried herbal wreath on the front door in the winter.

When he opened the door for Jake, he was acutely aware of the effort his mom went through to make the house a place of sanctuary. There was the tang of sandalwood incense in the air. Not a thick pall of it—just a faint lingering scent. The rooms were lit by Chinese lanterns and candles, producing a pleasant yellow-orange glow without harsh bright lights. You couldn't exactly read by it, but it was relaxing. The walls were decorated with prints from India and China, and the hardwood floor in the living room was largely covered by an Oriental carpet—fake, of course. His mom was far from wealthy. There was a low table in the center with a number of throw pillows surrounding it. Mom didn't really believe in sitting on chairs. And the fireplace had been lit.

"Wow," Jake breathed, as though afraid to disturb the peaceful atmosphere. "This is something else."

Danny's mother must have heard them enter, because she came scurrying out of Danny's bedroom, her caftan billowing around her small frame. "I thought I heard the door! Welcome to our home, Jake!"

Jake looked a little overwhelmed as she embraced him, kissed her son, and then took her guest by the hand to give him a brief tour of the house. Danny followed along, struggling not to laugh at Jake's bewildered expression while his mom jabbered on cheerfully.

There wasn't much to see. It was a single-story ranch with just a few rooms. But they were all clean and cozy. When they came to the sun-room, Jake noticed the tree in the corner and said, "Danny told me you don't celebrate Christmas."

Danny's mom laughed gently. "Oh, that isn't a Christmas tree, hon. It's a Yule tree."

Jake looked at her blankly.

Much to Danny's relief, his mother didn't go into the longwinded explanation. She simply said, "Let's just say it's a cross between the old pagan customs and the newer Christian ones."

"Okay."

The last room she showed him was Danny's bedroom. It looked exactly like it always had—except for the small basket full of condoms on the bed stand. That, and the bottle of lube next to it.

"Mom! For fuck's sake!" Danny went over to the basket and held it up. "Jake's going to think I host orgies here or something." He looked pointedly at Jake. "I do *not* normally have a basket full of condoms by my bed."

His mom shrugged. "I just want you boys to play safe."

All the blood had drained from Jake's face, and he looked like he might pass out. Danny decided to rescue him from further embarrassment. At least for the moment. "Thanks, Mom," he said with a wry smile. "Let me show Jake where he can put his stuff. We'll be out in a few minutes."

"All right, hon. I was thinking we could take Jake to the diner for dinner."

"Sure."

The look she gave them clearly suggested she thought they'd be up to something X-rated during those "few minutes," but she left them alone. Jake collapsed on the bed and buried his head in his hands. "Fuck me."

"If you like. We've got plenty of lube."

Jake groaned and sagged even further into his hands. Danny had to laugh. He sat on the bed beside him and said, "You knew it was coming."

"I didn't expect her to be so blatant about it," Jake protested. "She bought us *supplies*!"

Danny shrugged. "She's always like that. She sat me down for 'The Talk' before I'd even hit puberty. She wanted me to be prepared."

Jake raised his head and scrunched up his nose as if he smelled something disgusting. "Ew. My parents never even gave me 'The Talk.' I think they assumed the twins would tell me whatever I needed to know."

"Did they?"

He barked out a small, bitter laugh. "They taught me all the derogatory names for women they knew, and how to manipulate girls into putting out."

"Did it work?"

Jake gave him a look of disgust. "You don't seriously think I'd ever treat girls the way *they* did?"

Danny could see that Jake wasn't in the mood for teasing, so he backed off. Instead, he leaned forward and kissed him. "Look, my mom's just trying to show us she's cool. There are a lot worse things than your... friend's mom telling you it's okay to have sex with her son."

He'd almost said "boyfriend," and from the way Jake glanced at him, he knew it hadn't escaped notice. Fortunately, Jake didn't pursue it.

"Does she think we're screwing around right now?" he asked, looking at the closed bedroom door as if she might walk in at any moment with some sex toys she'd forgotten to leave behind.

"Maybe."

"How about we go eat some diner food?"

"Sure," Danny said. "But there won't be any avoiding things tonight." He waggled his eyebrows.

Jake sighed. "Yeah. I guess not."

CHAPTER TWENTY-ONE

DANNY'S MOTHER made it very clear that she was not to be called *Mrs.* Sullivan, because she'd never married Danny's father—"Thank the goddess!"—and she wasn't particularly fond of *Ms.* Sullivan either. She preferred Althea. "It's the Greek word for 'healing,' which is what I do!"

Jake suspected it wasn't her given name. According to Danny, it was common for people in the Wiccan religion to take on "craft" names—names they felt better represented their true spirit. That struck Jake as a little odd, but it was hardly the oddest thing he encountered at Danny's house. Besides, he thought the name suited her.

She was a vibrant woman and one who seemed fundamentally comfortable with who she was, or at least who she'd made herself into. Like Danny, she had flawless skin with a golden honey glow to it, and thick light-brown hair that shimmered like satin when she moved. Danny's mysterious father appeared to have contributed only one thing to his son's appearance—Althea's eyes were a bright, sparkling blue, instead of Danny's smoky gray. But if Jake ever met the guy, he'd have to thank him for that. Danny's eyes were the most beautiful eyes he'd ever seen.

Jake couldn't help but compare Althea to his own mother. Both were beautiful women, and he found them both admirable, but where his mother's strength seemed to be the ability to endure—until now, at any rate—Althea simply plowed through obstacles. Over the course of the evening, Jake learned details about her past that many people might have been embarrassed to talk about. As a young woman in college, she'd suddenly found herself with a newborn baby and no husband or family to rely on, yet she'd completed her liberal arts degree and worked whatever jobs she could find in order to support the two of them. At one point, she'd lived in some kind of commune in Vermont until the guru they all admired was accused of sexually harassing young women. He hadn't lived in that particular commune, but she'd left nevertheless. She had no tolerance for bullshit. But she'd never stepped off her path to spiritual fulfillment, and somehow she'd managed to survive and bring Danny along for the ride.

After they'd eaten at the Peterborough Diner—a great little place made from a 1950s train diner car—Althea drove the boys around town and gave Jake the two-dollar tour. It took about five minutes, and some of that was waiting for the lights to change. There were only a few streets. But they were quaint and beautiful under a thick blanket of snow.

"Danny had to go to high school in Keene," Althea told him. "And his friends always lived in different towns."

"That's because the guys in this town suck," Danny muttered darkly.

Althea's smile didn't falter, but she said, "Some of them."

This hint at some conflict between Danny and the local kids intrigued Jake, but there was no tactful way to ask about it and Althea was already talking about the other options for food in the area. "Danny will tell you, I'm not much of a cook."

"Come on, Mom. Your cooking's fine."

"Well I can cook a mean stir-fry and occasionally pull off a nice carob cake, but I'm nothing to boast about in the kitchen."

"My mom is a great cook," Jake said fondly, then wondered if he was being rude.

Althea didn't seem to take the comment personally. She smiled broadly. "That's wonderful. I do admire people who have that talent. Danny tells me you two are going to visit her on Christmas Day?"

"Yeah." He was actually a nervous wreck about it—having his sort-of boyfriend in the same room with his mom. But when Danny told him that he and Althea didn't do anything at all on Christmas, the solstice celebration being held on the twenty-first instead, he'd felt compelled to ask if Danny could come along. It was a little weird, under the circumstances, and he'd half expected his mother to say it was a bad time to have guests over. Especially since she herself was a guest in her sister's house. But she'd been okay with it. Of course, she didn't know that Danny was more to Jake than just his roommate.

Althea laughed. "I'm glad to hear it, because I don't have the faintest idea how to cook a turkey."

They returned to the house and spent a couple of hours chatting in front of the fire and drinking some kind of herbal tea Althea claimed to have blended herself. Jake had no idea what was in it, but she assured him there was nothing the federal government would kick the door down to get at. "It has a little valerian, which might make you sleepy, and a bit of lavender and rosemary, plus some spearmint. I call it 'Winding Down Tea.'"

All Jake knew was that it tasted minty and felt soothing.

When a strange pyramidal clock on the mantel emitted a quiet, barely audible chime, Althea rose and said good night. She kissed Danny on the top of his head and waggled her fingers at Jake. "Stay up as late as you like, but please remember to put the fire out. I'll see you both in the morning."

Once they were alone, Danny crawled across the short stretch of carpet separating him from Jake and began making out with him. It made Jake nervous to do it right in the living room—he pictured Althea coming out of her bedroom to get a glass of water or something—but he soon lost himself in the sensual feel of Danny's full lips against his own.

Then Danny whispered, "I've always wanted to make love in front of a warm fireplace."

"Jesus!" Jake gasped. Then he remembered to lower his voice. "Your mom could come out at any minute!"

Danny laughed quietly. "Dude, if having sex under the threat of being caught by a woman who'd just say 'oops' and run back to her room is too risky for you, you're in for a very dull life."

"Fine," Jake growled. "Fuck me in your living room. Tomorrow we can try the kitchen table."

So they stripped and stretched out on the oriental carpet, sixty-nining and—even though this made Jake far more nervous—rimming each other, while the warmth of the fire licked at their naked bodies. When they came, deep within each other's mouths, Jake felt grateful that Danny's cock prevented him from moaning too loudly.

They lay beside each other on the carpet, panting and enjoying the afterglow, until an unpleasant thought occurred to him. "Dude," he said quietly, "your house isn't… clothing optional, is it?"

"Are you hoping or dreading?"

"Kind of dreading."

Danny laughed, rolled over, and lifted himself up on his elbows to give Jake a kiss. "No. Don't worry, you won't wake up tomorrow to find my mom making pancakes in the nude."

"Good." Another thought occurred to him and he asked, "What about this solstice thing? You said some Wiccans like to do things naked."

"It's called 'skyclad,'" Danny said. "I shouldn't have worried you. Mom's friends don't really go in for that."

Jake hoped he hadn't said anything offensive. Dealing with people who had non-Christian religious beliefs was kind of new to him. But he was still relieved to hear he wasn't going to be surrounded by middle-aged naked people tomorrow night.

SO FAR, Jake seemed to be handling the solstice celebration fairly well, Danny thought. His eyes had gone a bit wide when Theron, the High Priest, donned his elaborate deer antler headband—Theron was straight, but he *did* love his pretty hats and gowns—but Jake kept whatever thoughts he might be having to himself. The ritual itself was only about an hour long, and Jake had said he'd participate. So he stood in the circle beside Danny, holding his hand and reciting the simple chants he'd been taught.

Afterward, during the Feast of Cakes and Ale, he seemed to relax, now that the "weird" part of the evening was safely behind him. He seemed especially delighted to discover that not everyone in the coven shared Danny's mother's devotion to vegetarianism. Theron had brought some venison stew.

"This is really good!" Jake exclaimed as he went back for a second bowl.

Persephone, the High Priestess, told him, "Theron's a hunter."

"Bow hunting," Theron chimed in from across the kitchen. "I prefer the bow. It's quiet. It allows me to be in tune with the forest."

"And kill things," added a voice heavy with disapproval. The speaker was new to the coven—an elderly woman who'd been introduced to Danny as Krauka. The name sounded oddly dissonant for a craft name—not that there were any real rules about it. She'd told him it meant "crow" in Old Norse.

"Hunters have been—"

"No debates, please!" Danny's mom interrupted before the conversation could blow up into an argument. "Let's just enjoy the holiday."

"Will you be greeting the dawn with us?" Persephone asked Jake.

"Yeah," Jake replied, glancing at Danny uncertainly. "I guess." Danny had explained to him that some—certainly not all—Wiccans liked to stay awake the entire night on the solstice, the longest and "darkest" night of the year, to herald the symbolic rebirth of the sun at daybreak. Again, he wasn't required to participate, but since Danny was doing it, Jake had decided to do so rather than sleep by himself. "I just hope I can stay awake."

Persephone laughed lightly and placed a hand on his arm. "Don't worry, I'm sure we can think of some way to keep you awake."

She was a bit younger than Danny's mother, and a little on the short side, with dark curls and rosy cheeks like a cherub. The straight guys in the coven all seemed to think she was cute. Now she was smiling at Jake in a way that looked....

Yeah, Danny was pretty sure she was flirting. But hopefully Jake could handle himself. He didn't appear to be in distress. If anything, he seemed happy to have someone talking to him about something other than pagan gods, magical elements, and psychic energy. Danny left him to it while he went to get another cup of wassail.

Sunrise wasn't until 7:16 a.m., so that left them with about nine hours to kill after they'd eaten. The entire coven wasn't staying the night—Krauka and some of the other older members had little interest in screwing around with their sleep cycles, and others had to work on Sundays and didn't think their bosses would be understanding if they nodded off halfway through their shifts. So that left seven people including Danny and Jake.

His mother didn't own a television, so they had no choice but to talk to each other. Danny and Jake were the youngest in the group by at least ten or fifteen years, but Danny had always found the coven members pleasant to hang out with. Raven and Hedda, a husband and wife, had been opera singers in a previous life—as in when they were younger, not when they were incarnated in the bodies of ancient Egyptians or something like that. So Danny accompanied them on his mother's upright piano, playing Puccini arias until it got late enough that neighbors might call the cops. Then he switched to quiet Chopin études and pieces by Debussy. Jake made him play *Clair de lune*, of course, and some others he'd grown fond of.

By four in the morning, they'd all grown fairly quiet. Danny was taking a break from the piano and lying on the floor with Jake stretched out beside him, much to the chagrin of Persephone, who seemed to have finally pieced together the nature of their relationship. She hadn't said anything, but Danny could tell by the way she smiled at the two of them.

He was actually surprised at the way Jake was snuggling up against him. He would never have done that a couple weeks ago. Now he was lying with his head on one of the throw pillows, nestled into the crook of Danny's armpit, half asleep and apparently unconcerned with how it looked to everyone else in the room. Danny found it adorable. And he was delighted that Jake felt so comfortable at his house, among these people who were closer to him and his mom than any relatives.

The sky began to lighten and Danny woke him. "It's almost sunrise."

Jake looked like a grumpy child being roused from a nap—he even whimpered a bit. But after Danny's mother thrust a cup of herbal tea into his hands—"This will perk you up, but there's no caffeine, so you can go back to sleep right after the sunrise"—he managed to sit up and glare sullenly out the window at the eastern sky.

Persephone passed around the last of the chocolate-and-whipped-cream Yule log cake and Theron distributed cups of wassail—cider mixed with beer he brewed himself, and spiced with cinnamon, clove, and orange peel. Then they all watched the sun peek its head above Pack Monadnock, while Loreena McKennitt sang "To Drive the Cold Winter Away" on the CD player. It was a peaceful, beautiful way to greet the morning and the beginning of lengthening days.

They were all looking forward to crawling into their warm beds, so things wrapped up quickly after that. Theron was too tired to drive home, so he asked permission to crash on the living room floor. The option was open to everyone, but the others were anxious to get home. So after hugging and kissing the guests good-bye, Danny steered Jake into his bedroom. They undressed in sleepy silence and crawled into bed. The sheets were cool, but they soon remedied that by snuggling their naked bodies together.

"Did you have a good time?" Danny asked, only half expecting Jake to answer. The guy was fast falling asleep.

"Hmm," Jake said. Then he smiled and nuzzled Danny's neck. "I wish I could stay here with you forever."

CHAPTER TWENTY-TWO

JAKE HAD been dreading Christmas ever since he'd made the arrangements to visit his mother. Not only would he be face-to-face with all the weirdness surrounding the divorce, but he'd also be dealing with his mom and Danny together for the first time. He'd have to watch everything he did or said, as well as everything *Danny* did or said. Though to be honest, he was much more worried about his behavior than Danny's. He'd been getting more and more open about his affection for Danny ever since the night of the snowstorm. It wasn't a big deal in the dorm, and apparently it was cool at Danny's house and in front of his mom's friends—nobody had complained about the way he behaved during the solstice party, at least.

But Jake's mom could have stepped out of a fifties sitcom. With a name like June Stewart, affectionate ribbing from Jake and the twins about her being a cross between June Cleaver and Martha Stewart had been inevitable, but it was much more than that. The way she dressed, the way she kept her hair, the spotless housekeeping, the fantastic cooking… it was all old-fashioned. And even though Jake had never heard her say a disparaging word about gays, he had to wonder if her attitude toward homosexuality would be just as old-fashioned.

Neither of the boys had a car, but Althea let them borrow hers for the trip. The distance wasn't too bad—his aunt lived in Derry, which was only about forty-five minutes away from Peterborough, going east on 101. Traffic wasn't bad—most people had done their driving the day before—and they pulled into his aunt's driveway just before noon.

Mrs. Stewart opened the door, all smiles at her son's arrival, and that was when Jake got his first shock of the day. She looked… different. First of all, she was wearing *slacks*, and her hair…!

"Do you like it?" she asked him, clearly nervous as she touched the hair cascading over her shoulders.

Jake realized with another shock that his mother had been dreading this meeting too. The changes she'd been going through were a little harder to hide than the ones he'd been going through, and she'd feared his rejection.

He smiled and said, "You look terrific, Mom."

"Really?" The relief was obvious in her voice. "Margie wants me to get it cut—something short and fashionable—but I don't think I'm ready for that yet."

"It looks great," Jake said sincerely. "I like the outfit too."

She made a dismissive gesture with her hands, but he could tell she was pleased. "That was her doing too. She practically dragged me to the mall last weekend, despite all the holiday shoppers."

"Mom, this is my roommate, Danny."

They shook hands, and Danny threw in a compliment about her hair, which obviously pleased her. As they followed her inside, Jake relaxed a bit. His mother had more to worry about right now than who her son was sleeping with. So maybe he could manage to get through one day without bringing the subject up.

Jake's aunt was younger than his mother, and she'd married a decent enough guy. Carl Gardner was a computer programmer at a startup in Manchester. They had one daughter named Becky, who was twelve. So their house wasn't nearly as loud and chaotic as Jake's house had been. That probably made it the best place for his mom to be right now.

Unlike Althea's house, the Gardners had done up their house big for Christmas, and Jake had to admit that he loved it. Althea's house was peaceful and wonderful in its own way, but he loved the smell of balsam that hit him as soon as he crossed the threshold, and all the paper and foil decorations on the walls, and the stockings hanging near the tree. The tree itself was glorious, with colored lights and tinsel and gold and silver garland—leaning a bit toward the tacky side, perhaps, but Jake loved it.

If Danny was bothered by all the Christian trappings, he gave no sign. He was charming to Jake's family, as Jake had expected him to be, and judging by Becky's shy smile, at least one person in the household thought he was cute. It was also a good thing he wasn't vegetarian like his mother, because except for the cranberry sauce and the apple pie, there wasn't much on the table without meat in it. Turkey, sausage stuffing, maple bacon green beans with pecans—which were delicious—and zucchini with some kind of chopped up cheesy bacon stuffing. Most of it had been cooked by Jake's mom, and it was amazing.

After dinner, they opened presents under the tree while Christmas carols played on the stereo. Jake had been tossing ideas around in his head for weeks, trying to think of something to get Danny. He knew Danny hadn't gotten him anything, and that was cool. But it had been really important to him that he get Danny something for their first—and hopefully not their last—Christmas together. Maybe Danny would think it was stupid. They weren't even officially dating. But Jake needed to do it. There were times when the love he felt for Danny seemed to fill his whole chest and he felt like he'd explode if he didn't do something—touch him, kiss him, say, "I love you...."

Or get him a Christmas present.

But what? What would a classical musician want? A CD? Jake had snuck a peek at Danny's music collection before they left, but he couldn't make much sense out of it. He could see what Danny *had*, of course, but that didn't tell him anything about what Danny *didn't* have. Why were there only four symphonies from some guy named Brahms, but nine from Beethoven? Were some of Brahms's missing? And would Danny want the missing ones, or was the reason he didn't have them because he didn't like them?

Jake had given up on that tack, knowing he'd never be able to figure all that stuff out in time, and skipped classes one day to take the Coast bus into Portsmouth. There were a bunch of touristy shops there selling quaint old-fashioned toys and candles and knickknacks that tried to invoke the feel of an old New England fishing port, and Danny had seemed to like them the last time they were in the city. Jake only had a hundred bucks to spend—his mother had slipped it to him on Thanksgiving, and he'd been holding on to it for Christmas presents—but he'd found something he could afford, along with the other gifts he'd gotten for his mom and his aunt's family.

When Carl handed Danny a wrapped bundle, Danny looked at him in confusion. "I didn't think to bring anyone presents," he said, as if that should disqualify him from receiving any.

"We figured that," Carl said.

Aunt Margie added, "It's nothing big. We just hated the idea of you sitting there bored, watching all of us open presents, so we picked you up a couple things. Of course, we didn't know anything about you, so they're kind of generic."

"Thank you."

Danny opened the wrapping to find a large, gray wool sweater inside. It looked a bit large for him, but at least it wasn't bright orange or fluorescent green. He seemed genuinely pleased when he said "thanks" again.

"Try it on," Jake's mother encouraged. She laughed gently. "We had no idea about your size, so it's probably a circus tent on you."

It was large, but not quite a circus tent. Jake thought Danny looked pretty good in it. It was hard to tell if Danny really liked it, but it was clear that he was pleased they'd thought of him. He took the sweater off and folded it neatly, then laid it beside him on the carpet.

It turned out they'd bought Jake an identical sweater, though his fit better, because his mother knew his size.

In the next round of presents, Danny received a twenty-five-dollar gift certificate to Stroudwater Books in Portsmouth, and again Jake received the same thing. That was it for Danny's presents, but he sat contentedly while the family opened the rest of their gifts until there were just a few left. Then Jake excused himself to run out to the car, where he'd hidden his present for Danny in his backpack.

He brought it back inside, while everyone watched him curiously, and stuck his hand out. "Here. There's one left for Danny."

He realized almost instantly that he'd made a mistake doing it that way. He hadn't intended it to be so dramatic, and now it clearly looked to everyone as if this was something special. The whole setup was practically screaming, "I'm about to give him an engagement ring!"

But it was too late to back out now. Conscious of all the eyes upon him, Jake walked over to Danny and extended his hand. The store had gift-wrapped it for him, so it was basically a cube with little snowmen all over it and a white bow. While Jake took his seat again, Danny unwrapped it and opened the cardboard box inside. Then he pulled out a snow globe.

Jake had always thought snow globes were kind of cute, but he'd never have actually bought one for himself. And he certainly hadn't gone looking for one for Danny. But the moment he saw this one, he'd realized it was perfect. There were two people inside, walking hand-in-hand through the snow, and thanks to their jackets and scarves, it wasn't really clear what their genders were. It was most likely a man and a woman, but it could easily have passed for two men. And with the snow falling around them, it had reminded Jake of the first night he'd held Danny's hand in the snowstorm.

Danny clearly got the reference. He shook it and watched the snow falling on the figures for a moment before he looked up and met Jakes eyes. When he spoke, his voice was unsteady. "Thanks. It's really—"

Don't say "sweet," Jake pleaded silently. *Please don't say "sweet" in front of my mom.*

"—nice." Danny smiled, but he was unable to hide the faint blush that had come into his cheeks.

When Jake glanced up at his mother, he saw that she was watching both of them with a thoughtful expression on her face.

Oh shit.

Later that afternoon, when his mom and Margie had been about to tackle the dishes in the kitchen, Jake went in to offer his help. His mother told her sister, "Margie, why don't you go relax in the living room. Jake will help me."

Of course, they all knew this was code for "I want to have a talk with Jake," so his aunt left without protest. Jake's mom handed him a dish towel and stationed him near the drainer to dry off the dishes she washed.

"I invited your brothers," she began as she scrubbed one of the dinner plates. "But they refused to come. I think they're angry with me."

Jake's first impulse was to say they could fuck themselves. But instead he replied, "They'll get over it."

"I hope so. This wasn't meant to hurt any of you—not even your father. I don't hate him. I just can't... live with him anymore."

"You don't have to explain that to me, Mom," Jake said, taking the plate from her. "I can't live with him either."

She smiled at that. "I know. I've always thought you and I were a lot alike. Not that you ever loved cooking, or I ever had your artistic talent...."

"Are you kidding?" Jake laughed. "Did you taste that gravy? That was a work of *art*, Mom. It should have been in a museum!"

She paused a moment, as if she were seriously considering the idea. "I guess I've never really thought of it that way, but cooking *is* a creative process. One might consider it an art form."

"Definitely!"

"I wonder.... Maybe one of the local colleges offers classes in gourmet cooking."

Jake was fairly convinced that his mom could probably teach those classes. But going to college might be a good idea for her. She'd eventually have to go to work, if she was going to live on her own, and there weren't many jobs out there for a woman who'd been a housewife and mother her entire adult life. "I think that's a good idea. Maybe you should even start thinking about a degree."

She turned to look him directly in the eye and gave him a warm smile. "Thank you, Jake. I don't think... well, a lot of people might have thought I was being ridiculous."

"You're not being ridiculous," he said seriously. "You're trying to start a new life. And that means thinking about jobs and careers. If you don't want to be flipping burgers somewhere, you'll need a degree."

"Yes." She turned back to the sink of dirty dishes, but she still had a smile on her face. "I think you're right."

They worked in silence for a while, his mom washing while Jake dried, until she said, "I've always felt we were pretty close, Jake."

All this personal talk was starting to embarrass him, but he replied, "Yeah, sure we are."

"I hope you feel you can tell me things. About things that are going on in your life, I mean."

He couldn't respond to that. A lump had formed in his chest, as if he'd forgotten to swallow a piece of the apple pie he'd had for desert. It just got worse when she turned to him again and held out a clean plate for him to dry.

"Jake… there have been things over the years… how upset you were when things fell apart between you and Tom… refusing to go to prom… never dating…. And now the look I saw passing between you and Danny today…."

Jake took the plate from her and his hand was shaking so much he was afraid he might drop it. He tried to swallow as he began to rub the plate with the towel, but his throat didn't want to cooperate.

"You know, don't you," his mother said, her eyes seeming to burn into him, trying to see inside, "that I would never turn you away, no matter what you told me."

A long silence fell between them. She was waiting for him to tell her what he knew she'd already pieced together. But it was incredibly hard to take that one tiny step.

He couldn't look at her. "Not even… if I said… I was… gay?"

Still unable to look up at her face, he felt her take the plate out of his hand. She must have set it in the dish rack, because a moment later her arms engulfed him in an embrace. "Oh, sweetheart," she whispered in his ear, "it's not a bad thing. I've suspected for a long time. I just wanted you to tell me."

He lifted a hand to touch her arm and felt the knot in his throat loosen enough for him to take a quivering breath. "Thank you."

THE DAY seemed to have gone pretty well, though Jake was oddly quiet on the way home.

"Are you okay?" Danny finally asked when it was clear Jake didn't intend to say anything without prompting.

Jake started, as if he'd forgotten there was somebody else in the car, even though Danny was the one driving. "Huh? Yeah." He was quiet for a moment. Then he said, "I just came out to my mom."

"Oh. I guess I missed that."

"It happened while we were in the kitchen doing dishes."

That would explain why Jake had seemed distracted all through the rest of the evening. "How did it go?"

Jake sighed and stretched his long legs as much as he could in the cramped passenger seat. "Good, I guess. She said she was cool with it. And she likes you."

Danny wasn't sure if he liked the idea of Jake's mom thinking they were a couple. Or *his* mom, for that matter. All the holding hands in front of people, and kissing in the lounge, and that snow globe.... It was all getting a little out of control. Not that he didn't like Jake, but....

"You don't seem very happy about it," he commented to cover up his own uncertainty.

Jake shrugged. "I just... I didn't plan on doing it today. It kind of took me by surprise."

"But she's cool with it?"

"Sure," Jake said. "Though she didn't think it would be a good idea to let my dad find out."

Danny couldn't think of anything to say to that, so he just nodded.

CHAPTER TWENTY-THREE

JAKE LIKED living at Danny's house. It was probably the most relaxing place he'd ever been. There was always a sort of hushed feeling, so different from the chaos and noise he'd grown up with. He could stretch out on the carpet in the sun-room with a throw pillow under his head and take a nap or read a book—he was finally on the last book of the Mercedes Lackey trilogy—or just stare up at the wall-mounted tea candles and listen to the ethereal relaxation music Althea liked and forget about everything except how happy he was to be there. It pained him to realize just how much this feeling had been lacking in his own home.

Danny seemed more relaxed here too. It was hard to tell if he was still having nightmares, but there was a subtle lessening of tension in him, as though this was the one place he truly felt safe. It was nice to see.

The remaining three weeks of winter break slipped by in a kind of ethereal haze. Not that Jake didn't want to go back to school. It was true that his business classes seemed excruciatingly dull these days, but he loved being in Eaton House. It would be nice to see Eva again, and even Paul. The guy was a dweeb, but Jake was starting to think of him as a friend. He just needed a little more coaxing to lure him out into daylight.

Getting laid might help him too. But Jake was hardly an expert. Paul would have to fend for himself on that one.

Speaking of sex, Jake and Danny were having a *lot* of it. Jake was still boggled that Althea was so easygoing about it, but he couldn't complain. It had been weird for the first few days, but he soon got used to it. They weren't having sex where she could *see*, of course. They hadn't even repeated the risky fireplace sixty-nine they'd had on their first night in the house. They kept it in Danny's room and avoided making a lot of noise, in case Althea might be wandering around in the kitchen. And if there was one thing he'd *really* miss about this place, it was that soft, queen-sized bed of Danny's. Dorm mattresses were thin, hard, and covered in waterproof vinyl.

One afternoon, when Jake was basking in a sunbeam on the floor of the sun-room, debating whether he should pick up his novel again, Althea announced that she was going to visit Krauka. "I'd invite the two of you along, but it's likely to be pretty dull—picking up prescriptions, doing a little grocery shopping, stuff like that. She's getting old and doesn't have any relatives in the area to help her, so people in the coven take turns."

Jake was feeling so lazy, he didn't even get up. He just waved at her and said, "That's cool. I hope you have a good time."

Danny came out from the kitchen to kiss her good-bye, and then he leaned against the doorframe of the sun-room while she headed off. When the front door was closed, he turned his gaze upon Jake and gave him a long look. Then he said, "I'm horny."

Jake tried to feign indifference. "I'm not sure if I'm in the mood."

"I've been watching the crotch of your sweatpants. As soon as I said the word 'horny,' you started tenting."

Betrayed by my own dick. "I should wear heavier clothing."

"Underwear might help," Danny observed. "You've turned into quite the libertine since I met you."

Jake didn't want to admit that he had no idea what a "libertine" was, since he was pretty sure Danny had deliberately used the word to stump him. Sometimes the guy made him feel like some kind of missing link. But he chose to ignore it. "About this 'horniness' you were referring to?"

"Oh yes," Danny replied in a fake British accent. "Quite. Well, my good man, I was thinking perhaps we could fuck."

"Yes, let's."

Danny led him into the bedroom, and it didn't take long to get naked and into the sixty-nine position they both loved. That soon progressed to mutual rim jobs, and Jake was in heaven. But then Danny lifted his head and said, "You think you're ready to try something new?"

So far, Danny had yet to lead him astray, but Jake couldn't help but feel a little nervous. "Like what?"

Danny stretched an arm out to snag the so-far unused bottle of lube off the nightstand. As he popped the cap, he said, "You just keep doing what you're doing down there. I'm going to introduce you to my fingers."

Jake felt a mixture of arousal and anxiety swirl around in his stomach, watching Danny dab some of the lube onto his index finger. He knew where this would inevitably lead, and he wasn't sure if he was ready. "I don't know if I want to be fucked...."

"Not even by a little finger?" Danny said, smiling as he flexed his index finger like a puppet.

"I don't... well, maybe a finger's okay."

Danny turned around on the bed so they were face to face. He kissed Jake tenderly and said, "I'm not doing this because I'm dying to get my finger up your butt. Though it does sound kind of hot. But anyway, it's mostly because I think you'll like it. You *really* get into anal play."

"True."

Danny smiled and looked directly into his eyes. "You can say 'no,' Jake. We'll just go back to what we were doing, and I'll love it— honestly. This is just something I think you'll like. But if you don't, you can stop it at any point, including right now."

Jake frowned. "Sorry, I guess I'm being a baby about it."

"It's not being a baby to say you don't want a finger, or anything else, up your ass," Danny said. "It's your ass. You don't have to do anything with it you don't want to do."

"But you think I'll like this?"

"I think you'll *love* it."

"All right," Jake said. "Do it."

He was relieved that Danny didn't just reach down and shove his finger in. They went back to mutual rimming, and he gradually relaxed into that. He *really* liked Danny's ass. It was amazing how smooth and flawless it was, even when he got this intimate with it. The musky scent he'd initially been a little squeamish about was now an enormous aphrodisiac to him. He could feel Danny's tongue, warm and soft on his own anus, and his thighs quivered with the need for more—a need he'd been experiencing often during their sex play, but he'd been uncertain what more he wanted.

Now he found out. As Danny slowly teased his index finger inside, Jake felt a thrill of sexual energy spreading out from his anus like lightning, yet somehow slower. It filled him up inside, spreading through his stomach and chest and out into his limbs, and then finally exploding like sparks in his head.

My God....

Danny moved his finger as if to pull it out, and Jake couldn't help but whimper.

"Did that hurt?"

"Put it back in," Jake begged.

Danny chuckled and did as he asked, but only as the beginning of a slow in and out motion that soon had Jake writhing underneath him. Jake moaned, grateful that Althea was out of the house.

He was so lost in the gradual finger fucking that he wouldn't have even noticed when the finger became two fingers, except that Danny asked him, "Are you still okay? That's two fingers now."

"Yeah," Jake moaned before burying his face back in Danny's ass.

By the time Danny inserted a third finger, Jake was surprised to find that his anus was no longer feeling any pain at all. The continual in and out motion had numbed it, in a way, though the pleasure was still there. And it wasn't long before he was craving more. Not necessarily more fingers, but... they weren't going in very deep. He wanted them *inside* him.

And he knew the best way to satisfy that craving.

"Okay," he said, so lost in the sensations he wasn't sure he'd be able to form a coherent sentence, "I think... I'm ready...."

"Ready?" Danny asked, sounding a little surprised. "You want me to put my dick in you?" Perhaps he thought they'd gone as far as Jake could handle.

"Yes... please...."

To Jake's immense frustration, Danny lifted himself off him and pulled his fingers out of Jake's ass. But it was only to retrieve a condom from the basket, open it, and roll it over himself. Then Danny climbed back onto the bed and laid his body down onto Jake's, but face to face. As he did so, he lifted both Jake's legs up over his shoulders, tilting his ass up. "Is this comfortable for you?" he asked.

Jake was so aroused, he could have been bent into a pretzel and he probably would have enjoyed it. "It's fine."

It was hard to get their faces close together in that position, but Danny managed to lower himself enough for a quick kiss. Being folded up *that* much made breathing a little difficult for Jake, but after the kiss, Danny eased off until Jake was in a more relaxed position. Then he reached down to adjust things until Jake could feel the tip of Danny's cock pressing against his sphincter.

He moaned his acquiescence and raised his hips slightly to ease access. Danny didn't thrust it in, but applied gentle pressure while he and Jake stared into each other's eyes with longing. Jake was frustrated that his sphincter didn't immediately open up and swallow Danny's shaft, but after a minute or so, it finally relaxed and Danny penetrated him. Even then, he moved slowly, sliding in an inch and waiting for Jake's body to adjust before he penetrated deeper. But eventually Jake felt Danny's pubic hair brushing against his ass, and then a final thrust brought their bodies together. It was amazing. Danny's cock felt warm and enormous inside his body, as if it were filling him entirely.

Then Danny began to move, and Jake found himself trembling head to toe with the electric thrill the movement sent through his torso. It was obvious Danny wanted to be gentle with him, but after several slow, cautious thrusts, Jake demanded, "Do it faster."

"If you say so," Danny responded with a gentle laugh.

Eventually, he had Danny thrusting into him so fast and deep that Jake began to worry his ass might not be able to take the pounding—literally. But it felt so good. He didn't want it to stop. He jerked himself off while Danny fucked him and timed it so that when Danny slowed and tensed for his orgasm, Jake released at the same time, dousing his stomach and chest with come. He could feel Danny's cock squirting inside him, even though the condom was presumably catching it all, and it felt as though their bodies had become one at that moment, as though Danny were coming through Jake's cock.

"Oh my God," Jake breathed when it was all over and Danny was softening within him. "That's the most amazing thing I've ever felt."

"I had a feeling you'd like it."

"I wish you had a detachable penis, like in the song. Then you could just leave it in there all the time."

Danny laughed. "Ew."

"Or maybe we could have an exact copy of your dick made in rubber, so I could carry it around with me."

"Again… ew. How about this instead. Whenever you want me to fuck you, you say, 'Fuck me, Danny,' and then I'll fuck you."

"Ah," Jake replied, nodding sagely. "A secret code."

DANNY STAYED inside until he softened enough to slip out and then collapsed on the bed beside Jake. "There are some other positions we can try too."

"Like what?"

"Doggy style," Danny replied. "Or with you sitting down on me. There's a bunch of positions. There's one called 'The Cross,' where you spread your legs with one leg up over my shoulder and the other lying on the bed, while I have one leg over that leg."

Jake quirked an eyebrow up, looking puzzled. "I'm having a hard time picturing that."

"It's easier to show you than to explain it. We can do it tonight."

Jake blushed adorably at that and covered his face with his hands. "Jesus! I never thought I'd do anything like this."

"Didn't you think you'd have sex someday?"

Jake lowered his hands. "Well, yeah. But the porn magazine I bought last year didn't go into much detail. It had one shot of a guy with his dick in another guy's ass. The rest was just blowjobs and jerking off."

Danny kept forgetting how little exposure Jake had had to gay… *everything*. "You've never seen a gay porn film?"

"No. I've seen some straight porn on cable. Bobby and Robbie kind of forced me to watch it and jerk off with them."

"Ugh!" Danny screwed his face up in disgust. "That's incest!"

Jake shrugged. "We didn't touch each other. And we only did it a couple times. Don't other brothers jerk off together?"

Danny had to admit he had no idea, not having a brother. He decided to get back to his original track. "I hadn't actually planned to go all the way to fucking this time," he commented. "I thought I'd just finger you until you came."

"Well, once it was inside me, I wanted more."

"I'm glad," Danny said, caressing his shoulder. "Watching you get turned on by something I'm doing is incredibly hot."

They ended up falling asleep, even though it was still early afternoon. Unfortunately, Danny dreamt of Steve Cory.

STEVE WAS a great kisser. But he could only kiss when he was drunk, which should have been a warning flag right there. That, plus the fact that he never went beyond kissing. They'd find themselves a secluded spot in the woods and hang out chatting, pretending they didn't know what was going to happen after Steve had a bottle of grape "Mad Dog" 20/20 in him. After a while he'd lean over and they'd make out. It was obvious that he had a hard-on the whole time, and sometimes he'd climb on top of Danny and hump him through their clothes. But nothing beyond that. After an hour or so, he'd just stop and say he needed to get home.

Still, he *did* kiss. And he kissed Danny, who'd had a crush on him for over a year. So Danny took what he could get. But he longed for more, and Steve seemed to know it.

They never talked in school. Danny was out, and Steve was absolutely *not*. When Danny had made a joke about blowing him a kiss in the hall on Monday morning, Steve's eyes went wide and he said, "Dude...."

The warning in his voice was clear. Danny quickly laughed and said, "Don't worry. I wouldn't do that."

"You'd better not."

It was Steve's idea for Danny to hang out with him and some of his friends from the wrestling team—Randy Woodman, Taylor Carmichael, Blake Harris, and Blake's younger brother, Alan. "Come on, you'll like them. We're just gonna get some Mad Dog and some beer and hang out at Randy's house. Just don't mention… you know."

Danny knew. What he didn't know was why Steve would risk his friends finding out by bringing Danny along, or why these guys would want the school "fag" hanging out with them. But he would have done just about anything to be with Steve, so he ignored the warnings in the back of his head.

When they got to Randy's house, it turned out everyone was in the garage, and the other guys had already been drinking a bit. Danny was nervous as hell going in, but he trusted Steve to keep an eye on him. After all, it wasn't as if these guys had ever beaten him up. They'd just been assholes to him, especially since he came out.

They seemed friendly enough. Steve told him, "It's cool. I told them how you helped me with my trig homework last week, and that you're okay—for a nerd." He laughed and gave Danny a playful jab to the shoulder. The trig homework was a lie, of course.

"Yeah, man," Randy said, handing him a beer. "If Steve vouches for you, you're good with me."

Danny took the beer. It helped ease his nerves a little, and he had a few over the next couple hours, while the other guys drank and talked shit about girls, teachers, and pretty much everybody. When Alan called Mr. Whitehouse, the physics teacher, a "fag," his older brother cuffed him on the top of the head and said, "Shut up, asswipe. You know Danny's gay."

"Yeah, whatever. I didn't say he was *gay*, I just said he was a *fag*."

"Nice."

Alan didn't bother to expand upon that little bit of reasoning, but Randy said to Danny, "Do you really suck on guys' dicks, man?"

Danny took a swig of beer to give him time to contemplate his answer. He didn't really mind talking about it, despite the fact that the question was pretty rude. But if he did, would he be inviting Randy and the others to give him shit over it?

Steve interjected, "Dude, that's pretty crass."

"What? I'm just curious. I didn't say it was bad. I'm just trying to imagine it."

"Don't strain yourself."

"Yes," Danny said finally. "I suck dick." Not that he'd done a lot of it. Just one guy during his freshman year, before he moved to Massachusetts. But they'd done a fair amount of fooling around together.

"Duh!" Taylor laughed. "He's gay! Of course he's gonna suck dick."

"Do you like it?" Taylor asked.

"Yes."

"I just can't imagine it," Randy said. "I mean, pussy, yeah—that's all soft and nice. But a dick, man… that's all hard and… I don't know… chewy."

Alan snorted. "You're not supposed to *chew* on it."

Danny laughed along with the others. It didn't seem like they were making fun of him, though he still wasn't sure.

"Whatever," Randy said. "If that's what you like, Danny, that's fine with me. The world needs more cocksuckers."

"*Yeah!*" Danny wasn't sure who shouted—it was sort of a general chorus of agreement—and then they all took swigs of beer or MD 20/20. But it was Steve who said, "I doubt it really feels all that different if a guy sucks your dick or if a chick does it."

"Hell, I'm drunk enough," Alan said. "Wanna suck my dick, Danny?"

They all laughed, except for Danny. He smiled and took another sip of beer, hoping the joke would die there. But he knew it probably wouldn't.

"Come on, I'm serious," Alan persisted. "Why not? I'm not afraid to try it."

Of course not, Danny thought, *since nobody gives a fuck if you're the one being sucked off. It's only the guy sucking you who's a* "*faggot.*" But he didn't voice the thought aloud. He had a sense that things could turn ugly very quickly if he didn't tread carefully. "I'm not really in the mood."

"I don't blame you," Blake said. "I've seen his dick. It's pretty gross."

"There's nothing wrong with my dick," Alan insisted. He grabbed his cock through his sweatpants and moved it to show everyone it was hardening. "And all of this talk about blowjobs has got me horny as hell." He appealed to Danny. "Dude! You say you like it. Let's help each other out."

Though Danny would never admit it to these guys, the thought of it did produce a mild stirring in his crotch. Alan wasn't bad looking. None of them were. The only one he *really* wanted was Steve—and he wanted Steve so bad he could taste it—but the thought of sucking off Alan wasn't totally disgusting.

Still, that didn't make it a good idea.

"Hey," Blake said, "if my kid brother gets to have a blowjob, I should get one too."

Danny frowned at him. "I didn't say I was going to give anybody a blowjob."

"Count me out," Taylor said, his face screwed up in disgust. "No guy gets to touch my dick, period."

"Fuck it," Randy said, "I'll do it."

Danny stood up, surprised to find himself unsteady on his feet. He'd drunk more than he realized. "Nobody's getting a blowjob, okay?"

"Why not?"

The sound of that deep, resonant voice brought him to a halt. He turned and found Steve smiling calmly up at him. Their eyes met and Danny felt himself falling into those pools of deep blue.

"I could go for a blowjob," Steve said softly. "Is four of us too much for you to handle?"

It wasn't. Danny knew that. Maybe some guys would hate it, find it disgusting, but he'd inherited a very casual attitude toward sex. And he loved it. The thought of having four guys at once, or one after the other, actually kind of turned him on. Why not? How many straight guys would turn down four women at once? It might be kind of fun. Especially if one of them was Steve....

His voice sounded small when he replied, "I don't want you to think I'm...."

What? A slut? A perv? He wasn't really sure. He just wanted Steve to like him.

"Do it," Steve said, his mouth opening slightly, as if he were panting with arousal. He slid his hand down over a noticeable bulge in his jeans. "I want to watch. Then I want you to do me last. It'll be fucking hot."

Danny grew hard at the sight of Steve touching himself, promising to give himself to Danny.

"You guys have fun," Taylor said. "I'm gonna do a potato chip run. Try to make it fast."

Danny would never really be sure, looking back, if he agreed to it or not. He didn't refuse. And when Alan pulled down the front of his sweatpants—he wasn't wearing any underwear—Danny just went along with it. It wasn't bad. Part of him enjoyed it, despite the alarms going off in his head.

Alan came in his mouth then stepped aside for his older brother to take his place. Danny kept glancing at Steve, watching him rub himself in his jeans, and the sight drove him mad with desire. Steve had always pushed him away when they'd been alone, afraid to go that far. But this was sanctioned by his friends. In this sleazy context, he could allow Danny to bring him off and his friends wouldn't think he'd done something "gay"—after all, they'd done it too.

It would be different for Danny, of course. But they were Steve's friends, and he'd kick their asses if they treated Danny badly.

Danny finished with Blake and moved onto Randy, but he was barely conscious of Randy's cock in his mouth. It was all for Steve. Once they'd done this, maybe Steve would be more comfortable doing it when they were alone together. That was what Danny really wanted, of course.

"Yeah... suck that cock, faggot...."

Danny tried to yank back at that, but Randy held him there as his come started spurting into Danny's mouth. When he was finally finished and relinquished his hold, Danny pulled away and snarled, "Don't fucking call me that!"

"Sorry, dude," Randy laughed. "I talk dirty when I'm about to shoot my load." He didn't seem sorry at all, and Danny glared at him. But fuck it. Danny hadn't really been doing this for Randy or any of the other guys.

He turned to Steve, ready to take as long as he could, to make this the best blowjob Steve had ever had. But he looked up at Steve's face and there was something there he'd never seen before, something cold. Those soft pools of blue had turned to ice, and Danny felt a shiver crawl up his spine. He had his hand stretched out toward Steve's crotch, but it froze there for a long moment, until Steve said, "You just sucked off three guys. Get away from me, you filthy cum whore."

Danny was so shocked he couldn't speak. Then Steve lifted his leg and kicked him across the floor while his friends laughed. They all began to kick him then, shouting "cum whore" and "faggot" at him while they laughed. It hurt, especially when Steve kicked him in the stomach, but Danny barely felt the blows and barely heard the epithets, as if he were somehow disconnected from the scene, looking down upon it. His mind was frozen in place at the moment Steve had spoken—at the moment the boy who'd practically been Danny's boyfriend for months had turned into someone else.

You just sucked off three guys. Get away from me, you filthy cum whore.

All those times making out in the forest together... how could that all have been a lie?

Some instinct for self-preservation kept his hands and arms wrapped around his head and his face to shield him from the kicks, but though it hurt, they weren't putting much energy into it. They weren't aiming for serious damage—just utter humiliation. At last, they dragged him out of the garage onto the back lawn, out of the light of any street lamps.

"Hold him down," Steve ordered.

Randy sat on his legs, his fly still gaping open, while each Harris brother grabbed an arm and pinned it to the cold damp grass. Then Steve straddled Danny's chest, unzipped, and started to piss....

DANNY WOKE up to Jake shaking him. "Danny! Danny! What's wrong?"

Disoriented, Danny felt Jake's hands on his shoulders and thought he was holding him down. He thrashed around, and fortunately Jake was smart enough to let go. Danny bolted out of bed and ran naked into the kitchen. He was only half awake and had no idea what he was doing—he just knew he had to get the taste out of his mouth.

"Dude!" Jake said in a hushed voice, looking around frantically, "your mother might be home now!"

Danny ignored him. He yanked open the refrigerator door, grabbed a bottle of orange juice, and chugged it.

CHAPTER TWENTY-FOUR

"A CYLON appears and kills you with a lightsaber."

Jake looked up at Paul in confusion. "Isn't that from like… *Star Wars*?"

"There are no Cylons in D&D," Eva said. She added to Jake, "And Cylons are from *Battlestar Galactica*."

"Whatever!" Paul threw his hands up in disgust. "We might as well be playing *Star Wars* or something, because these two aren't paying any attention!"

Danny and Jake exchanged sheepish glances, and Jake took his hand off Danny's knee, where it had been slowly creeping up under the leg of his shorts. Jake hadn't *intended* to feel him up in the lounge, but there were times when his hands seemed to have a will of their own.

"Sorry."

"Maybe you'd like to go to your room for an hour," Eva suggested, "and meet us back here, after you're all… tuckered out." She batted her eyelashes at them.

"Shut up," Jake mumbled, feeling the color rush into his face. Eva just laughed at him.

Danny kissed him on the cheek and got out of his chair. "As much fun as spending the entire day fucking sounds, I'd actually like to play this campaign. So why don't I move to another chair?"

Jake felt like crawling under the table and hiding for the rest of the game. Was he really that bad? "I'm sorry."

"It's fine," Danny said, tapping Wallace on the shoulder so he'd switch seats with him.

That put him on the other side of Eva. "We'll kill the cultists and steal the enchanted ruby. Then after dinner tonight, we can go back to our room and play dueling lightsabers."

Jake hadn't thought it was possible to blush when he was already blushing, but he felt another wave of heat wash over his face. "You all suck."

"Dude," Wallace said, smirking at him, "just keep your hands below midthigh. That's all I ask."

Jake made a noise that was halfway between a groan and a snarl, but he stayed put and did his best to focus on the game for the next hour or so. It was actually kind of nice to be teased like that, knowing that his friends were totally cool with him being gay—even Wallace.

The thing that was bothering him the most, though, was Danny. Not that Danny wasn't still terrific in bed and as enthusiastic as ever for sex in the morning, just before bed, and pretty much whenever Jake wanted it—except, apparently, during D&D—but he still felt closed off in some way. The nightmares were obviously continuing and he still refused to tell Jake what they were about. It was like a ghost story Jake had heard at summer camp about a guy who marries a beautiful woman with a velvet ribbon around her neck. She refuses to ever take the ribbon off or tell him why, and so he becomes obsessed with it. Then one night, he cuts the ribbon off her while she's sleeping and her head snaps off.

Jake was *trying* not to obsess about Danny's nightmares, but he was beginning to think there was something dark and horrible there he needed to know about if they were ever going to be happy together. At the same time, he was afraid to find out what it was.

The answer came less than a week later, so suddenly it broadsided both of them.

It was late afternoon on a Sunday, so there wasn't much going on. Danny was playing piano quietly in the upstairs lounge, and Jake was lying on one of the couches, listening and on the verge of drifting off to sleep, when Mark came in with a book and staked out the other couch. By now, Jake had pretty much written the guy off as a loser. He liked to drop an occasionally sarcastic line to see if he could get people worked up, and once in a while he managed to get in a good one and ruffle some feathers. But most of the time, Jake was able to ignore him.

Most of the time.

"Haven't you played that same song like ten times already?"

Danny stopped playing, but he said calmly, "It's called 'rehearsing.' But I can switch to something else." He began playing one of the pieces he knew better—by now, Jake could tell which ones he had down and which he still made mistakes on, though he never tired of listening.

"Yeah," Mark said in a tone dripping with sarcasm, "that one's *much* better."

Danny ignored him and kept playing, but Jake wasn't in the mood. He went to the piano and bent down to give Danny a quick peck on the cheek—he no longer felt self-conscious about doing that in front of people at Eaton House. "I still haven't showered today. I'm gonna do that now."

He thought that would be the end of it, but after he stripped in their room and wrapped a towel around himself, he walked into the bathroom to find Mark in there, taking a piss in one of the stalls with the door wide open. Even for Eaton House, that was kind of crass. A girl could walk in at any moment, and though she might not object to Mark toweling off after a shower, watching him piss was another matter.

Jake had gotten over his bathroom terrors, for the most part, so he walked past Mark to turn on one of the showers and then took the towel off. He hung it on one of the hooks and just stood there naked while the water heated up.

"So you two are an item now," Mark observed as he zipped himself up. He didn't bother flushing.

Jake didn't want to talk to him, but he couldn't think of an excuse to be rude. "Yeah."

"Well… if that's what you want."

Jake frowned. "Yeah, it's what I want."

"That's cool," Mark said. "I have no problem with gays."

"So I hear." It was impossible for Mark to miss the contempt in Jake's voice.

"Yeah, I know everyone thinks I hate gays because I couldn't stand rooming with Danny. But it's not gays in general—it's just him who grosses me out."

Jake could feel heat rising in his torso and neck. He finally turned to face Mark head on and said in a quiet voice, "Dude. He's my boyfriend. Why do you think I'm gonna put up with you talking shit about him?"

"Well, I'll say this for him," Mark said, apparently oblivious to the menace in Jake's stance. "He gives great head."

"You two can't stand each other. You expect me to believe he had *sex* with you?"

Mark snorted. "Dude! He has sex with *everybody*. In high school, he sucked off the entire wrestling team."

The rage boiled over. Jake was hardly aware of chasing Mark out of the bathroom, bellowing something incoherent. Somehow as they ran past the upstairs lounge, down the stairs, and through the downstairs lounge, they picked up a host of startled onlookers and people trying to halt what must have looked like a murderous rampage. Shouts of "What the fuck!" and "Jake!" and "Jesus Christ!' followed them as they burst out the lower lounge door into the freezing cold night air. Mark screamed as Jake tackled him at the edge of the walkway and sent them both sprawling into a snow bank.

"Jake! Stop!"

"What the *hell's* going on?"

"For fuck's sake!"

Jake got in one good punch to Mark's arrogant mouth before he was yanked backward by two people grabbing his arms.

"Jake! Stop it!" It was Danny's voice. And the sound of it brought Jake back to reality enough to realize that Danny was practically wrapped around his left arm, struggling to restrain him. His right arm was being held by Sonny.

"Get the fuck away from me, you fucking *psycho*!" Mark screamed at him, though his words were muffled by the hand clutching at his mouth.

"If you ever say anything like that again, I'll fucking *kill* you!"

"Dude!" Sonny snarled at him, "I don't know what the fuck's going on, but you need to calm down right now!"

"Everyone at Keene High School knew about it, you stupid gorilla!"

"Mark!" Sonny snapped. "Both of you need to shut up!"

"You're nothing special! Give him two beers and he'll fuck every guy in this dorm!"

Jake growled and tried to lunge at him again, but Danny and Sonny held him fast. Sonny was angrier than Jake had ever seen him—angry at both of them. "I swear to God, if you don't stop this, I'm gonna call the cops and get you both thrown out of the dorm!"

"Jake...." Danny's voice was the only one that seemed calm, and it drained some of the fight out of him. Jake looked at him and to his horror, Danny didn't look angry. He didn't look like he couldn't believe anyone would say this shit about him. There was no righteous indignation, no disgust, just... resignation.

This isn't the first time someone's said this about him.

"Jesus.... Danny...."

Danny looked at him with an expression of tremendous pain, and the words that came out of his mouth were the last words Jake wanted to hear. "I'm sorry."

NOBODY CALLED the cops, but that was only because Sonny didn't really want the hassle, and he spent a half hour talking Mark out of doing it. He'd ordered Jake to go up to his room and get some clothes on. Jake did what he was told, but Sonny was still furious with him by the time he came upstairs.

"You owe me, man!" he said, pacing back and forth between the beds. "He still might go to the cops and file assault charges in the morning, and if he does, that'll be too fucking bad for you. Nobody's gonna care what he said about your boyfriend. You're just gonna be out of this dorm and maybe out of school. And someone might get it into their head to file sexual assault charges against you too! There's not a goddamned thing I could do about it. That's what running around naked in public can get you, you stupid shit!"

Jake sat on his bed with his head between his hands, listening to Sonny's tirade. He didn't try to argue. And he wouldn't look at Danny at all.

Danny watched silently from his own bed, feeling like his whole world had just exploded. He remembered the kiss Jake had given him just before heading to the shower, and he realized that might have been the last time Jake would ever kiss him. The truth was out now. And the disgust in Jake's eyes when he'd realized it had ripped Danny's heart out. Jake hadn't said a word to him the entire time they'd been in their room, waiting for Sonny to come up.

He'd known it would happen, sooner or later.

You just sucked off three guys. Get away from me, you filthy cum whore.

"If you have any fucking sense at all," Sonny went on, "you'll go down there with me tomorrow and apologize to him."

"Apologize?" Jake said. He looked as if he'd never heard anything so insane in his life.

"If you want to stay in the dorm."

"Did you hear what he said about Danny?"

Sonny looked at Danny and asked, "Was he lying?" Danny knew he'd heard the rumors. Everyone in the dorm had, except for Jake.

Danny's hand was shaking, as he lifted it to brush his hair back from his forehead. "He exaggerated." He took a deep breath. "But no, it wasn't really a lie."

Sonny shook his head and let out a puff of air. "Look, I don't really care what you did in high school. But where I come from, you don't beat someone up for telling the truth."

He left them alone, and the silence that fell in the room when he closed the door felt like the silence at the end of the world. Judgment had been passed. Jake would never be able to look at him with the same adoration and affection he'd shown before.

"You sucked off the entire wrestling team?" Jake asked him, his mouth set in grim line. He was staring fixedly at the floor between them.

"I said he exaggerated."

"How many was it, then? Just *half* the wrestling team? Three-quarters?"

Danny didn't even know the answer to that question. How many guys had there been on the team? He'd never thought about it before. "There were three of them. And another guy was watching."

"Did they force you?"

"No."

"You wanted to do it?"

"I guess so."

Jake seemed to be chewing on that for a long time. Then he said, "Dickwad said you... did the same for him."

Fuck me. "The night the idiot stuck his tongue to the tracks. By the time we got back here, we were both pretty drunk. We got horsing around a little. It was the only time he was ever nice to me. When he said he was horny and asked me if I'd do it... I guess I thought he'd be less of a dick to me if I did."

Jake still couldn't look at him. "So... what? You just suck off anyone who sticks his dick in your face?"

"Maybe."

"Jesus."

There didn't seem to be anything to say after that.

CHAPTER TWENTY-FIVE

JAKE HAD never been so miserable in his life. Even losing Tom paled in comparison to how awful it was to no longer have Danny in his bed every night, to no longer be able to touch him. He'd had everything, and now he'd lost it. And Jake wasn't even sure who to blame. Mark for telling him? Danny for doing it? Or himself for not being able deal with it?

It wasn't just the wrestlers, though he had to admit that had wigged him out. He'd known Danny was casual about sex, but to just have a bunch of guys line up like that…. It was so sleazy. Was that really what Danny wanted? Did he *like* that sort of thing?

And to give *Mark* a blowjob, when the guy was such an asshole! The thought of touching Mark in any kind of sexual way nauseated Jake. It had been hard enough to go to his room with Sonny the next morning and choke back the bile enough to say, "I'm sorry." Mark had been a snot about it, of course. He'd threatened to call the police if Jake ever even looked at him again. It had taken every ounce of strength Jake had to keep his fist from reconnecting with Mark's face.

But no, the real issue was what Mark had said that night: *You're nothing special. Give him two beers and he'll fuck every guy in this dorm.*

He'd wanted Danny to tell him it was bullshit—the only guy he wanted was Jake. But he hadn't said that. He'd just confirmed that he would have sex with anybody who asked him to. Jake had asked, so no big deal. Just another guy to fuck.

They barely spoke to each other after that night. Danny hadn't tried to climb into bed with Jake when they turned the lights out, as he'd been doing for the past few months, and there had been no physical contact between them for days now. It wasn't that they were hostile. They didn't fight. They nodded at each other when they passed in the hall or the lounge. Jake just couldn't think of anything to say to Danny anymore. He'd thought they were in love, but he'd been wrong.

At least about Danny's feelings. He'd never said he loved Jake, and now it seemed pretty clear that he hadn't. It was just fucking around.

Once, Jake woke in the middle of the night to hear Danny crying softly in his bed. He'd wanted to reach out to him then, but when he called Danny's name, the crying stopped. Danny didn't respond, though he must have known Jake wasn't fooled into thinking he was sleeping again.

Just when Jake had thought things couldn't get any more miserable, his father came to see him.

"There's some guy looking for you," one of the girls watching TV told him when he returned from class through the lower lounge door. "He says he's your father."

"Oh Christ...."

"I told him he could wait for you in the upstairs lounge."

"Thanks."

Jake found his father standing in front of the painting of the nude girl. Jake knew who the artist was now—a girl named Sara who was in his oil painting class. There had been some progress made on it since he first moved in, and now it was pretty detailed. But for a straight guy, Mr. Stewart didn't appear to take much pleasure in the female form. His expression indicated he found the painting distasteful, at best. As far as Jake knew, his father hated art.

Mr. Stewart looked up when Jake opened the door in the glass divider that separated the lounge from the upstairs hall and stairwell.

"You could have waited here forever," Jake said. "Why didn't you tell me you were coming?"

"I was driving by the campus, and I took a chance. It's just before dinner, isn't it?"

"Yes."

"Then I thought you might go to your room to drop off your books or something."

It was true. Jake generally did do that. He dumped his accounting book on the table, as if to prove the point, and then closed the door behind him. He doubted this was going to be a pleasant visit.

His father didn't disappoint him. "I've had a call from the father of one of your dorm mates. Mark Peterson? His father was threatening legal action because you beat up his son—while you were naked, I gather."

"I was in the shower when he started the fight."

His father looked at him coldly. "I'm not concerned about the fight. Boys fight. It's how they become men. Mr. Peterson was bluffing, of course. I gave him the name of our lawyer and he immediately backed down. It's no wonder his son is such a pussy. But what I am concerned about is what appears to have started the fight."

Mr. Stewart moved closer, until they were looking eye-to-eye. They were the same height now. Jake might have even been a bit taller. But this man had hit him so many times as he was growing up, he couldn't suppress a twinge of fear in the pit of his stomach.

"I've always known you'd turn out to be a faggot," his father said quietly. "You've been a mommy's boy your whole life, no matter how much I've tried to beat it out of you. Are you going to deny you've been fucking your roommate?" The word "fucking" was already crass and obscene, but somehow he managed to fill the word with so much loathing it felt to Jake as if he'd just been accused of having sex with barnyard animals.

"He's been fucking *me*, actually."

He'd never dared say anything like that to his father before, but he no longer gave a shit what happened. His mother had found the strength to stand up to this bastard. It was time he grew a pair and did the same.

His father looked as if he wanted to kill him, but he'd never before struck out at one of his sons in front of witnesses, and it must have been the possibility that someone could walk by at any moment that stayed his hand now.

"I don't have fags for sons," he said. "Everything you own, every trace of you in my house, will be thrown in the dumpster tonight. If you want any of it, remember trash pickup is this Saturday. I'm not going to bother challenging the college for the money I've already paid them, but after this semester you'll have the fun of supporting a college education on minimum wage at Cumberland Farms."

He did strike Jake then, though just hard enough in the chest to shove him out of the way. Jake let him leave the lounge, slamming the door behind him, and then watched him walk calmly down the stairs as if nothing had happened.

Jake wondered if he should feel something, if he should be upset that his father had just disowned him. But he didn't.

He didn't feel a thing.

EVA DROVE the getaway car. And despite all the tension between them, Danny had come along to help with the dumpster diving. Jake was pleased that Danny still seemed to consider him a friend. Maybe they could at least salvage that much from this mess. Paul joined them, though he stated flatly that he wasn't going to crawl around in anyone's dumpster. He'd just go along for "moral support"—though how sitting in the car grousing about germs would support anything, Jake had no idea.

He wasn't really sure if there was anything from his house that he needed, but he wanted to check, just in case there was something he'd regret losing. Something he'd sketched, perhaps, or a present from his mother. Maybe nothing. But he knew his father was dead serious about tossing it all, and this would be his only chance to retrieve it.

The street was well lit, so there was little chance of getting in unseen. Jake didn't give a fuck. He directed Eva to pull up in the back of the house beside the dumpster and pop the trunk. Then he and Danny scrambled out with a handful of garbage bags each.

He'd thought he was fine with all of this, but the moment he peered over the edge of the dumpster and saw his entire childhood tossed out, it was like his father had been standing right there slapping him across the face. He felt tears sting his eyes, but he blinked hard to clear them. It was too late for that. Too late for anything.

Instead, he muttered "fucking asshole" under his breath and heaved himself up over the metal lip of the dumpster. Danny said nothing but followed him.

It was a miserable time. He found drawings he'd made in high school and stuck up on his walls, but his father had torn them up, so he left them. There were some notebooks and sketchbooks that had been tossed without being destroyed first, so he grabbed those. A couple of stuffed bears; he no longer slept with them of course, but they still stirred something in him. He rescued them. Some old Christmas cards from his mom. A birthday card from Tom. Some toy robots and a toy Starship Enterprise from *Star Trek: The Next Generation* that still had working lights. He left the clothes. He'd outgrown most of them anyway. It was the photos of himself at various ages, their frames smashed, the photos ripped, that finally forced the tears to come, but he ignored them and kept digging, hoping Danny wouldn't get cut on any of the broken glass.

At last, he signaled Danny to climb out and he followed. The surviving remnants of his childhood were contained in just two small garbage bags. They threw them in the trunk and closed it.

"Okay," Paul said, "Can we go now?" He hadn't even left the passenger seat of the car.

Jake turned for one last look at the house and saw his father watching from the window. Danny was still standing beside him and on a sudden, vindictive impulse, he said quietly, "I'd really like it if you could kiss me right now."

Danny looked at what had drawn his attention. Then he reached up and cupped the back of Jake's neck and drew him down. The kiss was weird—the same familiar lips and tongue, and Jake had to admit it felt good, but they weren't kissing for themselves, so there was no passion in it. When Danny let him up for air, Jake glanced at the window to find the shade drawn.

"Guys," Eva said nervously, leaning over Paul to talk to them through the passenger side window, "I hear sirens."

"Let's go," Jake said.

Fortunately, they were well away from the street before the police arrived. Jake suspected it hadn't been his father's intention to actually have him arrested. That would just force him to deal with his son a little longer. No, he'd just wanted to make it clear that Jake was no longer welcome there.

Not that Jake ever intended to go back.

CHAPTER TWENTY-SIX

BY THE time they got back to campus and made the long trek back to the dorm from A Lot, leaving Jake's stuff in the trunk for the time being, it was almost 2:00 a.m. Eva and Paul went to bed immediately. Danny wanted to crawl into bed too, but he and Jake were both pretty grubby from the dumpster. The lip of it had been caked with a residue of food and crap, and they'd had to put their hands on it when they climbed in and out. So when Jake stripped down and grabbed his towel, Danny followed suit.

Despite the fact that they hadn't had sex in almost a week and were no longer sharing a bed, they hadn't been shy about undressing in front of each other. So it wasn't particularly awkward when they hung up their towels in different stalls and turned the water on.

Then Jake said, "I'd like you to shower with me."

That threw Danny for a loop. He suddenly became sharply aware of the fact that they were both naked. "I'm not sure if that's a good idea...," he began, but Jake cut him off.

"Please. I'd like to talk to you."

"We can talk when we get back to the room."

Jake took a step toward him, until he was looking down into his eyes with a tender expression Danny had never expected to see again. "Is that what you really want? I won't force you. But I'd like to talk while we're showering."

He turned and stepped into the shower, pulling the curtain half closed—just enough to keep most of the spray from getting out onto the floor. Danny thought about it for a long moment. What *did* he want? The answer wasn't really all that hard. He was just afraid that if he stepped into that shower... if it led to sex... things would be even more painful than they already were.

But he turned off the shower he'd been about to use. Then he stepped into Jake's shower and pulled the curtain completely closed.

Jake smiled at him as he reached out to pull him close. Not really into a hug, but nearly, so he could caress Danny's shoulders with the castile soap they both liked. "Thank you," he said softly. "Honestly, I'm too tired and… fucking *exhausted*… to make a pass at you. I just want to… touch you. Is that okay?"

"I guess so. What did you want to talk about?"

"I've been doing some thinking," Jake said, "and I want to tell you a story." He slowly moved his hands down Danny's back, massaging the soap in as he spoke. Their fronts were so close it wasn't possible to disguise their arousal. Their rapidly hardening dicks were already rubbing together. "When I was in high school, I had a best friend named Tom. He was really smart and really cute and I secretly had a huge crush on him. And he had a crush on me too. I was too stupid to acknowledge it, but part of me knew. Unfortunately, when he finally worked up the courage to tell me he was gay—and that he liked me—I freaked. I wasn't ready to deal with it—not him being gay, and not *me* being gay. So I called him a 'faggot' and ran out of that truck stop diner as fast as I could go."

Danny flinched at the word "faggot," and Jake stopped caressing him, just letting his hands rest on Danny's shoulders.

"I refused to talk to him after that night, avoided him at school, stopped answering his calls. The poor guy used to walk up and down the street in front of my house, probably trying to figure out a way to patch things up. I watched him from my window, but I didn't have the balls to go talk to him. I was too terrified of what my father would do if he found out about… any of it.

"My father did figure it out eventually—at least, he figured out that Tom was pining for me. And he was so disgusted he called Tom's father and threatened to get a restraining order if Tom didn't stay away from me. That was kind of it. I avoided Tom for my last year of high school, and then my family moved down to Concord. I heard his family moved too, so I have no idea where he is now."

The story had killed the mood for Danny. He was no longer aroused. His stomach felt uneasy and he wasn't sure he wanted Jake to be touching him. "Jesus," he said. "The poor guy."

"Yeah."

Danny took a step back, though he couldn't move too far away without pressing up against the slimy tile wall of the stall. Jake took the hint and dropped his hands. "Why are you telling me this?" Danny asked. "Are you hoping I'll tell you it was okay to turn your back on someone you claim you cared about? To call him a *faggot*? Because I'm not sure if I can."

"No, I'm not asking you to say that, 'cause it would be a lie. It isn't okay. I was an asshole. And I was a fucking coward. Other guys would've found a way to at least meet up with him in secret, but I was too fucking scared. Hell, I was *still* scared when I showed up here last semester, even to come out to someone like you—someone who's gay himself and wouldn't care if I was."

"No kidding."

"I don't want you to forgive me for what I did to Tom. I don't even want Tom to forgive me for it. I want to remember for the rest of my life that *that's* what being an asshole feels like—*that's* what it feels like to totally screw up the best part of your life. 'Cause that's the only way I can stop myself from doing it over and over again."

"Jake… I'm way too tired to be having a conversation like this."

"Just give me a minute," Jake said, "please." He didn't have to take a step to move closer; he just leaned forward a little, but that put them only a couple of inches apart again. "I felt it again this past week. I mean, it *seemed* different, but it really wasn't, was it? I learned something about someone I cared about, and I didn't know how to handle it. So I ran away again."

"It *was* different, Jake." Danny was surprised at how adamant he sounded. "Tom was just telling you how he felt. I *did* things...."

Things I don't deserve to be forgiven for.

"Yeah, I get that," Jake said, reaching up again to touch Danny's shoulder. Danny didn't shrug it off. "And I'm still kind of a prude and not sure how I feel about it. But even I can see it was just—"

"Jake!" Danny cut him off. He didn't want to hear "it was just sex," or whatever Jake had intended to say. It wasn't that simple. It wasn't just a kink that he wanted Jake to accept and maybe try later with a bunch of their friends. "I really... *really*... don't want to talk about this at two in the morning...."

Jake looked at him for a long time, as if trying to divine what was going on inside his head. Then he said, "Okay. But will you do this for me? Will you sleep with me tonight? No sex," he added hurriedly when Danny frowned. "I just want you in my bed again. Then tomorrow maybe we can talk things out."

Danny wasn't sure what he wanted anymore. It was late and he was too tired to think. But his body knew what it wanted, and he found himself leaning closer, until he was pressed against Jake's hot, wet chest. Jake's arms engulfed him and Danny felt both their bodies relaxing into the familiar contact. "Okay."

CHAPTER TWENTY-SEVEN

JAKE WOKE in the morning to the feel of Danny's warm, smooth skin against his. It was such a comfort, after the tension between them the past few days, that he snuggled in closer to Danny's back and basked in it for several minutes, until Danny stirred.

"Morning," Danny said sleepily.

"Good morning."

Danny rolled over to face him. He looked into Jake's eyes and then slid a hand up to touch Jake's cheek. Then, without a word, he moved closer, until their foreheads were touching, and caressed Jake's neck and shoulder.

Jake took that to mean it was okay for him to touch Danny back, so he did, moving his hand across Danny's hip and around to his lower back. But it was Danny who made the first overtly sexual move. He slipped his hand down to Jake's ass and prodded his sphincter, causing Jake to moan with desire. If he hadn't been horny when he first woke up, he sure as hell was now.

"Is that what you want?" Danny asked quietly.

"Oh God. *Yes*."

They spoke very little as they made love, as if talking might disturb their tenuous connection. But the feel of Danny moving inside him was pure heaven to Jake. He hadn't realized how much he'd missed it. It had become a vital need for him in just the few weeks since Christmas, as important to his existence as food and water.

When their lovemaking was over, Danny lay on his chest and kissed him softly. "I've missed that."

"Me too. I've missed *you*."

Danny gazed into his eyes a moment, his expression affectionate but pensive. Then he said, "Let's talk later today, about where we want all of this to go."

"I already know—"

Danny stopped him with a finger to his lips. "I think I'll need to tell you some stuff before I can feel really comfortable continuing with this." When Jake couldn't stop himself from frowning, Danny added, "I think I want it. This isn't me shutting you down. I just need to wait until I'm more awake, so we can talk about some things."

"Okay." It wasn't really okay, but there wasn't much Jake could do about it. And things were at least looking better than they had yesterday morning.

Danny rolled off him and stood up, presenting Jake with a view of his beautiful, milk-and-honey-colored ass. Jake hadn't yet penetrated it, but he was getting a strong desire to do so. Being fucked felt so amazing to him, he longed to give that feeling to Danny, if he wanted it. But apparently, it would have to wait.

"I think I'm going to track down my advisor today," he said, "and see what it would take to change my major."

"Do you already have your gen eds done?"

"Yeah," Jake said. "I mean, I know it's kind of dumb to change things my senior year, but… it should be possible, shouldn't it? Why should I spend the next year doing something I hate? I don't have to answer to *him* anymore."

Danny sat down on the edge of the bed, his warm, naked skin pressing against the skin on Jake's belly. "You shouldn't. Do what'll make you happy." He gave Jake a wry smile. "Assuming you can find a way to pay for it."

Jake had been giving that a lot of thought, even before things blew up with his father. "I'm going to Financial Aid today too. I have a 3.8 grade point average. That should qualify me for some grants or something, shouldn't it?"

"Jesus! My mom would be dancing on the ceiling if I had a GPA that high."

Jake shrugged. "I didn't have a life until I came here. All I did was study."

Since they'd showered just before bed, they didn't bother to shower that morning. They just dressed to hit the dining hall before their first classes.

But when Jake walked out the door, he heard a familiar voice say, "There's the little faggot!"

Bobby slammed him against the wall before Jake even saw him.

"What the *fuck?*" The jolt caused Jake to drop his microeconomics book.

Both his brothers were there, and they looked like they wanted to kill something—him, most likely. The bizarre part was that they were both dressed in their business clothes. They were wearing slacks and button-down shirts and ties, as if they were about to head into a meeting.

"What the fuck?" Robbie said from behind his twin. "That's a good question. What the fuck is wrong with you? Dad says you're letting some guy pork you up the ass!"

"Fuck Dad!" Jake snarled. "And fuck you too!"

Bobby grabbed him by the collar and swung him against the opposite wall, causing his elbow to punch a hole in the thin plasterboard. Behind Robbie, Danny was standing in the door, watching the scene in horror. He shouted, "Leave him alone!"

Shit!

That was the last thing Jake wanted, for Danny to get involved in a fight with the twins. Danny had no idea what they were like. If Robbie and Bobby had consciences, Jake had never seen evidence of it. They never pulled their punches, even if someone was half their size— like Danny.

As if to prove his point, Robbie shoved Danny hard in the chest and sent him flailing back into the room. Jake couldn't see where he landed, but his initial anger instantly turned to blinding rage. "Don't you fucking touch him!"

Robbie was out of his reach, but he landed a good, solid punch to Bobby's gut. It wasn't the smartest move. Bobby barely seemed to notice the punch, except to be enraged by it. He yanked Jake forward and threw him back against the first wall, bellowing his fury.

Doors were opening as students poked their heads out to see what the hell was going on. Jake could hear Robbie yelling obscenities at Danny, calling him a "faggot" and a "cocksucker," but there was no way he could get to them. Not without getting past Bobby.

Jake lunged for the door of the room, but Bobby simply grabbed him by the waist and tossed him several feet down the hall toward the stairwell. Pain jolted through his entire body, as Jake landed near the open door and flipped over once before he came to a stop. Bobby screamed, "Who the fuck do you think you are, you little shit?" He grabbed Jake under the armpits and hauled him out across a short stretch of the hall and into the lounge, where there was more room to fight.

"You think you can take me, asshole?" Bobby shouted as he dropped him heavily on the carpet. "Come on! Let's see you try!"

Jake had never seen his brother so furious. They'd fought a lot when he was young—with Bobby and Robbie always winning—but there had never been this level of anger in it. For the first time, Jake was afraid for himself. But the thought of Danny alone with Robbie quickly drove that concern from his mind. He was terrified of what might be going on in that room.

DANNY HAD no idea whether it was Bobby or Robbie who'd come charging into the room and shoved him backward over the end of Jake's bed. He looked like the handsome redhead Jake had introduced him to before Thanksgiving—Bobby—but they were identical twins, so appearance wasn't a good guide.

The end of the bed had a short metal railing, which caught Danny painfully in the back of his knees before he toppled over it. Fortunately he landed on the mattress.

Jake's brother didn't immediately attack him—not after that first shove. He leaned over the bed, frothing at the mouth and jabbing a finger at Danny, while he went on and on in a practically incoherent stream of consciousness. "…fucking faggot who seduced my brother I should shove my dick so hard up your ass you'd taste shit if you ever touch him again I'm gonna bend you in two so you can suck your own dick you piece of shit cocksucker…."

Danny was terrified. But he was more terrified about what was happening to Jake out in the hall. He heard Jake shout something like "Don't you fucking touch him!" followed by an enormous crash that shook the walls. There was a dull thud, and Jake's brother shouted, "Who the fuck do you think you are, you little shit?"

Then the fight sounded like it moved down the hall and out into the stairwell.

"What the fuck is that?" Robbie or Bobby or whoever it was had just caught sight of Danny's nude male calendar. He stormed across the room and ripped it off the wall, then ripped it in half. "You're a sick fuck, you know that?"

"So you came here to kill us?" Danny asked him.

For a second, there was just a glimmer of humanity in those blue eyes so much like Jake's. He seemed confused. Then he threw the remains of the calendar at Danny's desk, knocking a half-full glass of water over onto Danny's music history notes. "Fuck you!"

Danny couldn't recall ever hearing the word "fuck" so many times in one conversation.

THE THROBBING in his arms and shoulders—not to mention his hip, where it had been dragged across the carpet—was starting to filter through Jake's anger. But he could still hear shouting coming from his and Danny's room, so he forced himself to ignore the pain. It sounded like Robbie was beating the shit out of Danny.

"Come on, you little fuckwad!" Bobby snarled, raising his fists. "You think you can take me? Huh, faggot?"

Jake gritted his teeth and spat back, "Just get the fuck out of here, Bobby! I don't want to fight you. I just want to be left alone."

"Get up!"

"Dad kicked me out and told me never to come back, so why don't you do the same? Just leave and you never have to look at me again."

"I said get up!" Bobby reached down to grab him by the collar and yank him to his feet. Then he let go and drove his fist into Jake's face, knocking him down again.

Jake hit the floor hard, pain once more shooting through his whole body—especially his head and jaw.

From down the hall, he heard Danny's voice faintly. "So you're going to kill us?"

Danny!

Jake heaved himself up and launched himself at his brother, barely able to stagger forward. He latched on to Bobby's waist and tried to topple him over, but he didn't have the strength. Bobby staggered slightly but didn't go down. He just leaned over to wrap his arms around Jake's waist from behind. When he straightened up, growling like a bear, he had Jake hanging upside down with his ass in the air and his legs flailing. Bobby charged toward the couch in front of the plate glass divider.

Perhaps he'd meant to throw Jake onto the couch, but if so, his aim was off. They fell forward together onto the seat, Jake's head mashing into the cushion. His stomach hit the back of the couch, and one knee smashed through the glass above it. Large pieces of jagged glass rained down upon them both.

THE SOUND of glass shattering in the lounge was enough to divert Jake's brother from screaming more obscenities at Danny. He stopped midsentence and ran out the door. Danny rolled off the bed and stumbled after him.

"Jake!" The other twin's voice was coming from the lounge, and he sounded panicked.

The scene they burst in on was nightmarish. Jake was draped face down over the top of the couch, not moving. One leg was completely through the empty space that had held one of the glass windows, his pants torn and bloody, and the other leg was bent at the knee, pressed up against the wooden frame. His face wasn't visible, since his head was wedged against the seat cushion at an awkward angle under his shoulder. There were shards of glass all over him and the couch.

Oh God! No!

Jake's brother was huddled over him, and he was bleeding from multiple cuts on his arms and shoulders. But Jake had gotten the worst of it. He was bleeding from cuts all over his body, and there was a particularly nasty gash on his back, where his shirt had ridden up and exposed bare skin.

"Jake!" his brother cried, tapping his arm. But Jake wasn't responding. "I didn't mean it! Jake! Come on, man, you can't die on me!"

"Don't touch him!" Danny's shout surprised even him. But he no longer gave a fuck about these two idiots. He wasn't afraid of them anymore. He just knew he had to get Jake to a hospital. "Get away from him before you make it worse!"

Both the twins looked at him in shock, but after a brief hesitation, they obeyed him. Jake appeared to be breathing, when Danny leaned over him for a closer look, but he was afraid to move him in case his neck was broken.

"Nobody touch him," Danny commanded them. "I'm calling 911."

He ran downstairs to the phone booth, praying he could hold himself together long enough to dial and give someone the address. Jake looked half dead, lying there in the shattered glass, his head wedged against the seat cushion at an odd angle. But he was tough. Now that Danny had seen what Jake had had to deal with growing up in that household, he realized Jake was even tougher than he'd appeared.

There was no way he could die.

CHAPTER TWENTY-EIGHT

"I'M SORRY," the EMT told Danny as he prepared to close the ambulance door, "we can't take you in the ambulance. You'll have to drive to the hospital."

Jake was strapped to a stretcher, but he hadn't moved and he looked deathly pale.

"What hospital?" There were two nearby—one in Dover and one in Portsmouth.

"Wentworth-Douglass."

Then the door slammed and the ambulance moved away.

Danny turned around in a daze and ran into Paul, who'd apparently been standing behind him. He gasped and tried to push away, but Paul wrapped his arms around him. Confused, Danny thought Paul was trying to restrain him for some reason, until it filtered through his muddled mind that Paul was actually hugging him. It was the first time Danny had ever known him to deliberately touch someone.

"He'll be okay," Paul said.

Danny hugged him back. "We need to find Eva."

When they entered the lower lounge, they could hear the twins upstairs reluctantly giving their information to the police who'd arrived with the ambulance, interrupted frequently by Sonny, who was having a fit about the damage to the walls and the glass partition.

The last thing Danny needed was to get snarled up in that mess. He led Paul back outside and up the hill and across the handicapped ramp to the side door at the end of their wing. Eva's room was right next to the door. If they were lucky, she'd be there and they could just grab her and sneak out again.

From the far end of the hall, they could hear one of the twins saying, "I need to go the hospital. I've got all Jake's insurance info."

"Were you involved in the fight?"

"I didn't hit him. That was Bobby."

"Thanks for throwing me under the bus, man," the other twin grumbled, but if Robbie responded, Danny couldn't hear what he said.

"All right. Give me your contact information and you can go. We have a few more questions for your brother."

JAKE WASN'T dead, or so Danny, Paul, and Eva were told at the ER. But that was about all anyone would tell them since they weren't relatives.

Even more infuriating, Robbie had arrived before them, and he *was* apparently being kept up to date, despite the fact that he and his brother had put Jake in the ER to begin with. Danny overheard the nurse at the desk tell him at one point, "Your brother is conscious, but they still need to do X-rays and stitches." That was something. Though he was puzzled that Robbie was still out in the waiting room—Danny had expected him to be allowed inside the ER.

Robbie spent several minutes on the phone in the entryway, arguing with his parents. Danny could overhear fragments of a conversation between him and his father—enough to reaffirm his conviction that Jake's dad was a complete dick and didn't care if his son died or not. Robbie, for all his dickishness, did at least seem upset about Jake being hurt. He hung up with his father and dialed another number. From what Danny could hear, he was talking to Jake's mom now, and she *was* upset, thank God.

"I don't know, Mom. He's being a dick. He told them not to let me in."

Well, Danny thought, *Jake's coherent enough to have some sense, anyway.*

After Robbie was done on the phone, he went up to the desk to pester the nurse again, but she kept pointing to the waiting room until Robbie gave in and took a seat, as far away from Danny and his friends as possible. He refused to make eye contact with them, simply glaring at the floor with his arms crossed over his chest.

About forty-five minutes later—the time it took to get from Concord to Dover, if someone didn't mind speeding a little—Jake's mother walked into the ER. She'd pulled her thick blonde hair back with a barrette, and with the expression of barely-controlled anger she wore, she reminded Danny of a pissed-off Lauren Bacall.

Robbie got up and went to speak to her. She made eye contact with Danny while Robbie was filling her in, and then she went to the desk to ask the nurse something. The nurse looked at her ID and, though she kept her voice too low for Danny to hear what she was saying, it looked as if she was insisting that Robbie had to stay in the waiting room. She pointed at him several times, and seemed kind of pissed off at him, which by now was probably the case. Mrs. Stewart held up a finger for the woman to wait a moment and then, to Danny's surprise, walked over to him.

"Danny?" she said, smiling at Eva and Paul but not taking the time to introduce herself. "I'm going in to see Jake now. Would you like to come with me?"

He jumped up from his seat. "Yes! Thanks, Mrs. Stewart."

"Mom," Robbie protested, "he's not gonna do any good back there."

"You're the one Jake ordered them to keep out," she replied coolly. "And I'm pretty sure he wants to see Danny. So you can either wait here or head home."

Robbie glared at Danny and set his jaw stubbornly. "I'm gonna go pick up Bobby. Then we'll both come back here."

"Fine. I'll ask the nurse to have someone flag me when you get back. Come along, Danny."

Now that he was with Mrs. Stewart, the nurse at the desk appeared to have no issue with Danny going inside the ER. They were escorted into a large room with a nurses' station in the center and rooms with curtained entrances along the outer walls. Jake was in one of these in the far corner, propped up in a bed, pretty much naked except for the sheet covering his waist. The cuts had been washed, stitched in a few places, and bandaged, but he still looked awful. The bandages were *everywhere*, and he looked ghostly pale.

"Hey," he said when the nurse left them to find the doctor.

Mrs. Stewart looked a little pale herself, but she smiled at her son. "How are you doing, sweetheart?"

"My head's killing me. Bobby didn't break my jaw, at least, but they won't give me any pain-killers until they can get an X-ray to make sure I didn't get a concussion."

"I thought he broke your neck," Danny said, his voice unsteady. Tears were stinging his eyes and he was struggling to hold them back. The last thing he wanted to do was break down crying in front of Jake's mom.

"Hey," Jake said, holding out his hand. When Danny took it, acutely aware of Mrs. Stewart watching them, Jake said, "I'm okay."

"Robbie filled me in on some of the… melodrama that's occurred over the past few days," Mrs. Stewart said. She appeared not to notice the handholding. "I'm disgusted with the twins' behavior, and I'm so furious with your father I can't even *think* straight!"

"Don't try to fix it, Mom," Jake said. "I'm done with him."

She nodded silently, looking as if she were struggling to hold back tears herself.

They waited with Jake until the nurse came back with an orderly to wheel Jake to X-ray. Mrs. Stewart asked her, "Is it all right if my son's boyfriend remains here to wait for him? I'd like to go out to the waiting room."

"Sure. It'll just be about fifteen minutes."

Mrs. Stewart smiled at Danny and left him. He sat down to wait, surprised that she'd been so straightforward about calling him Jake's boyfriend. Still, that was the least of his concerns at the moment.

When they wheeled Jake back in, he was still looking pale. "The headache's getting worse," he told the nurse petulantly.

"I'll talk to the doctor. Just hang in there."

It seemed as though it took forever, during which time Jake mostly sat with his eyes closed, holding Danny's hand but too miserable to talk. Eventually, the nurse returned with an IV. "The doctor will be in soon to talk to you, but he says you can have something for your headache now."

They gave him some kind of pain-killer injected into the IV, and Danny was relieved to see Jake relaxing as it took effect.

The doctor came in shortly after that. He introduced himself to both Jake and Danny as Dr. Prashad. "Are you awake?" he asked Jake cheerfully.

"Yeah," Jake said slowly. "Just sleepy."

"How's your head now?"

"Better."

"Do you feel nauseous?"

"Not anymore."

"Good. It was probably the headache making you feel sick to your stomach. You don't have a concussion. And you've pulled a muscle in your neck, but nothing's broken. I'll give you a prescription for a muscle relaxant and some pain-killers for a few days."

"I can go home?"

"Very shortly. Of course, you can't drive. Can your friend give you a ride home?" He smiled at Danny.

"We've got a car," Danny said quickly.

"Good." The doctor turned back to Jake. "You've had some nasty cuts. You were very lucky—falling through a window isn't like it is in the movies, is it?" He laughed gently. "Your injuries could have been much, much worse. So you'll have to be careful of your stitches for several days. It will all be listed in your discharge instructions."

CHAPTER TWENTY-NINE

AS VILE as the twins' behavior had been, and as angry as he still was with both of them, Jake couldn't quite bring himself to file assault charges against his brothers. Why he should feel any shred of affection for the two thugs who'd tormented him his entire life, he had no idea, but he did. Maybe it was Stockholm syndrome. At any rate, he just relayed through his mother that he needed them to stay the hell away from him until he was ready to deal with them. They'd sent him a dorky get well card but hadn't made any attempt to visit.

His father never tried to contact him at all, and for that Jake was grateful.

On the other hand, Jake had no qualms about giving Sonny Bobby's address to send a bill for the damages to the dorm. He'd taken a bunch of shit for it, including Mark trying to get him kicked out of Eaton House.

That had actually been a pretty serious situation, since Eatonites did *not* like fighting in their dorm. His fault or not, Jake's presence had brought more violence into their safe haven than they'd ever had to deal with before. A meeting was called that Wednesday, and the only dorm mates firmly on Jake's side were Danny, Eva, and Paul. Fortunately, Sonny had decided to step in and plead Jake's case, and he'd managed to convince the majority of them that Jake had done his penance for hitting Mark and he'd had no control over his brothers attacking him. So now Jake was merely on probation rather than out the door.

In the meantime, Danny and Paul put cardboard up over the empty space where the glass pane had been, so Danny could play piano in the lounge without the downstairs people complaining they couldn't hear Kyle MacLachlan say "Damn good coffee!"

But even though things were better between him and Danny, something still felt unresolved.

They'd continued to sleep together since the night of the Great Dumpster Dive, thank God. Jake would have gone insane otherwise. As it was, Danny refused to let Jake do anything athletic—like sex—until his stitches healed. The best he could get was an occasional blowjob or hand job, but Danny insisted he pretty much just lie there and take it like a man. Jake was allowed to cop a feel but not actually do anything to get Danny off. Danny did get himself off, but it was frustrating to watch without being allowed to participate.

That was all just temporary, though, and having a boyfriend who gave great head was hardly something to whine about. The problem was there still seemed to be a wall between the two of them, and Jake couldn't figure out why. He'd tried to be understanding, that night in the shower. Had he somehow fucked up his apology? Or had he hurt Danny so badly there was simply no way he could be forgiven?

Then late one night, after they'd been asleep for a few hours, Jake woke to find Danny sitting up in the dark beside him. He wasn't making a sound, so Jake couldn't tell if he was crying or not. Jake rolled onto his back and reached up to stroke Danny's back. Danny flinched at the touch but didn't move away.

"Tell me," Jake said in a whisper, afraid Danny would get out of the bed if he spoke too loudly. "Please."

There was a long silence, and then Danny began to talk. "One of those guys on the wrestling team… his name was Steve Cory. I had a huge crush on him. And I thought he liked me too. I mean, we made out all the time. If somebody likes to kiss you, doesn't that mean he likes you?"

Jake almost responded, but he stayed silent, afraid anything he said might make Danny go quiet again.

"I thought so," Danny said wistfully. "But he never wanted to have sex. I think somehow he convinced himself that kissing wasn't real—it was just fooling around. But sex… that would have been real. That would have been *gay*." He paused, as if uncertain he should continue, but then he went on, "That night in the garage… I didn't really want to… do what I did. Don't get me wrong. I wasn't freaked out by it. I wasn't forced. I just…. It was Steve's idea. He said he'd let me give him a blowjob if I did the other guys first. So I figured, why not? I mean, I didn't care about sucking off those other guys. But I thought maybe this could be the first step with Steve. Maybe if I did this, he'd be open to doing more with me...."

Danny took a long, quavering breath. "It didn't turn out like I thought. 'You just sucked off three guys. Get away from me, you filthy cum whore.' That's what he said. Then he and his friends kicked me around for a while, and... and then he pissed on me...."

"Jesus."

Danny shook his head, as if to clear it. When he spoke again, he sounded like he might be crying, though it was too dark for Jake to see. "The next day, Steve and his friends told everybody. And that was pretty much the end of any friendships I had, any respect anyone had for me. I was the faggot who sucked off the wrestling team. Nobody cared about their part in it—they were all drunk! I'd begged them to feed me their cocks and they were too drunk to care. That's what they told everyone. Someone wrote "cum whore" on my locker. Guys hid themselves when I went into the men's room or flashed their dicks at me so their friends could have a good laugh. Sometimes a group of them would follow me through the halls and spit on me, call me 'faggot' and 'cum whore' and 'piss-pig'—yeah, Steve told everyone about that part too. He said I asked him to do it in my mouth."

Danny swallowed. "There were a couple teachers who saw what was going on. Mrs. Kelly was cool. She shut it down when kids called me names in her art class, and eventually she told the guidance counselor. He called my mom in. And then he... made me admit in front of her that I hadn't been raped. I'd wanted to do it."

He was silent so long after that, Jake finally had to say something. "You just wanted this asshole to like you."

"It doesn't matter. I screwed my whole life up in one night, and there's no going back. Since then, I've fucked around a lot. Nothing like that night, but... there have been a lot of guys. Mostly one-night stands. The Dragon Con where I met Karl? That was a threesome. I don't even know who the other guy was."

Jake sat up so they could be face-to-face, even though it made him wince because the cut on his back still wasn't completely healed. In the dark, he could only see Danny in silhouette against the streetlight-illuminated window. "So what are you saying? You were a victim that night, but now you've gone completely over to the dark side?"

"I was never a victim. I knew what I was doing."

Jake groaned. "He manipulated you. And then he abused the shit out of you for doing what you thought *he* wanted you to do. That part about how you didn't think it was so bad at first? I don't see how that really matters."

"It mattered to you, when you found out about it."

"Yeah," Jake said. "I know. I guess it made me jealous. I was afraid it meant what you did with me was just… nothing to you. I'm sorry."

"Jake… guys like you and guys like me just aren't meant to be together."

That shut Jake up for a minute. It felt like Danny had slammed a door. At last, he said, "What do you mean by that?"

Danny didn't answer. He just lifted his knees and leaned his chin against them.

"You think you're too sleazy for me, don't you?" Jake asked.

"Yeah. I kind of do. I know some guys think I'm cute—"

"You're fucking gorgeous."

"—so I haven't had any trouble getting sex when I want it. But the guys who fucked around with me the last couple years of high school didn't come to me because they wanted a boyfriend. They wanted sex. I got pretty good at it, and everyone knew I was a good lay. I thought maybe I could get a fresh start here, since Keene is two hours away, but a lot of kids from Keene end up at UNH. Mark's not the only one in this dorm. He's just the only one who's a dick to my face."

"So what?"

"So?" Danny snapped. He appeared to be growing angry. "So I'm trying to tell you what everyone else already knows about me. I may be good-looking on the surface, but deep down I'm just a slut. A cum-whore. I'm sleazy and disgusting and—"

"Shut up! You're not any of those things!"

"How the fuck would you know? You've barely scraped the surface."

Jake sighed and frowned. "Let me ask you something. All of this shit about… threesomes and one-night stands…. Is that what you really want? Is that what gets you off? What makes you happy?"

"It doesn't make me happy."

"Could you be happy with just one guy? With *me*?"

"I don't want to sleep around, Jake. Sex with you is awesome."

"Then fine. Be my boyfriend. And we'll both be happy."

Danny was silent for a long time. When he spoke at last, his voice sounded small, like a child's, and frightened. "Every time you learn something new about my past…."

He trailed off, but Jake knew where he was going with it. He moved in close and placed his chin on Danny's shoulder, so he could whisper in his ear. "I'll tell you what. You're gonna start from the beginning. And you're gonna tell me everything you've ever done that you think is too sleazy for me to handle, even if we have to break for breakfast, lunch, and dinner. And then when you're done, you're gonna see that I'm still here. And I still love you."

IT WAS pretty ballsy, demanding his lover's entire previous sexual history like that. But Danny found he wanted to tell it. Deep down, part of him was still convinced Jake would bail, once he heard it all. So maybe Jake was right. Maybe the only thing to do was to lay it all out in the open.

He talked for a long time, making sure he got everything, with Jake eventually lying down to curl up around him like a big dog. Several times, he had to check to see if Jake had fallen asleep, but he hadn't. He was sleepy, but he could always repeat back what Danny had just said. Then, as the sickly gray predawn light seeped into the room, Danny said, "And then I started jerking off with my roommate."

"Mark?" Jake asked, confused. They'd already gotten past the drunken blowjob.

"No. This was a cute redhead who liked having his asshole licked."

"Sounds really sleazy."

"Yeah."

"I think he wants you to do it again."

Danny sighed and pushed Jake over onto his own pillow so he could lie down beside him. "I think he probably needs some sleep, considering how recently he got out of the hospital."

"Hmm. So was that it?"

"Dude, I've been talking for hours."

"It wasn't all that much. You just kept going into gory detail."

Perhaps he had. He'd felt compelled to tell everything and not leave the slightest thing out. "I'm sorry. I didn't mean to make you uncomfortable."

"You didn't. Some of it was pretty hot, actually. I'd like to try fucking on top of Garrison Hill Tower." He was talking with his eyes closed, as if he were about to drift off to sleep, and he looked adorable.

Danny smiled and leaned forward to plant a kiss on Jake's forehead. "Sure. Hopefully you'll be less afraid of heights than David was."

He wasn't sure if this had really accomplished much. He'd have to see how Jake reacted when he was fully awake, assuming he remembered it. But it did feel good to have it all out in the open, and he felt a small spark of hope deep in his chest for the first time since the first day they'd had sex. The instinct to stomp it out before it could get out of control was still there, but Danny resisted, letting the spark warm him as he drifted off to sleep.

DANNY WOKE to someone—most likely Jake—fondling his ass. He turned his head to look over his shoulder and immediately had Jake's mouth tickling the corner of his. Danny smiled at him. "I figured you'd sleep all day."

"It's almost noon. And I'm horny."

"You're always horny."

Jake made an attempt to climb on top of him but winced. Danny put a hand on his arm and said, "Lie back down, idiot. I'm not going to have you pulling out your stitches."

"I'm horny," Jake whined.

"Lie on your back."

Jake did as he was told and Danny rolled over to face him, reaching out to caress his naked skin wherever it showed through the bandages. Jake still looked a bit like a mummy, especially when viewed from behind, though a number of the bandages had been discarded as his skin healed. He'd have some scars, most likely, but fortunately nothing disfiguring.

"Do you remember anything I told you last night?" Danny asked, as his hand ventured lower on Jake's abdomen.

Jake's eyelids fluttered as Danny caressed him, and he didn't look like he'd be capable of coherent conversation for much longer, but he replied, "I remember all of it. And I don't think it was nearly as horrible as you were making it out to be."

That was good. "I never really said it was horrible," Danny said. "I don't think there's anything wrong with casual sex. I just...." He stopped, not knowing how to complete the thought.

"You just think it makes you unlovable."

Danny shrugged. *I guess that's it, isn't it?* "Well, since that... incident... nobody has ever wanted more than a quick fuck from me. A lot of guys have been attracted to me, but nobody ever wanted to stick around. Nobody wants a slut for a boyfriend."

"I'm sticking around," Jake insisted. "And stop calling yourself a slut."

"You're just saying that because I've got my hand on your dick."

Jake groaned, partly from arousal and, perhaps, partly from frustration. Danny knew he was being childish, but it was hard to let it go after all this time.

"How about you just shut up and fuck me," Jake said, "and we can talk about this in a few months, or a few years, when you see I know all the so-called sleazy things you've done, and I'm *still your boyfriend*?"

Danny laughed, but he was surprised to find his eyes tearing up. Embarrassed, he glanced away. Maybe it was time to change the subject. "Hold on."

He got out of bed and scampered across the room to his desk. Then he grabbed the bottle of lube and a condom out of his top drawer. He scurried back to the bed and climbed on top of Jake, who'd already grown impatient enough to start jerking himself.

"Would you like to try fucking me this time?" Danny asked, holding up the lube. "You can just lie there and I'll ride you." So far, it had always been Danny on top, because Jake loved—in an epic way—being fucked.

Jake looked up at him with eyes clouded by lust. "Okay."

He was so into what he was doing that Danny had to slap his hand away from his dick, but he groaned and let Danny take over. Danny rolled the condom over him and applied some lube. Then he positioned himself over Jake's cock and placed the tip against his anus.

"You aren't just going to shove it in, are you?" Jake asked, his eyes going wide.

Danny laughed. "No. I may be experienced, but that doesn't mean I can just do a high beam dismount and land on your dick. This works for me, though, if we do it slow."

He relaxed and allowed himself to open up as he pressed his sphincter down against the head of Jake's cock. The hardest part was getting the head of Jake's dick inside, but fortunately dicks were designed for penetration. After a minute or so of pressure, his anus relaxed enough for the lubricated head to slip inside. Danny gasped, but it wasn't pain he was feeling—at least not enough to override the pleasure. The temptation to simply slide down the rest of the shaft was strong, but he resisted, moving very slowly and pausing to allow his body to adjust. Jake waited patiently, caressing his sides and giving Danny's erection slow languid strokes to encourage him.

When Danny had settled down to the base of Jake's cock, feeling its comfortable warmth nestled deep inside him, he began to rock back and forth. Jake moaned and closed his eyes as he slid in and out of Danny's ass. "That feels amazing."

"I thought you'd like it."

It was hard to keep Jake from thrusting into him. Danny wouldn't have minded that—he would have loved it, actually—if it weren't for the fact that Jake needed to stay relatively still. The entire purpose of doing it in this position was to keep him from flexing his back too much.

Somehow, he managed to keep Jake still enough to get through it without pulling any stitches. At least, he didn't detect any signs of pain. There was no stopping the idiot from thrusting hard into him as he approached orgasm, and Danny enjoyed the way Jake hammered into him, until he slammed in as deep as he could go and scrunched his eyes closed to make a rather cute "orgasm face." Danny felt Jake coming inside him in powerful spasms, and the sensation resonated deliciously throughout his entire body as he furiously stroked himself off. He grunted and squirted come all over Jake's stomach and chest, and even managed to splash a little on Jake's chin.

"That was awesome!" Jake gasped when it was over, trailing his fingers through Danny's come on his stomach, the picture of wantonness. "But I miss you coming inside *me*."

Danny allowed Jake's dick to slide out of him as he lowered himself onto his hands and knees, hovering over Jake's wet torso. He cursed himself for being an idiot—he'd sprayed all over some of the bandages. They might have to change them.

Before he got up to get a towel, Danny licked his come off Jake's chin and then moved up to kiss him. When he broke the kiss, he said, "I never would have thought, when I first met you, that you'd be such a bottom."

"Is that bad?"

"Absolutely not," Danny said with a smile. "I can't wait to fuck you again."

Jake looked deep into his eyes a moment, his blue eyes clear and utterly without guile. Danny realized that he'd been wrong to compare them to Steve's eyes, when they'd first met. Steve's eyes had always seemed distrustful and suspicious. Jake had been closed off for a time, but he had always looked at Danny without deception, trusting him sexually and perhaps even emotionally. And his open gaze invited Danny to trust Jake back.

EPILOGUE

"I'LL TEACH you to make fools of us!" Jake shouted at Shane. Then he charged, his boffer hammer aiming to crash down on Shane's head. The theater major sidestepped, causing Jake to stagger as his hammer swung through empty space. His stitches were out now, thankfully, but he could still feel a tiny twinge in his back when he did it.

"With that," Paul announced, "Utgard-Loki vanished, along with his entire castle and all of its guests!"

Jake looked around in a comic parody of astonishment that drew guffaws from the audience. Well, he'd never claimed he could act. Danny, who was playing Loki, snorted and clapped Jake on the shoulder. "Come along, Thor, before you hurt yourself."

"How do you always manage to get us into these messes, Loki?"

"Skill."

When they walked out of the lounge together, the audience of Eatonites at the far end of the room, where the couches and chairs had been pushed, erupted into applause.

"That was awesome!" Sonny shouted above the noise.

Jake led the small band of performers—Danny, Shane, Holly, and a few of the other theater majors—back into the lounge for their bows. He was pleased to see Paul grinning like a goofball, looking surprised that his play had gone over so well. It had taken Jake forever to convince him to write up one of his original RPG games as a play for his dorm project. Then he'd gone around the dorm with Paul to recruit actors, since Paul was too shy to do it on his own.

Mark was in the back, rolling his eyes, but nobody paid any attention to him. The play had been very entertaining, Jake's "acting" notwithstanding. Paul had a knack for dialog and a better sense of humor than Jake, or probably anyone else, had given him credit for. He'd revealed to Jake a secret dream of becoming a fantasy novelist, and Jake suspected he'd be doing a lot to fan that little spark into a flame over the next few semesters. He wasn't quite sure why, but he seemed to have taken Paul under his wing.

Later, they went out for hot chocolate to celebrate Paul's first public accolades—Jake, Danny, Paul, and Eva. It was early May and though the night was chilly, it wasn't unbearably cold. Jake had his winter jacket on, but went without mittens so he could hold Danny's hand in his as they walked across the campus.

Jake purposely hung back a bit, letting Paul and Eva get ahead of them. Paul didn't even notice. He'd been babbling on a mile a minute ever since they headed out, thoughts of new plays bouncing around in his head and spilling out to anyone within earshot. Eva listened with an expression of amusement.

"You've created a monster," Danny observed, smiling.

"He deserves a pat on the back now and then."

"Yes. I suppose everyone does." They walked in silence for a while, enjoying the feeling of warmth between their hands, until Danny said, "There are only a couple weeks left 'til the end of the semester."

"I know." Jake also knew the real reason Danny mentioned it. Jake had been saying he'd find an apartment for the summer, but though he'd gotten a list from the Memorial Union Building of available apartments off campus for students and checked some of them out, he hadn't found anything. There was simply too much competition for apartments near campus. Plus he still didn't have a job. The Financial Aid office had managed to scrape up some grants and loans he qualified for, so it seemed likely he'd be able to pay for next semester and possibly the one after that. But changing his major at this point meant he'd have to take an additional two semesters of classes, and how he'd manage to pay for that was anybody's guess.

"You know Mom would love to have you," Danny said.

Jake sighed. "I've already been there for winter break and spring break. She's going to get sick of me."

"She loves you. You know that. We'll find some shit jobs in town, so we can at least help buy groceries."

"All summer is a long time for her to have me as a guest."

"I've managed to put up with you for almost nine months," Danny said, grinning at him.

"That's different," Jake replied. "You're madly in love with me."

Danny laughed and brought Jake's hand up to his mouth to plant a warm kiss on the back of it. "Yeah... I am."

Jake stopped walking, so Danny was forced to do so too. He pulled Danny close and wrapped his arms around his body, leaning down to bring their faces close together. "And I'm madly in love with you," he said, just before he closed the remaining distance for a kiss.

When he pulled away, Danny was grinning. He no longer turned away when Jake lavished affection on him or told him, "I love you." He could even say it back now.

"Are you guys coming?" Eva called out. "And by 'coming,' I mean walking this direction, not what you look like you'd like to be doing."

"Shut up," Danny told her affectionately.

Jake just rolled his eyes. But he took Danny's hand in his again, and they went to catch up with their friends. He knew he'd end up going to stay with Danny and Althea. It was, after all, what he wanted. He'd find some kind of job so he could avoid feeling like a deadbeat, and he'd visit his mom whenever he could to help her through the divorce. He might even agree to see the twins again, since they'd been calling him and trying to come to grips with his relationship with Danny, almost like real human beings.

And each morning he'd lie in bed, waiting for Danny to open his eyes, so he could see that Jake was still there... still wanting him... still loving him. No matter what.

JAMIE FESSENDEN set out to be a writer in junior high school. He published a couple short pieces in his high school's literary magazine and had another story place in the top 100 in a national contest, but it wasn't until he met his partner, Erich, almost twenty years later, that he began writing again in earnest. With Erich alternately inspiring and goading him, Jamie wrote several screenplays and directed a few of them as micro-budget independent films. His latest completed work premiered at the Indie Fest 2009 in Los Angeles and also played at the Austin Gay and Lesbian International Film Festival two weeks later.

After nine years together, Jamie and Erich have married and purchased a house together in the wilds of Raymond, New Hampshire, where there are no streetlights, turkeys and deer wander through their yard, and coyotes serenade them on a nightly basis. Jamie currently works as technical support for a computer company in Portsmouth, NH, but fantasizes about someday quitting his day job to be a full-time writer.

Visit Jamie at http://jamiefessenden.wordpress.com/.

Also from JAMIE FESSENDEN

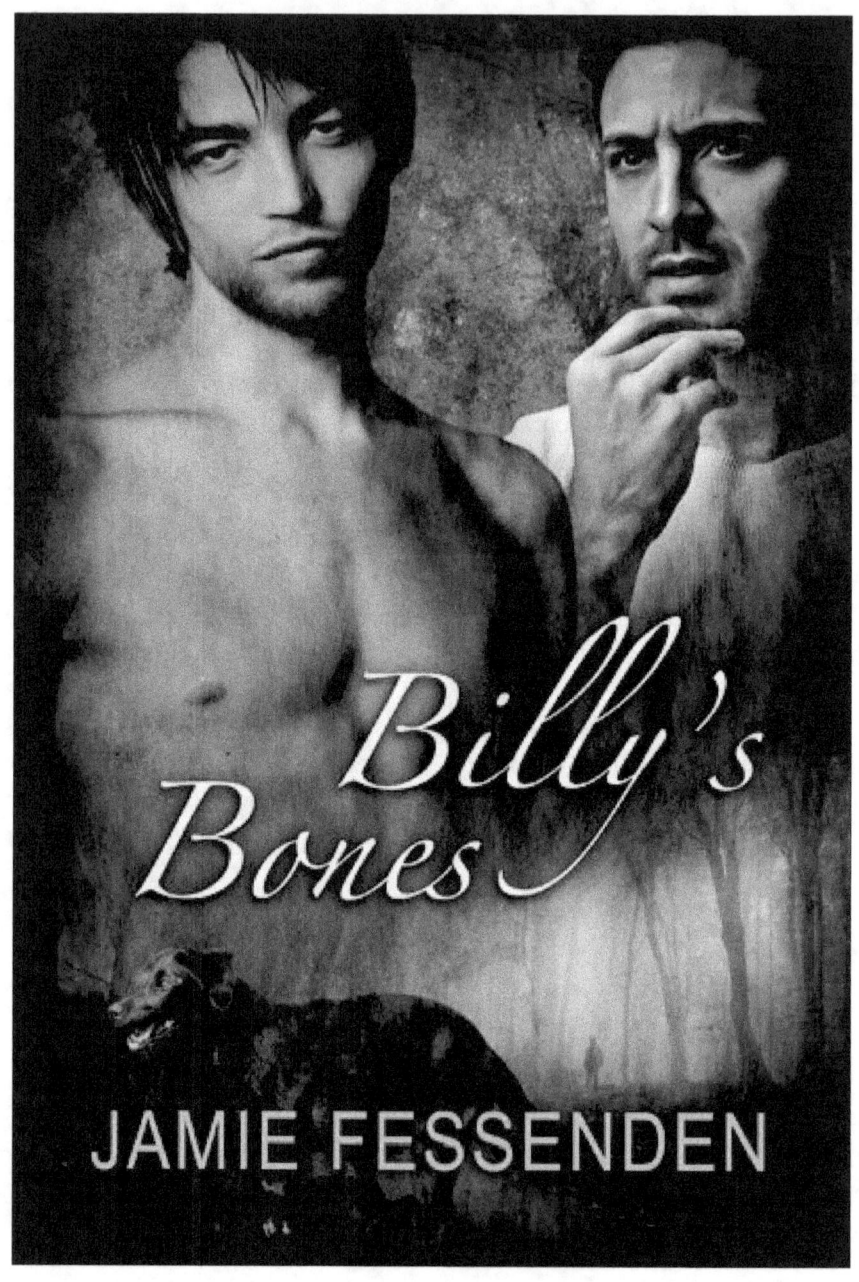

http://www.dreamspinnerpress.com

Also from JAMIE FESSENDEN

Jamie Fessenden

Murderous Requiem

http://www.dreamspinnerpress.com

Also from JAMIE FESSENDEN

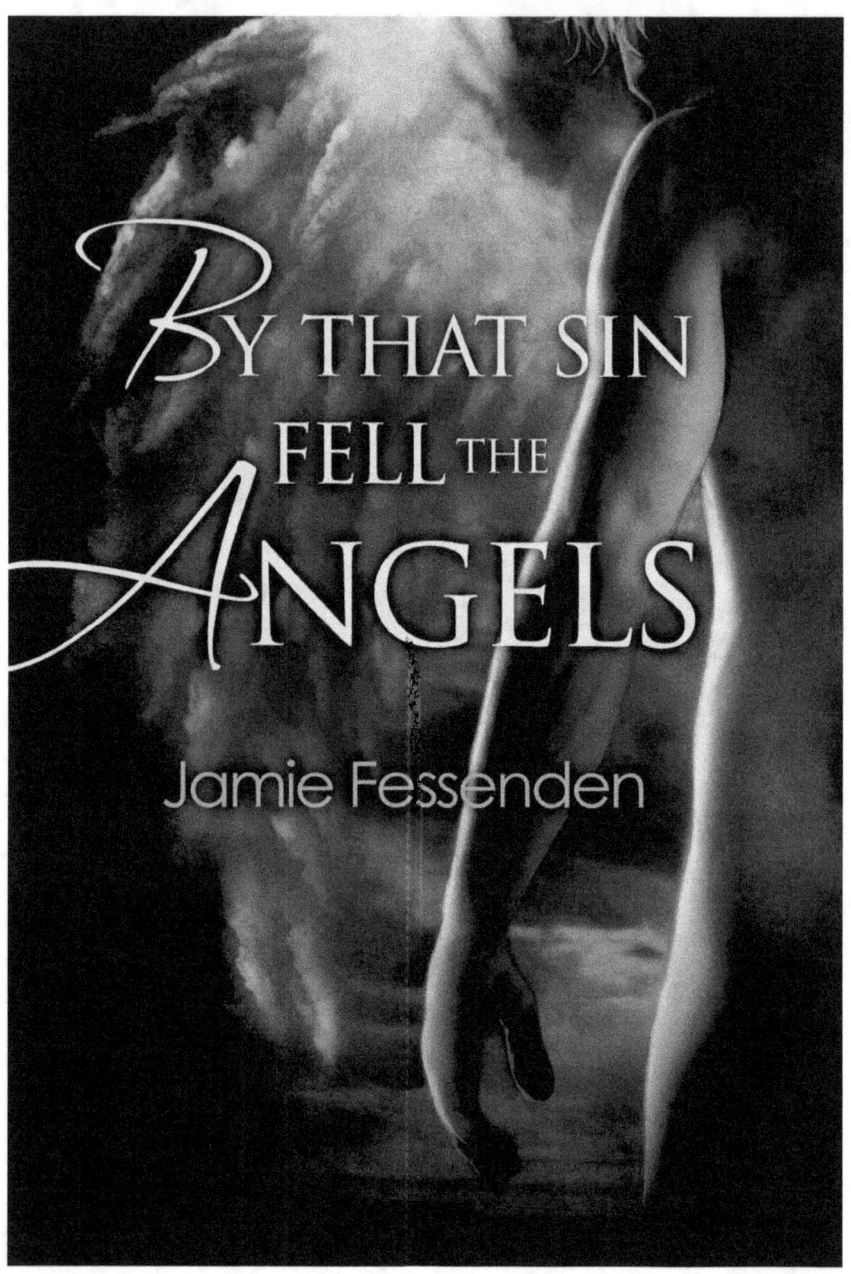

BY THAT SIN
FELL THE
ANGELS

Jamie Fessenden

http://www.dreamspinnerpress.com

Also from JAMIE FESSENDEN

http://www.dreamspinnerpress.com

Also from JAMIE FESSENDEN

THE Christmas WAGER

JAMIE FESSENDEN

http://www.dreamspinnerpress.com

Also from JAMIE FESSENDEN

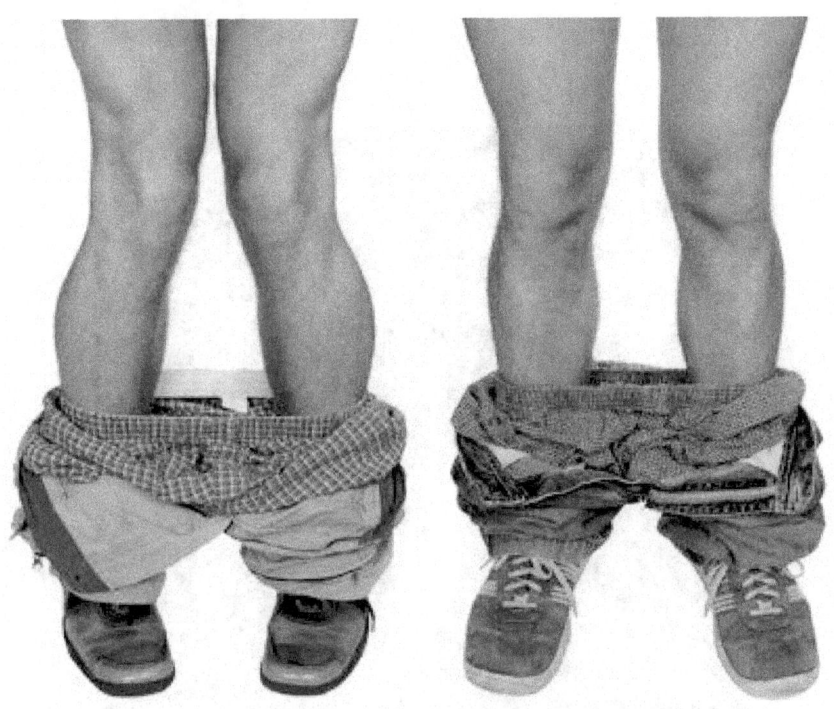

WE'RE BOTH STRAIGHT, RIGHT?

JAMIE FESSENDEN

http://www.dreamspinnerpress.com

For more of the
best M/M romance,
visit

Dreamspinner Press

www.dreamspinnerpress.com

www.ingramcontent.com/pod-product-compliance
Lightning Source LLC
Chambersburg PA
CBHW060052260626
47160CB00005B/1655